William Pleater Davidge

Footlight Flashes

William Pleater Davidge

Footlight Flashes

ISBN/EAN: 9783337250713

Printed in Europe, USA, Canada, Australia, Japan

Cover: Foto ©Andreas Hilbeck / pixelio.de

More available books at **www.hansebooks.com**

FOOTLIGHT FLASHES.

BY

WILLIAM DAVIDGE, COMEDIAN,

AUTHOR OF "THE FAMILY PARTY," (A COMEDY.) "THE DRAMA DE-
FENDED," ETC., ETC., ETC.

———— —•●•— ————

NEW YORK:

THE AMERICAN NEWS COMPANY,

119 AND 121 NASSAU STREET.
—
1866.

" THE DRAMA is the most perfect imitation of human life ; by means of the stage it represents man in all his varieties of mind, his expressions of manner, and his power of action ; and is the first of moralities, because it teaches us in the most impressive way the knowledge of ourselves."—*Hazlit.*

TO

EDWIN FORREST, Esq.,

THIS BOOK

Is Most Respectfully Dedicated,

BY HIS SINCERE PROFESSIONAL ADMIRER,

WILLIAM DAVIDGE.

BROOKLYN, N. Y., 1866.

ILLUSTRATIONS.

CONTENTS.

CHAPTER XX.

CHAPTER XXI.

FOOTLIGHT FLASHES.

CHAPTER I.

The web of life is of a mingled yarn, good and ill together.
—*All's Well that Ends Well.   Act 4, Scene 8.*

I**f** there be anything more detestable than writing one's
Autobiography, the individual who now essays the task,
would be glad to know what it is.   This assertion is made
fearlessly, and without dread of contradiction; but, if
one of my captious readers should consider me unworthy
of credit, let him, or her, try the experiment, and allow
me to sit in judgment on the document.

Everybody has doubtless heard the story of the man
who was suffering from a bad cold in his head, protesting
to his friend that "there was nothing in the world so bad
as a cold in the head!" The friend protested that he was
in error, and named as a greater affliction, "*two colds in
the head.*" The same may be said of an Autobiography.
Nothing can be so bad as *one*, except the perpetration of
two.

The life of an actor presents to the youthful and super-
ficial observer, charms of no ordinary degree of interest;
for there is no profession that holds so much sway, or
takes such firm possession of the youthful mind, as that
of acting. Well do I remember loitering when a boy, for
hours together at the stage doors of Covent Garden and
Drury Lane Theatres, to watch the actors arrive at, or
depart from, those temples of the drama. Little did I

then imagine that, in after life I should be on terms of professional fellowship with many of those I regarded (in my simplicity) as something more than mortal.

From the dreary and unpleasant prospect that has been, and still is, held out by some historians to aspirants for theatrical honors, and from the many hardships, and unpleasantries attending the pursuit of an occupation which in the end leads merely to an uncertain glory, it has proved a source of wonder in many reflective minds, that so great a number have been found bold enough to venture upon the culture of an art so fraught with disagreeables; an art in which so few of the great mass of actors ever render themselves decidedly eminent. And yet the number of youthful candidates who so incessantly stand forward to brave every danger attending a theatrical career, is immense. That an actor's life is one of great anxiety, cannot reasonably be doubted or disputed, when it is seen how quickly public taste and opinion veers. An actor for a time becomes the very idol of the public; he is flattered on all sides. His praise is resounded to almost every corner of the country, and his performances attended by all the beauty and fashion a gay metropolis can boast. But this lasts no longer than while his excellences are new, and possess the charm of novelty. When that is past, and public curiosity is gratified, we find him, (save in the rarest of instances), sink into cold and silent neglect.

Peculiar circumstances tend to give zest to theatrical anecdote, and as admiration naturally stimulates curiosity, the history of those to whom the mirth, or sensibility of so many pleasant evenings are due, must interest and gratify. The heroes and heroines of the buskin in their *real*, as well as assumed characters, experience that vicissitude and adventure to which the unvaried tenor of mechanical industry is an entire stranger. Their life teems

with incident which almost seems destined to realize the
fictions they represent. The early period of their professional career is therefore generally clouded with difficulties unknown, even in imagination, to those whose
pursuits have a different proclivity.

" The stage 'tis said, by right should be a school
To shame the guilty, and amend the fool."

So writes some one whose name " lives not in my memory," but the poet is grievously in error, if his couplet alludes
to the votaries of that enchanting of all professions, " the
stage." For no sooner does some ambitious youth, who
is perhaps partially initiated in the art and mystery of
spouting, and may have, at sundry times, and in divers
places, been allowed to deliver certain portions of the
inspired language of the " *bard of Avon*," determine (from
the ill-judging applause of his own companions perhaps)
to adopt theatricals as his future profession, than he
plunges headlong into folly. How far a dramatic performance may be allowed to arouse the dormant feelings
of benevolence, justice, penitence, or mercy, in the minds
of an audience, I leave to more able pens to describe; but
of this I am conscious from personal experience, that no
sooner does an individual indulge in ecstatic day dreams
(and night dreams too, occasionally,) of waving plumes,
glittering falchions, and spangled trappings — with all the
attendant additions of scenic castles, rocks, forests, &c.,
&c., than he pants ardently as lover ever did for the moment which shall give to his arms his well-beloved, for
that auspicious day which shall find him enrolled a wandering child of Thespis.

Oh! guardian angel of the respected and beloved, why
wast thou slumbering when thy child quitted the paternal
roof, to " strut and fret his hour upon the stage." But
suffice it, the profession hath its charms, and the love of

it once engendered in the youthful mind, never can be wholly or entirely eradicated.

I have been for many years the unworthy representative of all grades of human nature, from kings to beggars, and even now, at times experience as much pleasure as ever, and anticipate the hour when I am to appear in a favorite character, as anxiously as any amateur ever did. Even such an insignificant circumstance (though by the way not so insignificant either to an actor) as a round of applause, has entirely revolutionized my sentiments. Perhaps I was disgusted with the profession, and had resolved to relinquish it for ever, and return, like a prodigal son, brimfull of penitence. "And could a few unmeaning rounds of applause thus overthrow your intentions," I fancy I hear some sober-minded parent exclaim, with uplifted hands. 'Tis even so, and I have hastily resolved to pursue the enticing, though thorny path, which my sanguine hopes anticipated one day would lead to fame and renown.

But I am beginning to moralize, the which is not the purpose of this theme; further, what I have said applied to the state of the profession of the stage when I entered it, or rather, it might with truth be added, the condition of provincial theatres of the more minute class at that time. There was very little chance then of achieving fame or profit, without *roughing it*, and ascending, step by step, the round of the professional ladder. Now-a-days ladies and gentlemen, the former most particularly, cannot devote their attention to any less than the principal characters, and they will undertake the whole weight and consequence of a five act play with a temerity perfectly appalling to any one who is conversant with the difficulties of the operation. The gallantry of the public is of course, to a great extent, to blame for these futile attempts, by treating with favor and approbation what *they know* to be unworthy the attention they bestow upon it. It is as impossible to make an actress without experience, as it would be for a surgeon to qualify for the duties of *his* profession, without a thorough probation in the science of anatomy. This epidemic for stepping at a bound into the position of *Stars*, broke out with great virulence a year or two since among the fair sex, but I have not heard that the result, *in a single instance*, has been such as to justify the belief the ladies erroneously entertained of their histrionic skill, or to satisfy their friends that the monies invested in charges paid to managers for first appearances, have been wisely or profitably expended.

A terrible disease burst upon Great Britain immediately after the production of the "Lady of Lyons," and both sexes fell victims to the calamity with equal severity.

I am fully aware, while penning these lines, how impossible it will be to induce many of my readers — especially those who have fallen victims to an attack of the previously described malady — to give credence to my assertions, or place the smallest reliance upon this opinion. I desire, however, to adduce as an illustration of my views, the remarks of the late Mr. Harley, the celebrated comedian, which is pertinent to this very important question.*

" In the year 1840, I was a member of the Bristol theatre. During the season Mr. H. came from London to play an engagement. The conversation happened to turn upon the subject of "full blown artists," as he termed them, who hadn't patience, or industry, to wait till the "bud of their talent began to blossom."

" When I first acted Shakspeare's Clowns," said he, " I was a very young man, and felt quite satisfied that the rendition of those parts could not possibly be so well and truthfully presented by established actors of that period

* Mr. Harley died August 22, 1858, aged 68.

as by myself. I felt satisfied that I was the coming man who was to clearly define the great poet's meaning, and remove the veil of doubt that had puzzled so many brilliant minds. When I acquired a little more experience, I began gradually to realize the difficulties, and as I further advanced, became more involved, till. after acting them constantly for twenty years, I discovered, in comparison to their extreme excellence, I knew really *nothing about them.*"

CHAPTER II.

"How irksome is this music."
—*Second part Henry VI. Act 2. Scene 1.*

My *stern parient* was a merchant, of the city of London, (and not an actor, as some biographers have written,) in which ancient city I was born, or, as it is poetically termed, "*first saw the light*," on the 17th of April, 1814.

The author of my being, who had a *solidarity* of correcting his offspring which will not readily be forgotten, while

" Memory holds her seat in this distracted globe,"

had no dramatic proclivity. I am led, however, to the conclusion that he did not share in the antagonism for places of rational amusement indulged in by some of the "pater fami-li-asses" of the present day, who attend the representation of *Don Giovanni*, in its lyrical garb with a religious enthusiasm; but could not endanger their prospects of squaring accounts with the consciences, if they were to assist at a banquet of the intellectual food provided by the genius of Shakspeare.

My mother was devoted to her home and children — of whom there were three — (*children, not homes,*) casting a halo of goodness around the domestic circle, performing cheerfully, and with an unsparing amount of womanly benignity her mission of usefulness, tempered with the sweet smile of that natural instinct bequeathed by an all wise Providence, as a counter influence against the harder proportion of our common nature! For in those days the philosophy of woman's *rights* and other *phantasmagoria* of faith had not cast their delusive nets into the ocean of domestic happiness, sapping the vitality of that peace it is its duty to promote, and by a fatal and erroneous code of teaching, embittering the lives of those it should be its first desire to propitiate, by joining heart and hand in the common cause of mutual affection, confidence, sympathy, and love.

It so happened, during the tedium incidental to a boy's bringing up, that some one skilled in musical lore, made the startling discovery that I possessed a voice which might be attuned to harmony after the necessary probation had been gone through sufficiently to "ground us in the science,"—a favorite expression of the party in question.

Gentle reader, did you ever labor under the infantile affliction of a voice? Only those who have been attacked by that virulent disorder, can form the minutest conception of the suffering necessary to be endured. An hour's exercise on that vocal alphabet yclept *the gamut*, on the clammyest of mornings incidental to a London autumn, with a walk of a mile to the Cathedral of St. Paul, and there to find yourself habited in a clerical garb before a very limited quantity of early devotionals, is not an interesting proceeding for a youthful mind, whose only thought of the eligible future of such a probation is most probably centered in the protracted breakfast a ravenous appetite is anxiously waiting to pay court to, rather than the exercise of his vocal organ for hire and reward, when he shall arrive at the dignity of man's estate.

At the age of fourteen, the voice above alluded to, after the perpetual *grinding* process to which it had been so unremittingly and audaciously subjected, became so exquisitely tempered, that it either was ground down altogether, or, not finding the wear and tear upon its constitution likely to promote its ultimate usefulness, departed from its proprietary without the slightest intimation of its desire to peregrinate, or signifying its intention that it ever designed returning to its original location.

Physic was the next experiment proposed, as holding out great inducements for a youth to get well up in the world, and become a person of substance, (in pocket, not flesh,) but during a month's probationary servitude, I was very nearly qualifying myself for a landed proprietorship in the neighboring burial-place, by swallowing a copious draught of what I in the innocence of my knowledge of pharmacy, believed to be a mild decoction of peppermint, but which, from certain unmistakable internal misgivings, proved to be something of a less innoxious nature, requiring the aid of a stomach-pump to dislodge it. This ingenious device, assisted by gentle emetics, restored me to a state of convalescence.

Eccentricities of purpose, too numerous to particularize, beset me on every side, till, burning with dramatic ardor, I determined to shake the dust of London from my feet, and seek the provincial road to histrionic fame. A congenial spirit, with the same end in view, accompanied me on my probationary adventure. His proclivities were of a comic nature — mine, *darkly, deeply tragic.*

My store of worldly riches amounted to ten shillings and six pence sterling; my wardrobe did not much retard locomotion, and with hearts swelling with expectations of future greatness, we wended our way towards Brighton, fifty-one miles from the great metropolis.

CHAPTER III.

" I do wander everywhere."
—*Midsummer Night's Dream.* *Act* 2. *Scene* 1.

IT was the middle of the month of June, when nature was attired in her most gorgeous garb, we left Kennington Common behind us with a merry and elastic step. The delightful villas, and cosy dwellings, garnished with the choice perfume of rare exotics, and fashioned to meet the requirements of the man of wealth, who quits the bustle and din of business in the over-heated city, (that hive of commercial drudgery,) to luxuriate in domestic pleasure and social ease, meet us at every turn. In other spots, with their wants more economically considered, stand the homes of the less fortunate laborers in the world's vineyard, their youthful branches bearing ample testimony (if any were needed) by their buoyant spirits and ruddy looks, of the invigorating influence of their ample breathing-place. The cows by the wayside, and who are surveying the road from their pasture grounds, evidently believe that their natures have never been degraded, or their personal pride affected by any admixture of their lacteal fluid at the hands of the metropolitan milkman. They chew their cud of satisfaction as we pass, without exhibiting a fear for the presence of strangers, so common among their species who suffer the ignominy of a residence in the midst of a crowded populace. They wink, as their eyes follow us, till in looking back, we see them retreat to their pasture, leaving the frothy essence from their mouths upon the tops of the hedges, like hoar frost on an early winter morning.

We plodded on to Reigate, where the chalky cliffs and extensive fields of limestone, impart a sensation of partial blindness as you abruptly encounter the sight from the brow of the hill, with the meridian sun seething them after a heavy shower of rain. The town presented nothing to impress you with the belief that its residents had ever visited the great city.

We were nearly wet through, and by the time we reached the most business part of the town, the shades of night were creeping with a delicious twilight, gradually obscuring the spire of the Episcopal church, the only one of that form of worship the place could then boast. A couple of agricultural horses were enjoying their evening meal in front of the Green Dragon, and at the portal of that hostelry, assuming the character of a goodly pair of compasses, was the host, without his hat and coat. Probably an unnecessary piece of information, it being conceded as an established fact that that fabulous personage, *i. e.* " the oldest inhabitant," has not furnished the world with a solitary instance of an English boniface ever having been seen habited in outer garments of that nature.

Two sturdy fellows were superintending the ablution of the nether extremities of a splendid chesnut mare, whose expressive eye was turned winking an approval at the operation, while three or four of the juvenile population, paused in their conversation respecting the number of bushels of wheat to the acre Providence had in its bounty bestowed upon Farmer Stubble, to take a survey of the jaded travellers.

The pleasure derivable from certain scenes or incidents, in our career, affect us in proportion to the conclusions we can arrive at after forming a diagnosis of their usefulness, or adaptability for the several purposes of life, and if the minds of those youthful rustics could have been for an instant relieved of the bewilderment they had evidently fallen into by the sudden appearance of my friend and myself, it would not be difficult to believe that they entertained the most vague notions of our purpose and design. Petty larceny would have found few opportunities to exercise its prowess, if we had felt disposed to indulge in that fashionable weakness; for after we entered the Inn, and were enjoying our supper of bread, cheese, and ale, these inquisitive natives made numerous forays of enquiry, beguiling the early part of the evening with this congenial provincial habit, at times, in the most playful manner, landing one of their brigade in the most confused condition in the middle of the sanded floor.

Agricultural disquisitions are not particularly edifying to those whom fate destined to be ushered into life and reared towards man's estate within the precincts of great cities, it may, therefore, be readily supposed that when the usual occupants of the room began to assemble, that the quota of information we could impart on the subject, was not very extensive. It was somewhat of a relief when the landlord, for the purpose of drawing us out, went headlong into politics, in which my fellow-traveller happened to be so well skilled that we were soon perfectly at ease, and, after the roughest portion of the visitors had departed, we, in company with two congenial spirits, were invited by the boniface to a friendly glass in his private *sanctum* behind the bar.

What a cosy delightful place the bar of a country inn used to be to the tired traveller. The well polished pewter mugs depending from the brass nails garnishing the shelves, relieved here and there with bright tumblers, their thick circular pediments turned upwards, and sur mounted with large juicy lemons. The round of corned beef, what a size the ox must have been, you think, as you contemplate the huge platter of metal that seems almost to groan beneath the weight of a single joint! The buck-horned handled carver and fork, protruding from its sides, the parsley so plentifully displayed in its refreshing green to impart a zest, if any were needed, to the appetite. The home-made bread, not sparingly paraded, but of fitting dimensions to suit the most voracious desire, the pickles, also of domestic preparation; the whole surmounted by those infallible punch bowls of various sizes, from the quiet little revelry of a friend or two, to the annual Christmas cheer, when all available nature gives thanks to God for favors past, and invokes a blessing for the future.

It was midnight when the guests departed, and we ascended and descended several tortuous stairs and passages, to where we were to pass the night. The morning broke with nature's concert of feathered performers, cheerily carolling a welcome to the rising sun, each in ecstacy for the day-light, pouring forth a bright example to mellifluous mortals, who in operatic conjunction are seldom as harmonious as nature's choristers.

What a breakfast we eat too! The round of beef was a prominent performer at the feast. The smiles of the good natured landlady and her husband, who presided, had much to do with the comfort of the meal. We prepared to pursue our journey. We had serious misgivings that we had committed an act of impropriety by banqueting so lavishly at the commencement of our journey, with our limited exchequer, nevertheless proceeded to disburse. There is a rough delicacy amongst the unlettered, of conferring favors, which we not unfrequently look for in vain from those who are skilled in all the artificial refinements of luxury, education, and ease. This stalwart free-hearted boniface had listened the previous

night to our descriptions of the haunts and by-ways of
London. He had read with wonder how persons from
the country had been decoyed into the purchase of articles of apparently great value, the retailers having only
been induced to part with them from intuitive affection
they couldn't possibly repress for the purchaser, the
favored ones discovering when too late, that they had
invested about two hundred per cent. above their actual
cost. He had a boy who early in life displayed evidences
of a roving disposition which he had felt it impossible to
check, and from whom, during an absence of six years, he
had heard but once. He pitied us that we, so young,
were starting to seek, perhaps, a visionary glory — we
were welcome — very happy to see us; if ever we came
that way again, we must not forget to call, and many
more things in that delightfully awkward way in which
modesty so universally bestows a compliment. I met
this generous spirit some years afterwards. He had settled at Brighton. My professional position was very satisfactory, and I passed many pleasant hours with himself
and wife, including the smart son who had been to Australia, and amassed considerable money by the culture of
sheep.

We had calculated our chances of something turning
up, (like Micawber, though Mr. Dickens had not then
introduced that celebrated individual to an admiring
world,) from the fact that if that fashionable watering
place failed to offer us half, or the entire receipts of each
evening's performance for an unlimited period, there were
other temples of Thespis at various points along the sea
coast that would surely not be indifferent to their own
interests, nor insensible to our great dramatic skill.

Oh, delusive hope! We reached Brighton, that seat of
salt water, folly, and flirtation, two days from the time we
set out, weary, and footsore, with three shillings and nine-

pence in our pockets, and two bad cases of influenza equally divided.

We were, however, full of hope. We sought the manager next morning, and found he was full too, not only of hope — for he had been hoping on, and expected to "hope ever" — but he had, as he expressed himself, "too many bad actors already in his company, and had no desire, with bad business staring him in the face, to augment the number."

We took a stroll on the beach, where we held a council of war in relation to our future prospects. Our companion suggested that, as we were nearly financially exhausted, or "stumped," as he poetically expressed it, the most desirable plan would be to shape our course towards London. I felt inwardly of the like opinion; but my spirit was not so readily subdued, for I had determined to succeed, or perish in the attempt. We turned our steps, however, toward the point from whence we started, and enjoyed nine miles of cogitation, till we approached the delightful little town of Lewes. Here we learned, by an accident that sometimes did occur in those days of stage coaches, (we got sight of a newspaper,) that a small company, at a little town near Hastings, had been made smaller by the withdrawal of two of its members for a more extensive arena for the development of their powers. We determined to make a trial of our fortunes with the Mogul who exerted his managerial sway over the company's destiny, and when we had succeeded in delighting the inhabitants of that district, and our fame and attractiveness should reach the ears of the Brighton magnate, what ecstacy we should experience as we beheld him entering the town as rapidly as post horses could bring him, entreating and beseeching us to favor his patrons with a glimpse of our excellence, at terms to be named by ourselves.

Having settled this matter perfectly to our own satis-
action, we invested a small amount of our worldly riches,
in refreshments of as corpulent and nutritious a nature as
we could afford, and after wandering about the neighboring fields, took up our quarters on the outskirts of
the town, at a small inn, the like of which existed before
the iron monster of the rail-road closed 'em up by his
absurdly expeditious habit of never giving people time to
sleep on a journey.

The sun was waning, and its lurid glare fast travelling
out towards the sea with a diversified grandeur of color
when we came upon a rural resting place, lying in pic-
turesque beauty within the embraces of a cluster of large
elm trees.   The dwelling had no pretensions to architectural propriety, being entirely independent of any known
order, past or present, but there was a solid somnolent
satisfaction about it as if it would say, " Here friend, you
have good cheer, sweetened with a hearty welcome,"
which at once ingratiated itself into your good opinion.
A picture of the venerable uncle Toby, armed with his
pipe and foaming pitcher of ale, most boldly rendered by
the artist, swung upon the summit of a post, the lower
portion of which had suffered considerably by the impatience of the equine customers who had broken and
devoured its splinters, doubtless for the purpose of assisting digestion while waiting for their further allowance of
fodder.

A drowsy looking pony, profusely supplied with hair
about the legs, but lamentably deficient of that hirsute
luxury as regards the tail, was thus busily engaged as we
approached the spot.   Two or three teamsters were
smoking, and gaily preparing their cattle in order to their
departure, while the landlady — brilliant in cap trim-
mings — was within the porch to bid them an adieu.
The large black dog, who lay beside the horse trough,

casually glanced at us, as if he would say, "If you are in search of a first-class place for comfort, you've hit it this time," and the thrush hanging in his wicker-work tenement, poured forth his evening song with true content and happiness. The latticed windows of the sleeping rooms peeped out in various forms through the thickly clustered ivy in which the house seemed imbedded, and the smoke from the wood fire in the kitchen curled in fantastic designs, diffusing itself upwards amongst its native element, the trees.

If a man may be known by the company he keeps, the resources of his exchequer may, with quite as good a reason, philosophically, be fathomed, by the aspect of his exterior. It will be willingly conceded by the writer that the appearance of himself and friend was not such as to inspire the beholder with the conviction that we possessed a superfluity of the circulating medium at whose shrine all nature are, more or less, willing to bow.

The customary peregrinators who may be said to "live on the road," are easily distinguished by the practised observer; but an occasional adventurer turns up, now and then, whose purpose or destination will harass the mind of the most critical. It was our fate to considerably puzzle the shrewdness of the worthy landlady as we passed into the inn, requesting to be accommodated for the night.

CHAPTER IV.

" And should she thus be stolen away from you,
It would be much vexation to your age."
—Two Gentlemen of Verona. Act 8. *Scene* 1.

A VERY old man was seated beside the fire-place in the taproom, watching a black saucepan formed like a funnel, and for the most part imbedded in a pile of burning wood. He raised his head at our approach, returning his gaze upon the saucepan, which speedily began to simmer. He was plainly but comfortably habited in a long blue coat, of a rather antique date, with capacious side-pockets, a mixture vest, grey breeches and stockings, with very thick shoes, perfectly innocent of blacking, and secured to the instep by thongs of leather.

A shock-headed boy in velveteen, his shirt sleeves rolled up above the elbows, placed before him a long clay-pipe, and screw, or paper, of tobacco, and after emptying the warm porter into a pewter pot upon the table, withdrew to light up the premises for the evening.

" Good evening, Jacob," was the first sound that broke the silence, after the departure of this rustic retainer. The salutation came from a fine looking young man of some twenty-six summers, dressed in a shooting costume, his gaiters swelling almost to bursting with their well developed legs. Carelessly throwing his hat upon the table, he rang the bell, and ordered, of the buxom damsel who responded to the summons, a mug of ale and a crust

' of bread and cheese, requesting as a personal favor, that the Hebe who was to present the same would, prior to its delivery, cast one of her sweetest glances into the measure, in order to render it more palatable and delicious.

Pending the arrival of this refreshment, the young man availed himself of the customary forlorn hope of the British subject, when in need of a matter for discussion, and asserted it as his firm conviction that the then state of the weather was of the precise kind to suit the agricultural interest in that section of the country, being the only instance on record, within the writer's personal experience, wherein that numerous class have admitted the receipt of a satisfactory sample of the season's consignments.

The order for his repast was speedily fulfilled, and while in course of liquidation, afforded a favorable opportunity to express homage to beauty, the recipient coyly rallying with a charge of female artifice replete with resignation and approval.

The old man had finished his pipe, and now rose to depart; taking his hat and cane, he bowed an adieu, and quitted the room.

"A very fine looking old gentleman," I ventured to remark, as soon as he was fully out of hearing.

"Yes, pretty much so," was the rejoinder. "Not acquainted with him, s'pose?"

"Oh, dear no! we are strangers in this part of the country, and are on our way to Hastings. For my part I should think, if I were to take the liberty of forming a judgment, that he is better adapted for a listener, than a dispenser of knowledge."

"Aye, likely! likely!" responded the countryman. "He's lived here a good many years, old Jacob has; every body likes him on account of his curious history."

"Indeed! Has he endured hardships in defence of an

ungrateful country, and grown weary of presenting his claims to the notice of its insolent officials? "

"Oh, no! Would you like to hear his story? It's not a very long one."

"Much," I answered.

"Well then, let us fill up, and start fair." Our mugs were replenished, and after a repetition of the similar conduct before described, not in the least degree abridged or modified, he took a hearty draught, and composed himself to give us the

STORY OF JACOB MILLET.

"The night was mighty cold, when the guard's horn was heard playing one of its favorite tunes, descending the hill from London. I can only just remember the time; for I was not much above ten years old when Jacob Millet arrived here, as outside passenger on the Hope coach, dashing up to the inn in its usual jaunty style, with its expert coachman and musical guard. The Hope did all the best business; the squire and all his folks round the neighborhood, when they didn't use their own teams, used to patronize it. Jacob was rather a dashing chap, even at that time; but he seems to me to have grown old very rapidly, since, that is to say, within the last four or five years. Nothing particular was observed in his manner or appearance. At the time he alighted, he requested some one to show him to a room where he could take supper and pass the night. The doors of the coffee-room were open, and the customary meal smoking hot, awaiting the arrival of passengers — for the coach always supped here — but he refused to enter it; and, even preferred to wait till a fire was kindled in an upper chamber, sauntering up and down the road till the preparations were completed.

"The folks in the place who waited on him, couldn't

help noticing that he was much troubled in his mind and manner. When he retired to bed he was restless, and was distinctly heard pacing his room at short intervals throughout the night.

"In the morning there was no change in the style of his conduct from the previous night, except asking a few questions about the time the Brighton coaches passed. It was nearly a week before anything happened worth noticing; but at the end of that time, he received a letter which seemed to excite him terribly. He was out constantly on the road, and eagerly scrutinizing the passengers while the coaches changed horses. Well, sir, just as it was getting dark on a Wednesday night, the mail came rattling up with those celebrated four greys — thorough blood they were too, and very much admired. Folks used to say it was a pleasure to sit behind such cattle — as a dashing, handsome-looking man alighted from the inside, Jacob started and made a desperate blow at him with a pretty stout cudgel he always carried.

"The man reeled as soon as struck, and went in to defend himself; but Jacob was too quick for him, and kept following him up towards the coach-door, for which he tried to make. Loud and piercing shrieks were heard from a female, who was endeavoring to assist the beaten man into the vehicle. Scarcely a word was uttered during the time, except in broken sentences, such as villain! deceiver! false friend! and the like. The beaten man scrambled with difficulty into the coach, and after the ostlers had got the restive cattle a little quieted, the coachman let 'em have their heads, and away they started. You may be sure the neighborhood was terribly agitated; all manner of rumors were afloat as to the cause of the quarrel, and the man who used to do all the news at that time, for the Brighton paper, gave a very animated description of the whole affair, as from an eye-witness, how Jacob had charged the man, who was represented as holding a very fine office under government, with running away with his wife, and forging his name for some large amounts; how the lady, whose personal appearance was fully described, had sprung from the coach and thrown herself between them, calling for help; how she fainted, and was carried into the inn, and was brought to her senses by the worthy landlady and her charming daughter; how it took the coachman, guard, and four stablemen to prevent Jacob inflicting more punishment upon the destroyer of his domestic peace, who lay covered with blood in the middle of the high road, from whence he was removed with difficulty to the coach, where the lady was afterwards placed upon two feather pillows; that Jacob was with great difficulty dissuaded from mounting a swift horse and following in pursuit. It all ended with a perfect history of the private affairs of all the parties from their youth, with several very amusing incidents which befel the lady while at a fashionable school in the south of France; the amount of dower her husband received with her, the name of the firm where he kept his banking account, and every particular thing that was like to interest the reader, which everybody at a distance fully believed, while it was well known here that on the night of the occurrence, the writer of it had been taken home by one of the waiters in the Blue Lion, very much intoxicated, after enjoying the good cheer of the annual feast of the churchwardens, who met to devise means and raise funds for the benefit of the poor during the following winter.

"In a few days Jacob went to London, and remained for about two months; when he returned, he was so dejected and unhappy, that his strength gave way, and was followed by a violent fit of illness, which confined him to his bed for a long time. In his wanderings he uttered charges of great ingratitude against some one that had basely wronged him ; the landlady, who watched him with most unceasing care, bore with his whims, and fancies, to such an extent, that he couldn't help confiding to her one evening, the story of his grief.

"Then he told her how he had lost his wife many years ago, leaving him with an only child — a daughter — how much he doated on her ; how he had expended large sums of money on her education ; how she had, in the bloom of youth, listened to the addresses of one who was a *roue*, and unworthy of her. How she had eloped with him ; how they were on their way to London, when he surprised them ; how, when he had discovered the cheat the seducer had played upon her, she had died while giving birth to a child, leaving him solitary and alone in the world. He admitted that he had never met with so much disinterested friendship as he did here at the hands of the landlady, and he would feel happier to locate himself near such kind and considerate people for the rest of his days.

" He took a cottage, (the one just over the hill,) where he beguiled his time, attended by a single servant, digging and planting in his little garden, or playing on the violincello, on which instrument he is a very skillful performer. He strictly enjoined the landlady, when he found, by the questions she would occasionally put to him, that he had, in a moment of thoughtlessness been betrayed into a recital of his story, that she must consider it in the light of a secret, and never reveal it to any one. It oozed out, however, somehow, ' women are not good hands at keeping a secret, you know, sir.' And here old Jacob comes every evening to take his warm ale, and pipe of tobacco, and seems to have little spirit for any other pastime, save his passion for music.

" Taking his hat, he wished us a good night, pausing at the door with a request that, if we should see Jacob again, we wouldn't mention that he had dropped a hint about the matter, because, ' It is a secret you know.' "

CHAPTER V.

" For beauty is a witch,
Against whose charms faith melteth into blood."
—*Much Ado.*　*Act 2.*　*Scene 1.*

THE BEAUTY OF THE INN.

SHALL I ever forget the snowy whiteness of my bed, and its appurtenances? Much less shall I ever forget the radiant beauty of the landlord's daughter, who prepared, with her own fair hands, a delicious supper of ham and eggs in the private sanctum behind the bar, and shall I ever forget how much I was struck with this maiden, her rosy lips, and the transparent texture of her skin, glowing with health such as the pure country air only can impart to those who pass their time continually inhaling its invigorating perfume? The recollection haunts me still. I remember I would have offered to marry her on the spot, if my exchequer could have warranted me in indulging in such an expensive luxury!

What a night I passed! Sleep was out of the question; but when I did get into a state of unconsciousness, I had an insane notion of stealing cautiously to where her aged father slumbered, depriving him of his brief existence, carrying off his charming daughter to some remote Indian settlement, where to pass the honey-moon on buffalo humps, with bear-steaks for Sundays, would have been the *acme* of human felicity.

At length I fell into a profound, unmistakable sleep, and believing I had carried my design into execution, and while in the act of masticating my first meal of buffalo, the war cry of justice came howling down upon me, tear-ing me with a fiendish triumph from the arms of my lady love, and consigning me without remorse to the chilling embrace of the county gaol, on a charge of murder and abduction.

I felt certain I had heard the tramp of the horses that were to convey me to a boat that should return the idol of my soul to the paternal roof, and myself to the less pleasing dwelling above mentioned; and I breathed vengeance on the cruel heads of those who could, in spite of entreaties, remorselessly tear asunder such fond, such doting natures, and I uttered imprecations of a most uncomplimentary-character against the world in general, and my pursuers in particular. Nay, I even, in the excess of my rage and indignation, seized a tomahawk and felled the most athletic among them to the earth, planting my foot upon his prostrate form with the satisfaction of a conqueror against one of an adverse tribe, and would have devoured him on the spot, if my early taste for luxuries had not rendered such savory nourishment unpalatable.

This was my frame of mind as morning dawned. It may, therefore, be readily understood my feelings were not in a very quiescent condition, as I believed I had duly qualified myself for an illustration of capital punishment, when I was suddenly aroused by my companion to the fact that he regarded me as a public nuisance, and found it impossible to sleep in the same room with one who didn't enjoy his repose like a decent Christian. Before I had time to dispute or question this conclusion, we were summoned to breakfast.

Our toilet was not very extravagant. It was soon completed, and while waiting to be apprized that the morning meal was on the table, I sauntered to the back of the inn, and there leaned, in what I conceived to be a very graceful attitude, against the pump, gazing most

2

earnestly at the windows of the second story, the top one
in this particular instance, not from any known conviction
that my soul's idol occupied one of those apartments,
but from an intuitive belief I have always entertained
that all landlords' pretty daughters sleep in the back
parts of inns — probably placed there by a dispensation
of Providence, to be ready for an elopement without being
observed by the private watchman or legally qualified
guardian of the public peace.

I had not been long in contemplation when my ears
were assailed with the following colloquy :

"Betty !"

"Yes, Miss."

"Is them two London chaps up yet?"

"Yes, Miss: I seed one on 'em in the coffee-room just
now."

I was all attention. She was surely going to make a
confidant of the domestic, and confess the impression that
I had made upon her susceptible nature, when she proceeded:

"I hope they ain't stole nothing, and runned away
with it. It's a pity somebody don't send 'em up to town,
to their friends; for I do think they are respectable
chaps — but the one in the drab coat, is the biggest fool
I ever did see. Last night I gave 'em both some supper,
'cause they looked so very wretched, and all the time
that chap was eating it, he was looking at me in the
spoonest way you ever did see. I was watching him
through the looking-glass over the fire-place. I thought
I should have died with laughing at the fool! Men must
be scarce indeed, for me to fancy such a scarecrow sort
of chap as that."

My self-esteem sank a long way below zero immediately upon hearing this distressing admission, and as I
shrank away from the spot, felt an inward conviction

that I might then and there be purchased like goods out of season, at an alarming sacrifice! I told this tale afterwards, but did my travelling-companion the honor of making him the hero of the story.

"THE COUNTRY MANAGER."

WE soon took a hasty farewell, and proceeded on our journey. By dint of some exertion, we reached the location we proposed to astonish, at about five o'clock in the afternoon, and immediately sought the manager. The handmaiden who admitted us to a small, but particularly neat looking cottage, inflicted another wound upon our feelings, by announcing us as "two boys," as wanted to see the manager. We were ushered into the presence of "the last glimmer of the great Kemble and Siddonian era," as he used to designate himself, and shall not be going far out of the course of my narrative, if I give the reader some account of his appearance and habits.

In person he was large, in appearance benevolent. In height he had as much as most men can boast of, while in rotundity he possessed more than actors with tragic proclivities care to be encumbered with. Not to be ungenerous, he was what is usually designated as a fat, podgy man. In fact, his circumference had increased so much within the last few years, that he found himself at times subjected to impertinent remarks from some of the choice spirits among the audience who couldn't bear with his increasing bulk in the heroes of the Shaksperian drama, and who would insinuate as much from the pit of the theatre, when he was endeavoring to illustrate the last moments of the poet's choicest creations.

His face was ruddy, almost amounting to a purple hue; even in its quiescent state, when under the influence of artistic inspiration, it assumed a cerulean intensity positively distressing to witness.

His costume was airy, and worn with a negligence which ever distinguishes great master minds from the common every day mortals, being a mixture of the dramatic with the social, so happily blended that the combination was rather agreeable than otherwise. His feet were encased in slippers of purple velvet, such as the monarchs of tragedy are wont to indulge in. His pantaloons were of a pepper and salt color, with a larger proportion of the latter seasoning than the former. The buttons, or fastenings with which they were moored to his waist, had long ago burst from their anchorage, and the canvas that had originally aided in their security, now hung from their apertures with a forlorn aspect of untidiness and neglect. His linen might have impressed the casual observer with the conviction that a heavy tax had been most remorselessly and suddenly placed upon soap, whereby his acquaintanceship with that necessary article of domestic consumption had been, in consequence of his very limited exchequer, for a length of time suspended.

Such was the manager, as he sat in a large easy chair, indulging in the luxury of a pipe of huge dimensions, with mountings of silver, a plate of which precious metal acquainted the curious in such matters, that the same had been presented on the interesting occasion of his benefit, and performance of "Octavian," by a few admirers, in testimony of his great worth as a man, and his unapproachable ability as an artist.

His peculiarity was that he had a veneration for ancient tragedy, which nothing could subdue. I have seen him enact "Cato," in the play of that name, to only a few shillings, with a vigor quite astonishing! But to our interview. The manager admitted, and he did so with great regret, that his business was not at that time profitable — for the season was antagonistic to the best interests of the drama. The parliament were in session in London, and consequently many of his wealthy patrons, some of whose names you will find inscribed here, said he, pushing the pipe towards us, were attending to their duties as guardians of the rights of their constituents; and he was further grieved to admit, as a result thereof, that his income did not at present keep pace with his outlay; therefore, it behoved all lovers of the true and classic drama, among whom he was proud to name himself, to put their shoulders to the wheel, in order to propel the dramatic vehicle into the haven of safety.

He was exceedingly fond of flattery as regarded his position as a manager and actor, and so proud of being known as the former, that he invariably caused to be printed in significant type, at the head of each play-bill, " Sole proprietor, Mr. ——."

We speedily came to business. He did want artists, he said, with a strong emphasis on the last word; inquired what we could do, where we had come from, and what salary we expected to receive. We assured him that we were in possession of the usual modicum of talent necessary for the most faithful delineation of any and every species of character, within the range of the ancient, or modern drama, which is generally the impression entertained by novices, in a profession of which they are totally ignorant; that we were from London — had been at Brighton — but didn't care much about effecting an engagement there, had preferred seeing him, knowing the interest he took in the proper cultivation of his art, and would be happy to place ourselves at his disposal, with a view to progressive excellence, which we were satisfied could no where be so well and efficiently attained as at his establishment, and under his personal supervision. This tickled him amazingly; he laid down his pipe and gave a cough that had a tone of satisfaction about it. As

to emolument, we left that entirely to him, and would
readily be guided by his better and more mature judgment, and place ourselves at once at his disposal.

The bargain was speedily completed : we were to receive
fifteen shillings sterling per week each, and commence
operations at once, if we thought, after partaking of a
little refreshment, we could manage to play that evening,
we would extricate him from a most embarrassing dilemma. Of course we could! Could I play "old Norval,"
in "Douglas?" and "Sir Jacob Jollop," in the "Mayor
of Garrat?" and could my companion go on for "Lord
Randolph?"

My vanity felt a sudden and a chilling check when I
heard the proposition! "*Young* Norval," I had long
believed I could distance all competitors in, but the parent
of that young gentleman, with my youthful ardor and
juvenile bearing, was a blow I was not prepared for.

As for the part in the farce, the very idea made me
feel as if I had swallowed a dose of his namesake. However, I was compelled to yield, and after partaking of the
proposed refreshments, we started to find some economic
dwelling place, with a promise to be prepared for action
in the evening.

The appearance of the theatre was somewhat startling,
being extremely primitive, both in design and decoration.
Four walls, or sides, there were to be sure; but in the
auditorium, one end seemed to have had a piece unceremoniously lopped off in such an ungraceful manner that
it entirely destroyed its identification for any specific
purpose. It was spacious enough to accommodate a very
considerable number of persons ; but either the merit of
the performances were too æsthetic for the matter of fact
inhabitants of the district, or they entertained an enmity
towards our exertions, and remained away in consequence.
Certain it is, its capacity for large numbers was never
sorely tested by the generous multitude.

I had, prior to the rising of the curtain, on this, our opening night, signified to the manager a distaste that I should be called upon to represent a character very much below the standard of histrionic consequence in which I felt assured nature had destined me to occupy amongst the great names of dramatic history; but was somewhat appeased by the knowledge that he, the manager, had once reduced himself to a secondary position, and enacted "Macduff," to Edmund Kean's "Macbeth," who was at the time playing an engagement at one of his city houses, as he called theatres in towns of any magnitude, and this too in a locality where he was well known and appreciated as the only living "Thane of Cawdor," that had received the unqualified plaudits of an audience, distinguished for its poetic and literary attainments; in proof whereof the editor of the *Snifflebury Chronicle*, a writer with a mind finely tempered to the impressions of the most delicate manipulations of art, had considered the matter of such vital importance, that he devoted an entire column of his paper to an analysis of the two interpretations of the character, approving Mr. Kean's rendition in many places; but for subtlety of purpose, with a scholarly delineation of the idiosyncrasies of the part, yielded the palm to the worthy manager, than whom no man was socially and professionally more respected.

We got along pretty well with the performance, considering that we didn't know the words of the author, but substituted something of our own when we were at fault. The dressing-room was in the cellar under the dramatic temple, the which had in its early history been used as a malt-house, and was still tenanted by some of its original settlers, "the rats," who must have keenly felt the altered destinies of the establishment.

The convenience for the operations of the toilet were not of a very extensive or costly description; and as no member of the company boasted the possession of a mirror, we painted our faces over a bucket of clear water.

It would be impossible to recount a tithe of the troubles and difficulties that the tyro in the dramatic art had to pass through in those days, and it might appear strange how young men of tolerable education, and friends willing to assist them, as many of us had, should encounter such scenes; but such is the infatuation, or call it what you will, of the lovers of the drama, that any one of us would have passed through any description of misery, rather than our friends should awake to the conviction that we were not on the high road to histrionic excellence.

One of our company gave us the following anecdote that had occurred in his presence; and as it will afford a good illustration of the general style of theatres of that class, it will serve as a fair sample. "Chance threw me," said he, "in the way of L——, the celebrated strolling manager, who was about opening at Walton in Surrey. He proposed to us a sharing scheme, with the stipulation of two shares for himself as manager. This we agreed to, and on the following day we started for this charming village, and the hills over which we trudged echoed again with the speeches we expected would electrify the good people of Walton.

"The appearance of the theatre rather damped our ardor. It was nearly outside the town, in a very tumble-downish kind of a barn, in the yard of the Plough inn. The way to the stage door was through a cow-yard, and the door itself was a hole barely three feet square, cut on purpose, which led to a trap-door that brought you at once on the upper corner R. H. of the stage.

"The stage itself was about eighteen feet wide, eleven feet long, and eight feet high. The proscenium of colored paper took off five feet on each side, so that the actual stage was only about eight feet wide. The audience part was very dilapidated, but very extensive, thronged with a number of wide seats, and parted off into pit and gallery by a long pole. The boxes were divided from the pit by a long strip of canvas, ornamented by numerous harps, Apollos, and other tasteful designs, illustrative of the muses. The foot-lights consisted of ten dazzling halos of tallow candles, eight to the pound. The scenes were painted on tick, (I mean the materials for coloring etc. were obtained on credit,) and they consisted of a splendid modern chamber, excessively pink in tone; on the reverse, a kitchen equally ingenious in color and design, and a representation of a wood in a frantic state of exuberant foliage, laid on with no sparing or niggardly hand upon the back wall. The wings were movable, and corresponded with the proscenium; flies · or borders we had none, so there was little chance of the roof taking fire from the carelessness of scene-shifters. It was light and airy in consequence of several tiles being missing. The orchestra consisted of a blind fiddler, a trumpet, and a drum.

"After working for about a week, the theatre was completed, the actors perfect, and the town well billed. The opening play was Richard the Third; the night arrived, and the house was full to overflowing.

"The play proceeded quite satisfactorily till the fight, in the fifth act, between Richard and Richmond. In consequence of the very contracted space, it was absolutely necessary to pursue the combat from the top to the bottom of the stage, and while Richard was driving Richmond up with a splendid show of head blows, he (Richmond) suddenly vanished from the sight of Richard, and the audience.

"In vain did the crook-backed tyrant call for Richmond to come on, if it was only to kill him. No! Richmond

2*

was too much disconcerted by his sudden mishap, and
Richard determined not to be cut out of his die, cast
himself on his own sword, spoke his speech and expired.

"The manager of whom I speak, and whose description
is here attempted, was a man of the most liberal principles, with an affection for his company that amounted
almost to parental solicitude. He was extremely susceptible to grief, therefore was often the victim of a distressing recital, related for no other purpose than to act upon
his sympathetic nature. He was afflicted with periodical
attacks of gout, and occasionally, when recovering from
that distressing malady, would imbibe a little too much
stimulant; then it was no difficult matter to deluge him
with tears with a well-timed and heart-rending story.
He was seated one evening in a portion of the building
facetiously termed the 'green room' just recovering
from one of his attacks of gout, and had evidently indulged in alcoholic fluid during the day. The play in
course of representation was the 'Stranger,' at which
he was shedding tears most copiously; in fact he was
what might not inaptly be termed, 'crying drunk.'
'Good heavens,' said I 'Mr.——can anything have happened?' 'No,' said he, wishing to disguise his real condition, 'but I am always thus affected whenever that
pathetic piece, the "Stranger," is performed.' 'Yes,' said
I, 'but it surely cannot distress you so much when you are
not witnessing the representation.' 'What does that matter,' returned he bursting out into a fresh flood of tears.
'Can't I conceive what is going forward?'"

CHAPTER VI.

"I am Sir Oracle, and when I ope my mouth let no dog bark."
—*Merchant of Venice. Act 1. Scene 1.*

THE aspirant for dramatic fame will peruse with wonder, not unmixed with incredulity, the incidents related in the previous chapters, of the primitiveness of the places set apart for the exposition of the drama in England. There is scarcely a town of any pretensions in America, that is not well provided with a properly appointed hall, or lecture room, with ample facility for some kind of dramatic performance. The peculiarities of some of the members of their several companies will appear in due course in these pages.

The successive changes consequent on the attempt to ascend the several rounds of the ladder of fame in every profession, particularly those of an intellectual character, bear such a similarity to each other, that it would be a useless task to enumerate them at every step upward toward the goal of excellence! Therefore the author of these pages may be pardoned if he abstain from boring the reader with every little incident of his career, except to touch upon those which present features of a nature peculiar, or in any way unusual. It is, however, needless to say, that the life of an actor presents a very dissimilar aspect from the impression entertained of it by the public at large. To the auditor, and casual observer, it is an avocation of the most alluring kind, indeed some minds cannot resist the temptation of believing that the natures of actors and actresses assimilate themselves to the peculiar temperament of the parts they represent.

One particular instance in support of this fact was during his masterly performance of Luke, in "Riches" by Edmund Kean. A lady of great wealth, who had regularly attended all that fine actor's representations, became so appalled by the hideousness of the picture, that she immediately took a distaste for the man, and had a codicil inserted in her will rescinding a handsome legacy she had bequeathed him as some acknowledgment of the pleasure she had derived from his previous unapproachable efforts.

Many of the drama's patrons are fully persuaded in their our minds that the hero and heroine of the play have, or entertain some affinity of the elements towards each other they so graphically express in their professional vocation. It is needless to say this is a great mistake; indeed, I have met with several cases where the sexes have most happily commingled professionally their adoration for each other; but, who never exchanged the salutation of a vocal compliment, from a settled antipathy they could not suppress. True, there are instances where marriages, and a long life of happiness, have resulted from such an association, but they are certainly not more frequent than might arise from the mixing of the sexes in any other close proximity of business necessity.

THE ORACLE OF THE VILLAGE.

Every town, village, or hamlet, however limited its population, can proudly boast of the possession of some master spirits in matters of art and politics, the former most particularly, who exercise an influence on those who surround them at their social gatherings. They are the oracles who proclaim to the little world in which they move, their plan for the amendment of the constitution under which they enjoy their proud position in the scale of civilized nations. Who regulate the quality and number of ounces avoirdupois of solid food necessary, upon scientific principles, for sustaining the pauper population in such a condition as will inevitably compel them, in order to satisfy the cravings of exhausted nature, to pause ere they accept the munificence of parish accommodation!

They not unfrequently enjoy the proud distinction of having the pages of the *Meagreville Gazette* placed entirely at their disposal in all matters of public interest, assign causes for the conduct of officials for whose positions they have been unsuccessful candidates; and readily play the jackal to assuage the sufferings of some wounded lion who has been drawn into a conflict with public opinion, entirely through their own instrumentality.

It is not to be expected that a dramatic company who may pay brief visits to one or other of these places, can easily escape being taken under the special care of one of these ogres, whenever opportunity presents itself. It was my fortune to meet with a capital specimen, at a town of small significance in the county of Lancashire. He was a good type of the class who desire to regulate the internal business of the theatre according to his own infallible dicta. He was a man of commanding presence, a brewer by trade, and had once seen Mrs. Siddons, (in the street.)

The party consisted of the brewer above named, the postmaster of the town, the tailor, who also added the stationery and millinery business, (the two latter presided over by his wife,) the landlord of the Goose and Gridiron, a maltster of plethoric pocket and person, a commercial traveller, attached to a London glass firm, who had seen something of the drama, and a sallow-faced man who acted as parish clerk of the church, and who was chiefly remarkable for extreme baldness, and a capacity for hot drinks.

The company had not been long assembled before the *Oracle* was intruded upon in the middle of a learned disquisition on a past political crisis, by the addition of the writer and the gentleman who assumed the position of principal tragedian to the theatre. Our presence threw a sudden gloom upon the scene, but the Oracle speedily rallied, and after asking a common-place question or two relative to the nature of the patronage bestowed upon our efforts by the public of the town and neighborhood, proposed as a personal obligation, that our friend should favor the company with an exhibition of his vocal powers. The delineator of the poet's choicest effusions looked with a scornful aspect at the mention of such a profanation, and gave a stern, and positive refusal. In this case the tragedian was never addicted to vocalization, though it is not an uncommon case to find actors of the serious drama the most jovial and entertaining in social gatherings.

The tailor came to the rescue, and expressed the pleasure he had derived from being present at our performance of " Venice Preserved " the previous evening. He also attempted an analysis of the representation of " King Lear " he had once seen in London; though he couldn't tax his memory with the name of the theatre in which the same was acted, but he particularly remembered it from the desperate conflict in the very last scene between the King and a man in armor who conquered his majesty, and who didn't make his appearance till the thing was nearly all over; he also considered the scene very good where the King fancies he saw the daggers hanging in the air, with which he had previously killed a king whose throne he wanted to occupy, and was sadly troubled with a guilty conscience, and a wicked woman for a wife. Proving incontestibly that the name of the building in which he beheld this multiplicity of events transpire, and the incidents connected therewith, was not very clearly registered upon the tablets of a memory distinguished for its reliability.

"Sir," said the Oracle, "the drama is a great moral engine for the advancement of the human species. There are some pretty keen judges of good playing here, sir, I assure you. Indifferent acting may do for London, Liverpool, or Manchester, but I can tell you there is a fine, pure taste for the proper thing in this town."

"Aye," chimed in the parish clerk, he believed there was, when they really gave 'em anything good, not that he had ever seen much of tragedy himself; but he always made one of the Rev. Mr. Sniffin's party, and took charge of two of the children, when the singers with their faces blacked came along; or the learned dogs; and a pig that could spell out the name of any of the company, which he thought was very clever, and seemed to afford a great deal of satisfaction.

The landlord considered the downfall of the drama was to be attributed to the vanity of actors, who thought too much of what they called position. Now, for his part, he couldn't see what difference it could make in the quality of the parts they played ; that's what he had always been given to understand by what he had read in the papers, some of which came out pretty strong upon the subject. One case he recollected, a year or two ago, wherein a manager had refused to pay the salary of a member of his company because he declined to appear in a style of character for which he was not engaged.

The Oracle here broke in with—

"Yes, yes, it is a notorious fact, and I explained it fully in an essay I did some three or four years since, for the *Monthly Gooseberrybush,* a very ably edited work on fashion and the arts. I had hoped to have broken through the absurdity, for the article was very elaborate, and embraced all the points of the subject thoroughly, and, I believe, was extensively read, but it's a deeply rooted evil, sir, and will take a long time to eradicate."

" Yes, sir," said the tragedian, who had been writhing for some minutes, " it has existed for some time — if we believe the press, or take their definition of a matter which doesn't, to my thinking, exactly concern them,— ever since the time of Garrick, who refused to play Hotspur more than once, because he found Quin's Falstaff eclipsed him. I have been nearly twenty years, sir, in the profession, and remember very few instances wherein I have not been dealt unjustly by, by the manager. I once gave great offence, because I declined to appear as Harlequin in a pantomime, merely to gratify his desire to have my name in the bill of performance; the press of course took it up, and my private business soon became a matter of public censure. Very few can realize the discrimination necessary to a profitable position in the profession. The world is too ready to condemn an actor who objects to appear in characters which he may consider unfitted for his style or temperament, on the plea that they have a right to demand that the plays presented should be cast in the strongest possible manner, irrespective of the claims of the artist to his, or her, definite position, in obedience to the terms of their agreement. I am satisfied that there are very few of our professional brethren who would not be ready, and willing, to cheerfully assist in the representation of parts out of their proper calibre, if their pecuniary position would not be affected thereby; but when it is notorious, that the paying portion of the public, with very few exceptions, regard those who enact the prominent characters as the most talented of the company, it must be obvious that a system such as this, if persevered in, would soon reduce the market value of the individual, who would thus have to suffer for the perpetuation of a principle in which the manager himself is never ambitious to become a shining example.

"There are rules and forms of government in all positions of life. We understand those appertaining to our craft as well as the physician, the lawyer, or the printer; and surely no one would expect an editor, who was retained in an establishment for writing leaders, to distribute copies of the paper to the several subscribers. Yet this is not more unreasonable than some of the requests frequently made in reference to us; nay more, we are even sometimes elevated to the dignity of a partnership when a sacrifice is to be made in times of distress. The actors are expected and compelled,— or quit the scene of their occupation, which they are seldom able from lack of funds to do,— to make a reduction in their incomes in order to shield the manager from loss; but the business unity never extends to a moiety of the profits in times of commercial prosperity, or even the liquidation of a previous defalcation. This, I admit, is not always the case where managers have been, or are themselves, members of the profession, but with those who embark in the *sale of the drama*, as they would a branch of trade, for the sole purpose of acquiring means; their ignorance and selfishness is akin to their love of gain. Why, sir, I once knew a man who was connected with a profitable theatre in the metropolis of the country, who positively refused to accept a play tendered him, assigning as his reason, that he didn't like it, it was too much like Shakspeare."

The traveller here expressed his belief that our friend had defined his position in a thoroughly business-like manner; and positively refused to permit the subject to be further discussed till he had done himself the pleasure of contributing towards the hilariousness of the entertainment by becoming responsible for a repetition of bumpers to the entire party. A proposition in which the landlord, with that alacrity for which his class are distinguished when there is a goodly profit to be acquired by the operation, readily concurred, by conforming to the request with an amount of expedition extremely praiseworthy for a person of his corporeal capacity.

"There is a point that has always puzzled me," continued the traveller, when the company had expressed their acknowledgments to the donor of the feast, "I have frequently met with most flattering notices of persons of whose superior ability I had never heard; and when I have seen them could never discover a scintillation of the merit the gentlemen of the press had led me to expect. Now, if the authors of these puffs, for they are nothing less, either have not the knowledge of the drama necessary to write a sound, and scholarly article upon the subject; or having it, do not exercise it, why will they always assume a paramount dictatorship over the actor who has made his profession a matter of business and study for years?"

"I think I can enlighten you, sir, a little upon that subject," said the tragedian, just as the Oracle was endeavoring to plunge into an explanation.

"Newspapers have frequently a job printing office attached to their business, and many persons who think it desirable to try their fortunes as features, or stars, as they are usually termed, are very liberal in their patronage; upon the principle that it is money profitably expended, as they will be sure to get lengthy notices in the paper, which they can dispatch to the next town or city, prior to their appearance there. They will even carry their system to such an extent that I, myself, knew an instance where a conscientious reviewer, who knew more than the ordinary class of writers, penned two, or three severe articles on the style of a performance he considered not entitled to approval; when he was met by a request in writing from the injured party to amend his style of criticism, as they had claims upon the establishment for long notices of the most eulogistic character. Upon declining to have his department supervised either by right or intimidation, he was met by the proprietor of the paper, who readily admitted all he had stated in reference to the worthlessness of the performances, that he could speak from personal experience, for he had once sat out a representation, with no desire to repeat the infliction; 'but we receive a large amount per annum for printing their bills and posters, it is a good advertisement for us apart from the profit we derive, because it exhibits our work in distant cities and places where it would never otherwise be seen; therefore all we can do is to push their interest in every way, regardless of truth.' The gentleman was obliged to retire from the department which treated upon theatricals, rather than appear to indite what he knew to be false."

The company all expressed their surprise at this system of conducting business; and the tragedian becoming, under the influence of argument, more and more sensitive to the cruel acts of tyranny and injustice levelled at his race, cited the incident of Kean's distress at some articles in a London paper denunciatory of his acting, to Mrs. Garrick, who advised him to spare himself the pain of any annoyance, and for the future to do as David did, i. e. " write the notices himself."

"And she was right, gentlemen! it is the only way to have them done properly, take my word for it."

We parted with the Oracle, whose massive mind has doubtless long ere this bequeathed to an admiring pub-

lic his views of the base ingratitude of two members of
a profession he had striven, (with a devotion almost
amounting to impiety) to elevate in the scale of art and
social usefulness, but whose distaste for literary guardianship have placed them beyond the conviction of well-
tried experience and intellectual brotherhood.

CHAPTER VII.

"And let those that play your clowns speak no more than is set down for them."
— *Hamlet. Act* 3. *Scene* 2.

STORIES innumerable are told of *serious* dilemmas into which *comic* actors are, from lack of numbers, in small companies, occasionally thrust; but we know of nothing more ludicrous than the following. The affair happened some time prior to the date of my acquaintance with its hero, but among all the extraordinary beings it has been my lot to encounter in all my Thespian wanderings, none certainly exceeded Berry, "facetious Tom Berry." ·

Berry was one of those light-hearted originals that occasionally cross our path during our journey through this world of pleasures and disappointments — well educated, but of an unsettled disposition. He embraced the profession of the stage very early in life. His first attempts were marked with tolerable success; but finding practice necessary, he was very properly advised by a theatrical friend to place his foot upon the lowest round of the ladder. He took his friend's advice, and after much trouble accepted an engagement at the Haymarket Theatre, London, then under the management of Morris, for general business.

He remained there six seasons, when change of management threw him on his own resources. This was in the season of 1836. Barnet of the Oxford circuit was in London engaging a company, and by the intercession of some friends Berry was enrolled in his corps, to make himself useful in any parts he might be called upon to play. It so happened that Hamlet was the piece fixed upon for the opening night, the part of the Priest by facetious Tom Berry.

It was a great misfortune that our friend never could get over the difficulties of blank verse, and further, a much greater misfortune that he should, when he had any to speak, invariably take a trifle too much alcoholic stimulant, with a view to keep up his courage for the event. He was fully conscious of this defect, and solicited a member of the company to give him the words from the side scenes. On his first appearance in the funeral throng, a slight uneasiness of gait in walking, and a swaying of the body on taking his position at the grave of the drowned Ophelia, could be easily perceived, though this might have passed as an artist-like delineation of the infirmities of age. His features, naturally extremely comic, were on this occasion, " screwed to the sticking place " of solemnity, although the scalp designating the " shaven monk " placed a little awry, and suffering a straggling lock to escape, blended with the vermilion intended to color the cheek, being by some accident communicated to the extreme tip of the nose, slightly deteriorated from that expression.

He turned his head, and looked imploringly at the side from whence he expected to be supplied with the words, while his friend, book in hand, keeping faithful to his promise, had mixed in among the group surrounding the grave.

" Her obsequies have been so far enlarged as we have warrant," whispered the prompter, close to his ear.

" Her obsequies are large enough, I warrant," commenced the Priest.

Again the text was poured into his ear in continuation.

" Her death was doubtful."

" 'Tis doubtful if she's dead," said Tom, now wishing to cut the matter as short as possible.

The prompter proceeded with—

" She should in ground unsanctified have lain till the last trump—"

" She should not trump in sanctified ground," replied the hero.

" Here she is allowed her maiden struments," shortly, and rather indistinctly continued the prompter, who was now getting somewhat angry at the evident hopelessness of his task.

" Here she is allowed her pails and stew-pans," responded poor Berry, who had caught something like the sound, but not the sense of the last phrase. This was too much. Shouts of laughter mingled with hisses, now so overcame our unfortunate hero, that he dropped his book.

" Take him off," was shouted on all sides, but there was no necessity for that, for in stooping to recover the said book, he suddenly disappeared as if by magic, from the sight of his indignant patrons, having by the effort precipitated himself head foremost into the grave of the dead Ophelia.

The curtain fell on the scene, and the reader may rest assured it was the last appearance on the Ryde boards of " facetious Tom Berry."

Whether I was one of fortune's favorites I know not; but I *do* know that I worked " most vigorously " to advance my professional usefulness, and soon rose to some amount of prominence. I had to play anything and everything. As a proof of this, I may instance that while attached to the Kent circuit, I played in one evening the characters of Banquo, and Hecate in Macbeth, and sang all the music. In Hamlet, I had to do duty for Polonius, the Ghost, Osric, and the first Grave Digger.

Managerial Wives.

I have often asked myself the question, why managers, dramatically, have wives! Domestically, I am willing to admit they are as much entitled to that coveted luxury as the members of any other profession or calling, but in a business point of view they are, save in very rare exceptions, institutions of a grave, and serious import.

I adore the sex in general, and our wife in particular. But if ever, for some unatoned crime committed in my boyish frivolity, I should be consigned to that pandemonium of dramatic life, the "managerial throne," and the partner of my bosom exhibited the slightest propinquity for the buskin, I should, without the smallest compunction of conscience, retain the most skillful in legal manipulations, with the benign determination of dissolving the nuptial tie.

I say this unhesitatingly, because I am, and ever have been, opposed to all feuds, whether domestic, dramatic or editorial, and as one, or all these would be the inevitable consequence of my wife's embracing the stage, I would, as I desire to exist in the most perfect amity with all mankind, much prefer that such an ebullition of affection should be monopolized by myself without let or hindrance of any kind whatsoever.

These reflections have forced themselves most unceremoniously upon my cogitations, as I look back to the drudgery of my novitiate when I formed one of a company in the west of England, the manager of whom had a wife, whose chief diversion seemed to be to convince her husband of the great sacrifices she had made when, in an outburst of virginly magnanimity, she bestowed upon him the honor of her hand. Such is, however, the extreme selfishness of human nature, that the fortunate possessor of the treasure evidently took a different estimate of its value.

The field of action in which this lady distinguished herself, prior to her entrance into marital array, was a seminary for the instruction of young persons in all the polite accomplishments indispensable for their advent into the social circle ; and it was during her *espionage* of the said charges at the theatre of the locality in which they studied, that her heart was made captive by its present owner, while he was engaged in the representation of Romeo. The most full-blown amongst the young ladies was, on retiring on that eventful night, admitted into her confidence and sworn to secrecy, and in little less than three months had the honor of assisting at a surreptitious marriage ceremony, in addition to three professional associates of the hero of the adventure, who had been expressly chartered for the purpose.

The most casual observer could easily credit the fact, so often referred to, that at that period of her history the lady was physically presentable for the adoption of the profession she was not slow to enter; but it did so fall out that the embodiment of the principal female characters in the works of the best authors required some initiatory experience, which she, in the excess of her vanity, never seemed to contemplate ; and if at any time, the which frequently happened, an unlucky contributor to the weekly paper, in an insane desire, as he imagined, to manifest his affection for the progress of art, should delicately suggest that the wife of our worthy manager was scarcely up to the mark for the rendition of Queen Catherine, such a character requiring a depth of thought and intensity of expression not usually possessed by a lady whose forte lay in the exposition of soubrettes of a vivacious nature, the unfortunate husband was compelled to place himself in instant communication with the proprietors of the journal that had " thus gone out of its way to offer violence to a sensitive lady's feelings," at the same

8

time insinuating that if the delinquent correspondent again exhibited such unheard of malevolence, he, the manager, would be compelled to withdraw his advertisements, and furnish his establishment with programmes of the entertainments from the office of the rival journalist over the way.

The very desirable advantage of youth and beauty, our heroine had no respect or sympathy for whatever; indeed, the possession of either of these pleasing qualifications was, in her estimate, rather an objection than otherwise; in proof of which she declared instant warfare with any lady who could, by her personal attractiveness on the stage, secure the approval of the public, and should she add to her enormity by presuming to obtain an *encore* for a song, a gentle shaking was the certain result, as a just and proper penance for such a flagrant act of impropriety.

It may very readily be supposed that the theatre over which this ogress presided, was no very agreable place for one of the female gender under such a course of tutorage. Resignations were in consequence not unfrequent; every secession invoking the pretended ire of the very person who had been the sole cause of its consummation.

This antagonism arose from the serious conviction the good lady entertained, that the juvenile heroines of comedy or tragedy could find no such fitting representative as herself; for even her increasing age and rotundity of form failed in dispelling the pleasing delusion. Should she be now in existence, we feel assured she still clings tenaciously to the hallucination.

Alas, poor lady! she is but one amongst the many of both sexes who ignore the potency of that universal leveller, *Time!* and who prefer to exist upon the delicate disguise of stubborn facts.

It is well to bear kindly with these weaknesses! it is

exciting to be button-holed by one who was once the *beau ideal* of the man of fashion and faultless symmetry on the stage, and who has just had his feelings deeply lacerated by the receipt of an offer from a manager, who would like to avail himself of his services for the ensuing season, to take charge of the representation of the heavy fathers of the ponderous drama.

In the seclusion of private life, it would be well the world should know, that however intoxicated with the success of their early career, there are many not unlike the wife of our manager here represented, whose charity, in its quiet, unobtrusive delicacy, has shed a cheering ray of atonement for years of professional vanity, and whose memory may occupy a niche in the kindly remembrance of many a grateful heart.

THE PHENOMENON.

In the year 1837, I was a member of a company in Kent, presided over by a gentleman who, with his daughter, has been photographed by a great writer, presenting as he never fails to do, a most pleasing. and droll portraiture; but in no single instance is this like the originals. This must have arisen from the author's reliability upon the representations of others, without availing himself of the facilities for personal observation.

'Twas here that I first heard that most popular of comic songs, "Jim Crow," not by my dear old friend "Daddy Rice," but warbled by the Phenomenon.

There was a ponderous attempt at grandeur about the parent of the novelty above named, that had for its object a desire to impress the company with its great magnificence, but which generally had a contrary effect.

It was a custom to give single performances at adjacent towns on the off play nights; which the choice spirits of the company used to designate the "Waterspout perfor-

mances " so called from the fact that the scenes used in
the representation were so constructed they would pack
into a long box, which receptacle, when emptied of its
contents, was placed across the front of the stage, and
formed a very good temporary float-light guard.

We made a foray into the town of Ashford, and took
possession of the hall wherein all the public business
appertaining to the place and neighborhood was conducted.   It was a large room, with portraits of celebrities who
had devoted the best energies of their parochial nature
to the perpetuity of measures for the welfare of their
fellow townsmen, and whose facial monuments, albeit
not rendered in a flattering aspect by the artists who
had handed them down to posterity, glared out upon you
with a severity which impressed you with the conviction
that you were on trial for some heinous offence, and need
expect no mercy at their hands.

It was well lighted with oil lamps, and capable of
seating one thousand persons without much inconvenience.
We boasted not of raised platform, or stage; the box
before mentioned divided the actors from the audience,
while draperies of various colors filled the spaces between
the canvas proscenium, and the walls.   The pieces for
the evening's entertainment were the tragedy of Douglas, a song and dance, and the farce of Popping the
Question.   The manager played Glenalvan; his wife,
Lady Randolph; the Phenomenon, young Norval; and
the writer, old Norval.   The Highland fling between
the pieces, by the exotic, who also enacted one of the old
maids in the farce.

The attendance was very good, and the performance
satisfactory, but when, at its conclusion, we were about to
depart, the conveyance in which we had made our
triumphal entry into the town was no where to be found ;
after considerable delay it was discovered locked up in

the churchyard, and no one could find the key. We had another temporary attachment for a hotel beauty here, and were rather pleased at the delay than otherwise.

The performances were under the patronage of the "Chummy, and Fish Clubs" a bill of which is before us as we write. The manager impressed the public in every town he visited, with the belief that Edmund Kean had, in a burst of admiration for his daughter's ability, present-ed her with what, in theatrical parlance, was called a battlefield hat; whereas the true story was, "that the identical head gear was found among some odds and ends in the property room of the Richmond (Surry) Theatre, and its ever having been worn by the great tragedian, was at best doubtful!"

I allude to these peculiarities of gaining popularity in no spirit of spleen, or mischievous desire to cast a stigma of any kind upon the talent of a lady who has most de-servedly risen to the highest point of dramatic ex-cellence. No one cherishes a greater regard for her than he who now alludes to a single instance only, of a career that, by clever business management during its nonage, planted the seeds that have since blossomed, and present-ed to an admiring world the most luscious products of the Thespian garden.

A heavy calamity has lately befallen this distinguished actress. A few years since she quitted the sphere of professional greatness, and bestowed her hand and heart upon a brave and gallant soldier. Now the nation mingles its sorrow with the bereaved widow for the loss of him who, in the pride of manhood, yielded his life to sustain the honor of his country.

After many years, when fortune had not been a niggard with her gifts, I met the father of the subject of these remarks in London, and he remembered me with much gratification; which is not always the case with many who recoil with horror at a retrospect of the days when the season's exertions would terminate, and leave their exchequer in so needy a condition that a pedestrian expedition became a matter of absolute necessity.

After one or two attempts, at divers places, similar to those recounted in the preceding chapters, where I distinguished myself in (as, I then believed) the rendition of the heroes of tragedy, I took flight to Nottingham, where I commenced the assumption of aged characters, in the part of Adam Winterton. This was in the month of June, 1836. My stay here was very brief, for in the month of September of the same year I received an offer for the Queen's Theatre, London, where I made my Metropolitan bow in the Baron of Oatland in the opera of the Haunted Tower. Mrs. Waylet, George Stansbury, Mr. Manvers, and Mr. Conquest were in the cast. I played Simpson in Simpson & Co., Sir Peter Teazle, and many parts of a like nature to the popular Mrs. Nesbit, and remained a member of the company till the close of the speculation, when I removed to the Victoria, where I speedily discovered the fallacy of remaining in London with my then limited experience, and departed for Worthing, in Sussex, in August 1838, from thence to Sheffield and Doncaster with Hammond, Reading with Barnet, and Bristol with Mrs. Macready, the step-mother of the great tragedian.

While at Sheffield I may recount an act of assurance I committed which, for effrontery, has seldom been excelled.

It happened that the celebrated Mr. and Mrs. Wood, the vocalists, were announced to sing La Somnambula, but on the morning of the expected production of the opera, the gentleman who was to perform the part of the Count Rodolpho, was taken with a severe attack of sickness, and compelled to keep his bed. What was to be done ? The box list was full, and to substitute another opera would give great cause for dissatisfaction. It took very little persuasion to induce me to try to get through it; and, with the leader of the orchestra, worked at the score all the afternoon so satisfactorily, that, when the evening came I received *two encores ;* and, with the aid of Mr. Wood, who gave me all the starting notes of the several solos in the second act from behind the curtains of the bed, got along in a way that seemed to afford perfect satisfaction to a densely packed house, and repeated the part on two or three subsequent occasions.

In 1840, I went to Norwich, Yarmouth, Cambridge, Bury St. Edmund's, Ipswich, Colchester and Lynn. These several towns formed one of the most delightful circuits that can be well imagined. Though so many years have passed, I look back to that happy period of my career with feelings of pleasure and delight. The Norwich circuit was celebrated for its matrimonial attacks upon the members of the dramatic company both male and female, therefore I am not reprehensible for being caught in its toils at Bury St. Edmund's on the 30th Nov. 1842. Indeed, so contented am I to bear, with uncomplaining fortitude, the penalty of my rashness, that I seriously recommend all youthful dramatic artists to emigrate there, in the hope that, should they connubialize, (which almost amounts to a certainty,) they may be as fortunate as I was in the selection of a partner, who by unwavering faithfulness to her domestic mission, has illumined the dark horizon of professional turmoil; and shed a cheering influence of content and happiness upon all around her.

In 1842, Mr. Robert Roxby became the manager of the Theatre Royal, Manchester. The principal members of the company consisted of S. Butler, C. D. Pitt, D. W. King, (Tenor), Munyard, J. Jonstone, Woolgar, C. Bass,

C. F. Marshall, R. Roxby, Bellingham J. Howard, Barham, W. Grisdale, Miss S. J. Woolgar, Miss Walcott, Miss Angel, etc. etc. and Mr. W. Davidge.

In 1844, the Manchester Theatre was destroyed by fire. I went to Brighton, and at the end of the season to Edinboro', where I found E. Glover, Lester Wallack, Leigh Murray, Couldock, Ray, Parselle, Mackay, G. Honey, Lloyd, J. Moore, Miss Nicoll, Miss Macready, etc. etc.

I received the kindest consideration from the Scotch critics, as well as the inhabitants of the capital city; and quitted the scene of my labors to return to Manchester, for the opening of the new theatre in September, 1845, having previously made my first visit to Plymouth in August, where I met the Misses Cushman.

During the vacation of 1847, I played an engagement at the Queen's Theatre, Dublin, where the production of " The Fair One with the Golden Locks," with other light pieces of a similar character, afforded an opportunity of my being seen to some advantage, and was a source of great profit to the management.

The following year I made a second visit to Dublin, with, I am pleased to say, the same satisfactory result.

As an illustration of the exteme length to which prejudice or caste could in those days affect an actor, I remember meeting the lessee of the Theatre Royal, who inquired if I could recommend the name of a comedian I considered sufficiently up to the mark to suit the patrons of his establishment. I thought for a moment, and recollected I had lately seen at the Grecian Saloon in London, a gentleman who would be precisely the person he wanted.

" What's his name ? " said the manager.

" Robson," said I.

" Robson ! " echoed he ; " where did you see him ? "

" At the Grecian Saloon," I replied.

"Ugh! wouldn't have him if he'd come for nothing!"

Since the date of the above, Mr. Robson, prior to his death, rose to the highest grade in London, and able reviewers claimed for him a position as an artist second only to Bouffe, of the French stage.

I have seen the time, now happily past, when an actor of either of the patent theatres, as Covent Garden and Drury Lane were then termed, would with reluctance address a brother professional who might be employed at an establishment not legally entitled to that proscriptive distinction. The Hon. T. Duncombe broke down this barrier, when he introduced his bill permitting the representation of the standard drama at every theatre, without distinction of caste. Whether the drama as an art, by being deprived of its surroundings, has been benefitted thereby, is a question I am not disposed to discuss in this place.

Mr. Robson died in London, much regretted, on the 11th of August 1864, aged 43.

CHAPTER VIII.

" A merrier man,
Within the limits of becoming mirth,
I never spent an hour's talk withal."
—*Love's Labor Lost. Act 2. Scene 1.*

A CONSECUTIVE chain of events form no part of my purpose in these pages, neither do I propose to solicit the company of my patient readers through engagements at places where the styles of people are merely a reflex of those met with before; but shall in pursuance of this intention, pay little regard, if any, to data, but present the " Footlight Flashes" from the crucible of memory in such a manner as will produce the most luminous and pleasing effect.

Long ere I became a professional actor I beguiled my leisure evenings with a probationary element of the drama at an amateur theatre in Catherine street, Strand, London; a nursery from whence many of the brightest lights which now adorn the histrionic art first passed through the trying ordeal of facing the enemy in the auditorium; a more difficult task, I am advised by those skilled in the science of warfare, than encountering your antagonist in the din and deathful clamor of the battle field.

BEN SMYTHSON, THE DRAMATIC AGENT.

Some of my professional brethren, for there are a few in America now, (1866) who graduated there, will recollect with feelings of respect Ben Smythson, the dramatic agent who, for several years, leased the theatre for the purpose of amateur performances. Ben was a retired actor who had once held a fine position in Ireland when the great Talbot, the light comedian, was in his zenith. He was a man of much information, and geniality of manner, very grandiloquent in conversation, and totally regardless of his personal appearance, in the matter of costume.

He had a wife of herculean mould, and a constantly increasing family of children, all of whom are now in good positions in music and the drama. Prior to his tenancy of the place above mentioned, he kept a tavern, a general resort for all actors who were seeking engagements, and who congregated there to possess themselves of all the current news of the day.

Mrs. S. had but recently presented her lord and master with the customary annual offering, when I did myself the pleasure of calling for the purpose of expressing my congratulations on the event of an increase to the family significance; and expressed a hope that the offspring, with its mother, were progressing favorably, at which he placed himself in a pantomimical attitude, "a la Don Juan," and began—

Tum, te tum, te tum te tum, tum, te te te te, tiddle tum te tum te tum te tum te tum!

The last sentence brought him into a final and imposing position, with his right hand extended, and pointing to a large placard over the bar door, on which was written in capitals, for the benefit of all enquirers.

"*The hostess and her offspring are as well as can be expected.*"

His pompous style was well exemplified on one particular occasion. Calling to indulge in a cup of coffee, the following dialogue took place.

W. D. "I think I'll take a cup of coffee, Ben, if you please."

Ben. "Certainly, my boy. (*Opening a door leading to the kitchen.*) Rosabella."

Servant. (*In the extreme distance.*) "Yes, sir."

Ben. "A vase of the sedative."

W. D. "Won't you take one?"

Ben. "Thank you, my boy, I will." (*Turning to us,*) Do you take sugar?"

W. D. If you please."

Ben. Rosabella. Two vases of the sedative, one with the saccharine, and one without."

Great men in whatever way distinguished, have at all times a peculiar charm for the youthful mind; and in no case more evident than in contemplating the performance, or presence of a great actor.

Though mournful the occasion, I can well remember being in the midst of a galaxy of the greatest names associated with the London stage.

In the year 1831, died the most perfect actress of her time, the unapproachable Siddons; she, before whose youthful efforts even Garrick quailed. The concourse of mourners, and the aspect of woe each countenance wore, bore ample testimony to the position the lost one had occupied in the public esteem; while the numerous representatives of her family, from the classic and elegant gentleman, Charles Kemble, to the most accomplished of dramatic managers, William Murrey of Edinburgh, poured out their grief as an offering of regret to the social excellence of the departed.

Similar emotions impressed me when, two years later, Edmund Kean was summoned to "another, and a better world" and the town of Richmond, in Surry, paid the last tribute to the matchless tragedian, by suspending its daily avocation, and, in company with sorrowing spirits from afar, mingling their tears of anguish for a nation's loss.

The former of these world-renowned artists I never saw;

with the latter's acting I was perfectly familiar. I have decamped from the paternal roof with the certainty of a sound thrashing and the deprivation of my evening meal when I returned, to see the great actor in his several parts. I have been rammed, jammed, and trodden upon, till I became callous to consequences, waiting to obtain an entrance into the gallery of Covent Garden Theatre. I have watched for him in the streets for hours; have followed his carriage, have jumped up behind it, and been most ignominiously cut down by the coachman's whip. But my first practical and demonstrative acquaintanceship was at Drury Lane Theatre, where by virtue of the favor of Tom Cooke, the leader of the orchestra, I managed to intrude behind the scenes. There I received my

FIRST IMPRESSION OF EDMUND KEAN.

At the time of this adventure, the actor was at the meridian of his professional glory. Not to have seen him in his most powerful and unapproachable delineations would have stigmatised you as beyond the pale of civilization. It cannot be wondered then that the youthful, as well as the adult mind, should have thirsted for such an intense enjoyment. Having the opportunity to avail myself of a peep behind the scenes, I never overlooked the privilege, and ensconced in a secure retreat, awaited the performance of Othello thus cast: Othello, E. Kean; Iago, C. Young; Cassio, J. Cooper; the after-piece was a spectacle of gorgeous magnificence, requiring a large amount of scenery for its representation. Kean had retired to his room during a wait in the second act, and the writer, (emulating the example still adhered to by fashionable visitors to places of amusement when the favorite quits the scene,) vacated his little standing place near the wings, and prowled about amongst the mysteries of castle walls, oaken chambers, palace gar-

dens etc., and was returning, attracted by the bell peeling
forth its solemn and ponderous thunder of mutinous discontent. I heard a rapid tread behind me. "Go on," said
a voice, with great impatience, and in an awfully distinct
tone. I did "go on," I thought.

The passage way was so crowded with scenery that it
afforded space for but one person at a time. Suddenly I
became aware of the extreme impulsiveness of human
nature in general, and the proprietor of the voice in particular, by a powerful shock inflicted on that part of my
person that looks north when the face is to the south,
which threw me most unceremoniously far beyond the
contracted pathway; and before I had time to request to
be made acquainted with the nature of the services I had
performed that should entitle me to such an unusual and
exclusive mark of recognition, I heard the unmistakable
burst of Kean's voice, and caught sight of him rushing
with cimeter in hand through the centre gates, shouting
"Hold for your lives" etc., etc. I then made the discovery that I had, unconsciously, nearly made the stage wait
for the great tragedian.

I did *not* insist upon an explanation. It is even
probable I might rather have felt *painfully* flattered by
such an unmistakable mark of distinguished recognition.

I was a great patron of the several theatres at about
this period; indeed, no new and startling drama could
possibly be presented to the public without my sitting in
judgment on its inaugural presentation. The incidents
both before and behind the curtain are so peculiar, as to be
embodied in a separate sketch; it is to be hoped that
many who have listened to the peculiar badinage of the
London mechanic and other patrons of the galleries of
the minor theatres in the great metropolis, will discover
some resemblance to the reality in the following description of,

THE FIRST NIGHT OF A NEW PLAY IN LONDON.

The production of a new play at one of the minor theatres was, and still is, a matter of most intense importance to that portion of the building yclept the gallery, where the freedom of costume and expression affords ample scope for the study of the curious.

Time, 5.30 P. M. Scene, the New Cut approaching the gallery doors of the Victoria Theatre. Dramatis Personæ, the Gamins of London, with a plentiful sprinkling of adults, whose pursuits being of a mechanical nature, are by no means inconvenienced by the pushing and crowding they have to encounter; but seem rather to regard it as a pleasing relaxation from the dull routine of the work shop.

As the time for opening the doors approaches, the crowd increases to an extent by no means agreeable for those who find themselves beyond the possibility of securing a front seat, or even one in an eligible position.

It is then that the young gentleman who has divested himself of his jacket as an unnecessary article of wearing apparel in such a temperature, indulges in pleasant little sallies with those who are less fortunate in location than himself:

" I say old 'un," bellows the young gentleman alluded to above, to a staid looking old play-goer, whose chance for a good seat is extremely remote.

" Hi!"

The old gentleman purposely turns a deaf ear to the salutation, and refuses to recognize it.

" Hollo ! you in the blue choker, and downy caster!" perseveres the youth.

" Well, what now ? " cries the individual, whose personal identification has been thus positively defined by the above inventory of his head gear.

"Vill ye stand a ke-vorton, two outs, if I carries ye in in my harms as my own babby?"

At which the old gentleman looks exceedingly wroth, and intimates his conviction that his interlocutor is an impudent young puppy, and he would like to indulge in the luxury of boxing his ears. A threat that rather seems to fail in its intention; for the urchin invites him to " send an express messenger for his father and all his relations of the male gender, the whole of whom he is ready to take his affidavit he will despatch to that ' bourne from whence no traveller returns;'" and in consideration of his opponent's pitiable condition as an occupant of a back seat, he will generously undertake to provide for the feminine part of the household, by taking the most prepossessing one to wife, and disposing of the balance, in the most sumptuous manner, for the balance of their natural lives.

"Now, then, take care, will ye, stupid?" says a gentleman in a paper cap, and whose jacket is strongly impregnated with the odor peculiar to those who pass their time in converting deal boards into articles of domestic use.

"Jest you keep off my corns, or you'll hear from me by the werry earliest conweyance."

"How can I help it, when that ere chap will keep a shoving me behind in this way?"

"Now you keep tight hold o' me, Mary," urges a young man gotten up with some amount of care and attention, to a pretty looking servant girl, with very bright ribbons in her bonnet, and cheeks to match, whose readiness to comply, rather ignores the impression that her sex are prone to a contradictory code of principles.

"Now, then, look out! steady! Oh, don't shove so! Oh! keep your elbows out of my ribs, will ye?"

A large bolt is withdrawn, and the mass of human beings begin to move slowly upwards. The first six or eight who effect an entrance, charge furiously towards the money taker, whose box is garnished by two policemen of forbidding aspect, and herculean proportions ; the duties of whose office is to marshal, without favor or affection, the several patrons in proper file to receive their checks, and to preserve the peace generally.

Presently a boy tries an artful bit of generalship to gain admission ; it is done in this wise. While placing his hand, as if in the act of depositing his money, upon the pay place, he affects to have dropped the coin at his feet ; to search for it is, of course, impossible at such a time ; the guardians of the public peace instantly pounce upon the unlucky delinquent, and ho is speedily deposited in a corner, all the time protesting that his bob (shilling) slipped out of his hand, and "they might let a cove in afore all the best seats is gone, for he's been waiting there, ever since three o'clock in the afternoon, and the tin will be sure to be found arter the crowd has gone in."

Sometimes ho will begin to bellow most lustily, when he sees an elderly man with two boys approach, hoping to excite the compassion of the *pater familias ;* but the *ruse* generally fails, and may be remembered with the *street-door key* and *basket* delusions, which have, years ago, lost their fascinating qualities. The result is almost certain to be disastrous to the principal performer, whom, when time and opportunity serve, is most unceremoniously propelled, by one of the stout boots of the policeman, with alarming rapidity to the foot of the stairs.

Save the several and frequent admonitions for the visitors to take personal care of their pockets from the attentions of the light-fingered gentry, there is little to occupy your thoughts till you find yourself deposited in the gallery, where a scene presents itself both animated, and variable.

The *genus artful*, again exhibits its prowess with the laudable design of procuring for itself a comfortable location from whence to view the performance. This is accomplished by feigning to recognize some friend in the second or third row from the front, and begging permission of the occupants of the upper seats the privilege of passing down. Sometimes the *ruse* succeeds, and he will manage to squeeze himself into a sitting posture. This, with the invitations from those who have really secured seats for their friends, beguiles the time till the lights are raised, and the orchestra begins the overture.

The first scene, (being new for the occasion,) or so much of it as to destroy its identification with a landscape painted for a new piece gotten up in the early part of the previous season at considerable expense, and which was seriously intended to run three months, but " shuffled off its mortal coil," in a like number of nights, is received with that applause which its merits deserve, and the actors also are favored with a recognition so pleasing to those who are in constant receipt of such compliments, and so inconsistent to others who never obtain any notice whatever, and the act terminates to the satisfaction of the most exacting critic.

"Apples! Oranges! Ginger-beer! Bill o' the play!" cries a sturdy female, with strong, muscular development, as she grazes the shins of the occupants of each and every seat with a basket of unusual proportions containing the aforesaid luxuries.

" By your leave, young ooman, if you please ; and she dabs the basket into the lap of a female, who, in company with a congenial spirit, is taking her second sandwich, a large bundle of which nourishment she has armed herself with, as a set-off against her afternoon meal which she has been deprived of by her presence there.

" It's my opinion," says the young woman addressed,

after having plentifully fortified herself against the attacks of hunger, "that these 'ere women with their baskets is a confounded nuisance, and ought to be put down."

Similar scenes are repeated in pretty much the same style at the end of the several acts, during which it is more than probable we are favored with an interlude not provided by the management, but none the less amusing.

A young lady in a faded pink bonnet and shawl, with a profusion of border of a crimson tint, inadvertently replies to a question propounded by a gentleman in a colored shirt, embellished with studs of a dazzling splendor; the which excites the ire of the lady's *chaperon*, who threatens, without fee or reward, to pitch the said individual into the pit. He, of the studs, while treating the compliment with disdain, consoles himself with a promise to wait favorable opportunity, during the absence of the fair sex, and thrash him to his heart's content.

As none of us are proof against the blandishments of the softer portion of creation, it is no wonder that the female with the prettily formed mouth, which she keeps in a perpetual giggle, should secure the admiration of the susceptible youth with curly hair, who fixes his eyes upon her with an expression of fervor too significant to be mistaken for the result of accident; so evident, indeed, is the action, that her cavalier, with a frown, requests he will direct his gaze in some other direction; an admonition that only meets with the rejoinder that,—

"He belives his heyes is his own, and he shall use 'em as most convenient to his own fancy, without consulting him, or any of his friends as he knows on !"

Meanwhile, preparations are proceeding on the stage for the "great third act," (vide bills,) wherein the Duke, surrounded by his officers, habited in his robes of state, seated upon a raised dais, issued a decree of outlawry against a poor but honest peasant, whose only perceptible crime appears to be, a secret affection conjointly existing between himself and the pet daughter of the aforesaid ducal despot.

As the play proceeds the audience entertain a personal admiration or antipathy for the several personages, in proportion to the phase of character they represent ; and when in the fourth act, the heroine, attired in garments of snowy whiteness, with her back hair streaming to the winds, encounters her obdurate parent, while he is chafed with the affairs of state, and acquaints him with her firm determination to linger out her virgin existence within the close confines of a dungeon's walls, sooner than be immolated upon the hated affections of that "fiend in human form," (as she styles the lord and princely owner of a neighboring domain, to whom her father is preparing to dispose of her,) the audience are in ecstacies of delight at her personal courage, and devoted affection for the friendless, but virtuous peasant.

A confidential interview between the dignitary so highly complimented, and the Duke, speedily discloses the deep subtlety of the dramatist in the conduct of his plot: these worthies not only propose to carry off the heroine aforesaid, with the aid of two hired ruffians (whose very appearance is a stamp receipt for cruelty,) but they also design, when this little bit of paternal beneficence shall be consummated, to divide the worldly wealth to which the lady would be entitled on reaching her majority, between them, which very equitable disposition of the property is only prevented by the startling discovery that one of the gentlemen detailed for this pleasing office, is none other than the humble peasant before alluded to, and whose appearance in such a character without being very clearly defined how he could possibly get there, secures for the drama a powerful and brilliant *denouement*, and contributes a wholesome lesson of retributive justice to the delighted auditory.

The audience retire to dream of the fascinating scene; the actors wend their way homeward weary and fatigued with their night's exertions; the ladies of the ballet emerge from the stage-door bearing curiously shaped baskets or parcels supposed to contain small articles of wearing apparel indispensable for the next day's use. As they draw their scanty shawls about them, and the night air pierces into their very bones, cast a thought of womanly sympathy, ye choice daughters of affluence and comfort, whose very atmosphere shields ye from the breath of calumny, and know that beneath those cheap, but tastily made habiliments, beat hearts as pure from guile, or sin, as many who luxuriate on the downy couch of indolent ease, or indulge in the freedom of fashionable folly.

The night watchman relieves the day porter, and, as he wanders through every nook and cranny of the building, bears an apt resemblance to the troubled spirit of some departed gnome, searching for something he cannot find.

CHAPTER IX.

BENEFIT MAKING.

THIS is a science achieved only by a limited number of the profession. It is impossible to describe its *modus operandi* with any amount of accuracy. Some there are who deluge every friend, or acquaintance, no matter of how long standing, with tickets, who are often compelled to dispose of, or pay for them, for very shame. Others there are who, in the exercise of their desire to uphold the dignity of the profession, content themselves by simply notifying the public through the medium of the daily papers that "they beg to present . their claims for the kindly consideration of their indulgent patrons, hoping to be favored with a small modicum of their usual affectionate regard."

The profits derived from these transactions are not as advantageous as the public, in the innocence of its good nature, mostly believe! indeed, we once knew an actor who refused most postively to permit his name to be used for a benefit, under the plea, that with a rapidly increasing family, and a sick wife, he couldn't possibly afford to run the risk of the speculation.

Another congratulated himself on his increasing popularity in only losing ten dollars at his last benefit; whereas, on making his appeal the year preceding, he was minus twenty dollars, showing a clear gain of ten dollars in his monetary significance with the public.

The most successful manœuvre within my recollection was perpetrated in the county of Norfolk, where we had a very useful and pains-taking actor, whose name was Baker, but who never had been able to muster a tolerable assembly at his benefit. On the occasion to which I here refer he was much in need of money, and hit upon the following plan. A wealthy man in the neighborhood had an only child, whose custom was to wander about the fields plucking flowers. A river with a rapid stream skirted the field, terminating in a dam of great depth and difficult of approach from the shore. Suddenly a shriek was heard, the child was seen struggling in the water, and being carried with great velocity towards the dam. Baker was on the spot; quick as thought he threw off a portion of his garments, and regardless of danger, (he was an expert swimmer) dashed into the current! The cries of the child had brought numbers to the place, among them the frantic parent of the little one, whose almost suffocated form was thrown to and fro, at the will of the turgid element. The excitement was terrible, as the bystanders were unable to assist in the slightest degree from their point of sight the intrepid youth, save with their encouraging plaudits. At length he seized the drowning one by the back of its little neck, and tenderly elevated its head to such a position as to afford its fastly ebbing nature the advantage of respiration, and sustaining himself as best he could, made for the shore; where, amid the shouts of a gratified multitude, and copious flows of tears from the joyous parent, he laid his little treasure at his feet, and walked triumphantly to his lodgings, a "*wetter*, but a happier man!"

The journals throughout the whole county indulged in panegerics without number, of the most laudatory kind, and his benefit came off under special patronage of the Mayor and corporation; the house was crowded to excess, and when Baker came forward in all the agony of evening costume at the end of the play, to return thanks for the distinguished honor conferred by the attendance of the aristocratic visitors, two old maiden ladies, whose heads were surmounted with formidable battlements of pink gauze and white roses, and who came to the theatre because everybody who could lay the slightest claim to being anybody was to be there, sobbed audibly, when the actor briefly alluded to the touching incident that had, in so providential a way, directed attention to one so unworthy their esteem as himself; that, when in after life, should he be spared to witness the time when the young lady he had had the happiness of rescuing from a watery grave, should attain the dignity of lovely woman's estate, and be blessed with maternal charges, it would be the proudest moment of his varied career, could he be on the alert in the event of a similar catastrophe happening to one, or all of them.

The young lady, who occupied a conspicuous place, and was gotten up with great care, in virgin white decorated with blue ribbons, became suffused with blushes, at this perspective view of her future position in the social scale; while her parent, with his massive iron-gray head, obliquely cut whiskers, and very stiff white choker, could hardly suppress the feelings of pleasure and pride that swelled beneath the ample folds of his plaited shirt bosom.

Presents of all kinds poured in upon Baker; from the silver pitcher with an inscription on its stomach detailing all the incidents of the affair, to the embroidered pen wiper, and illuminated vest pattern.

Jealousy, with its hydra-headed, and venomous conceit, looked distrustfully upon the hero of the above drama, and, in one instance, offered to prove by undoubtcd authority, that a similar incident had happened a year or two prior to that date, but in a different part of the country; and further, that there were those who were prepared to show that the accident was the result of a well devised plot, artfully invented by the said Baker.

The late Mr. Burton once told me a good benefit story. Many years ago, he played a star engagement at the town of Napoleon, on the Mississippi river; it had not been very profitable, and his only chance of retrieving himself, was by personally beating up for the benefit; with this object in view, he deposited a goodly bundle of tickets with the bar tender at the hotel where he was staying, with a polite request that he would use his best endeavor to get rid of them. The benefit came off, and the attendance was very flattering. After the play, the comedian invited several friends up to the bar of the man who had so liberally patronized the drama, and there had the satisfaction of learning that he had managed to get rid of all the tickets entrusted to him. This was very gratifying, but no offer of liquidation for the same met his expectant gaze, whereupon, as he was on the point of quitting the city, he ventured to suggest that he would like to have the pleasure of receiving the insignificant amount of seventy-five cents for each piece of pasteboard deposited.

It takes a great deal to astonish a bar keeper in Napoleon; it is no ordinary feat to take one of them thoroughly off his guard, but this one was evidently distanced. He surveyed Burton with surprise not unmixed with credulity. Finding the comedian didn't relax a muscle of his very expressive countenance, he said—

"Look here, Mr. Billy Burton, none of your infernal Northern tricks here; it won't do, no way! no how! You told me to get rid of them tickets for you, and as I had

4

promised, I was bound to go right straight through with it, *and by thunder, I was obliged to stand drinks to every man to take one.*"

THE STAGE DOOR KEEPER.

["No admittance behind the scenes, under any pretence whatever, without the express permission of the manager.]—*Vide Stagedoor.*"

Probably the above prohibition is the incentive to that curiosity invariably manifested by the youthful mind, to catch a glimpse of the workings of the mysterious machinery within the magic circle of the dramatic temple; or, it may be that, as in every sphere of our chequered existence, the antagonism to authority engrafts a two-fold desire within our breasts to arrive at the interdicted goal, whether it be in the perusal of a volume, the peering into private closets, where niceties are heartlessly sealed, or the love of ruminating in the proximity of a neighboring brook; such an endless source of anxiety to the stern father and affectionate mother, that makes us thirst for the forbidden treasure.

If we experience an intense pleasure in opposing the will of others in the domestic circle, how natural it is for us to desire to violate the chilling manifesto of the Cerberus who lounges through his monotonous existence, holding watch and ward over the swing door, crowned with the above proscription. How we wonder what he does with himself at night; where he goes to, when the individual with thick boots and scarlet comforter, who is frigidly taciturn, relieves him, and begins his peregrinations through the building.

I remember in my thirst for knowledge, once attempting to obtain the personal history of a stage door keeper, I mean one attached to a regularly well-organized establishment in a populous city, not one of an exotic nature, where the lessees start with the praiseworthy intention of resuscitating the much abused drama, and as an earnest of their intention assume the entire responsibility of the act, by personating all the *best parts* themselves.

The natural instinctiveness for divining the occupations or early habits of people is not very sorely tested if the party of whom we desire to collect information should have been engaged in the defence of his country's cause, either by land or sea. If the former, there is invariably an erectness of bearing, a respect for those in authority, and a positive regard for duty and obedience, which so strongly prove the sternness of military tactics. If the latter, it is easily discernible by the possession of the very opposite attributes which marks the soldier's identification. His conversation is so constantly impregnated with expressions of a saline flavor, that it would be perfectly unnecessary to worm yourself into his good graces for the purpose of learning his previous occupation.

The one of which I speak, had been consigned in early life to the service of a grateful country. He first saw the light in the barracks at —— during a morning parade, and the interesting event was conveyed to the paternal author of his being by his eldest brother, who was a fifer in his father's company, while he was exercising the duties of his office as corporal in the —— regiment of foot.

When, in course of time, our hero had grown to boy's estate, he was duly instructed in the art and mystery of that very necessary, but somewhat emphatic musical instrument yclept "The drum." As time marched on, waving its variegated plume of riches and wretchedness, the father of our hero passed away, covered with his country's glory, and the gashes of an obdurate foe; and, while his life's blood oozed out amid the din of battle and the shrieks of the wounded and the dying, his mind

wandered to the wife and little ones he was bequeathing
to his country's care. And when all became a misty vision and his fine, manly heart had ceased its beating and
was ushered into the presence of the Supreme Conquer-
or, the clamorous joy of the victors, whose prowess
loomed amongst the greatest of military exploits, shed a
halo of imperishable renown upon all who took part in
the conflict.

It was then the bursting heart of the corporal's widow
received its quota of thanks,— a sorry equivalent for so
great a sacrifice ; but, alas ! all her country had to offer.

Trained and nurtured under strict military supervision,
our hero devoted the sunshine of his days to the only
duty he had ever known, to find himself in the evening
of his career in receipt of a scanty pittance, doled out under the dignified appellation of a " pension," by no means
sufficient for his daily wants.

Thence it was that he now added to his little store of
weekly wealth by mounting guard as above stated. If
it yielded little in the way of remuneration, it sometimes
carried him back, (in a minute degree) to a like position
while guarding the outposts in the battle-field.

He will delight to descant on his perilous campaigns,
with illustrations, amid the roar of cannon and all the
frightful paraphernalia of war ; but he fashions his dis-
course to the social status of his inquirers. The supers
he looks upon with great distrust ; he often considers
they display a large amount of presumption in propounding questions relative to sorties, charges, and other war-
like mysteries, and half suspects that these worthies are
addicted to the vice of practical joking.

The leading lady of the establishment is an especial
favorite with the door-keeper. Only watch him as he
marches out to assist her from the carriage. And if the
weather should happen to be wet, see how he will dive

precipitately into the little den at the extreme end of the porter's hall, and speedily appear with an umbrella of huge proportions, holding the same over the lady's head with a grace which many might envy, but few could imitate.

The gala-time for the stage-door keeper is pending, the production of a "Military drama of intense interest, embracing startling and thrilling effects never before attempted upon such a scale of magnificence."

Then he is in great request — he drills the supers for the various conflicts with which the piece abounds. We have seen our hero equipped with side arms, going through the mystic manœuvres of charge and retreat, with an earnestness worthy of a better cause.

Perchance the leading lady above mentioned may have valiantly to defend herself at the sword's point against two ferocious monsters (as she has several times stigmatized them through the three preceding scenes,) it is then that the talent of the old soldier presents itself in its most interesting aspect.

The bravos that resound through boxes, pit and gallery, at the *defeated fiends in human form*, as the retainers of the usurping Baron are usually designated by the author of domestic drama, are nothing when compared to the feeling of pride that fills the breast of the door keeper, as he considers himself as an accessory before the fact in all the successful hits of the evening.

Did ever one of our masculine readers, after the production of a piece of the above description, fall desperately, head over ears, in love with the fair heroine of the play? and would he not have given, (figuratively of course) one of his ears to pour forth in person his passion to the idol of his soul, (figuratively again) and has he not urged, begged and entreated of our friend, the private residence of his best beloved, and did he ever succeed in getting it?

The stage-door keeper is always distinguished for extreme taciturnity on all matters relating to the private abode of the company, the ladies in particular. His constant reply to all enquiries is,—

"Don't know, sir; leave a letter here, sure to get it; send it up by the first person going in, can't leave the door myself."

This is another of the strong peculiarities of our friend. Although so closely connected with dramatic matters, it is very rarely that he witnesses a performance. I well remember a very old and faithful servant in the Edinburgh Theatre, who had been at his post for thirty-six years, and during the whole of that time had never once seen a play performed.

Our old soldier is an important item toward the proper conduct of a theatre; and whether he be of the nature herein described, or of a loquacious turn of mind, trained in early life to mechanical usefulness he is invariably distinguished for honesty to his employers, always evincing a prudent regard for the secrets of the establishment, the keys of which he will often exhibit with an air of pride and satisfaction.

CHAPTER X.

In 1845 I gave, for the first time, an entertainment on the works of Charles Dickens. Manchester, Liverpool, Birmingham, all through the midland counties, Perth and Edinburgh were visited for this purpose. The press of every town or city paid me some very flattering compliments, in connection with our "Evenings with Charles Dickens," but a writer in the North British Review, made some rather savage attacks upon the author, the nature and tendency of his works, &c., insisting that he was a gross caricaturist; that such people as Mrs. Gamp and Pecksniff never existed in real life; and falling back, as is customary with Scotch critics, upon the usual literary comparison with Sir Walter Scott.

The writer did himself the pleasure of replying, at one of his entertainments in the "Modern Athens" of the North, to the above named article, and on submitting, by request, an outline of the argument, received the following, from the great novelist in reply.

(*Copy*).

1 DEVONSHIRE TERRACE, (York Gate, Regent Park.)
22d *December*, 1815.

" Dear Sir :

"I beg to thank you for your obliging note, and its enclosure, which shall be disposed of as you desire, and as it deserves.

"Let me assure you that I fully appreciate the honor you do me, not only in making my books the subject of your lectures, but in entering into your theme with so much warmth and earnestness.

I am, Dear Sir,

Faithfully yours.

CHARLES DICKENS.

" WILLIAM DAVIDGE, Esq."

The Scotch mind is usually too metaphysically constructed, to appreciate a writer like Dickens. There is a ponderosity, (so to speak) about the literary tastes of many of our very dear friends " t'other side the Tweed," at variance with the sparkling and life-like pictures presented by him whom I regard as the greatest social reformer of his time.

Where is the generous soil that yields the like marvellous variety of tempting products? Talk of the fruit of Hesperides, or the nectar of Jove! the one falls, and the other is insipid, when brought into comparison.

In his books, a spirit is abroad whose effulgence has penetrated the hearts of susceptible humanity, and opened the floodgates of inestimable treasures, that ages cannot exhaust. To the man with desires properly tempered and guided, life is not wholly the career of hard portions and depressing cares, or a medium solely for the gratification of hot passions and ill-neglected powers, as it is to many who possess the means, but ignorantly and foolishly reject the more lasting and healthful pleasure which is nowhere so readily found as in his pages. He is one of those who have caught the light of that magic spirit which has dispelled darkness, doubt, and despair; and still ministers, a high priest, at its shrine. The light that has beamed upon his own soul he has given reflected, not concealing or keeping it from his less fortunate fellow creatures, but sharing it with all; and as his path is illuminated, so would he illuminate the high road of the world. He is the humanizer before whose magical wand the evil that is in human nature crouches, subdued and overthrown.

If ever a writer lived who could nightly place his head upon his pillow with a firm conviction that he had never recorded a sentiment he need recall, it is Charles Dickens. A charge against him, (especially in Scotland) which has been made to assume the shape of a most serious accusation is, that his scenes and characters, either from congeniality or predilection, are invariably drawn from middle, or lower life; — that the exquisite tone and refinement of fashionable society, are above his conception or ability to portray. But Dickens, like a true student of nature, knows that if his subject require strong and powerful interest he must not seek it in those grades where the passions and feelings ever act under the disguise which the position of the individual casts around him. In search of native wit, humor and force of expression, the writer of fiction must stop long before he reach the circumscribed circle within which the high and mighty invest themselves with the artificialities of their station. Who, let me ask, when dwelling with rapture upon the wondrous fidelity of a painting by Tenniers, or Wilkie, allows his judgment to be warped, or his admiration to be suppressed by the homeliness which those great artists delighted to depict. And so, like them, only in another sphere of art, Dickens raises an everlasting monument to his own renown, by selecting materials that are durable and efficient.

Imbued with this estimate of the author's works, my readers may judge the state of my feelings when, during the most prosperous period of the season, I determined to impart the peculiar excellence of his books to the pub-

lic of Glasgow, the second city of the country that proudly boasts having given birth to Scott and Burns.

DICKENS IN GLASGOW.

It was a fine starlight evening in the month of April,
when, after due process of advertising, posting, and all
the accessories of diurnal attention, I presented myself
white-gloved and chokered, at the Music Hall, to perpe-
trate my "Evening with Charles Dickens." The door
keepers duly arrived with checks, and a heavy amount of
specie for change, posted themselves in orderly array,
waiting the rush of the expectant multitude. The hall,
a most beautiful one, was brilliantly illuminated, and two
rows of extra chairs placed in convenient proximity to the
rostrum. At the specified time the doors were thrown
open with the customary bang, and from the partially
opened door of the retiring room, I listened impatiently
for the approach of my patrons. A painful propriety pervaded the passage way, relieved at brief intervals by one
of the attendants who, with his finger nails, extemporised
a medley composed of the popular airs of his native land,
upon the capacious tin box provided by the establishment
for the receipt of tickets.

. At length, the delicate step of one of the fair sex,
accompanied by the more amply provided tread of one of
the opposite gender, assailed my ears. The audiences are
very fashionable, mused I, and come late here; the rust-
ling of silk approached nearer and stopped in its progress
towards the money taker. I listened, then peeped out. A
lady and gentleman were surveying a formidable bill of
fare hanging in the hall. They perused it with evident care
and circumspection. I felt flattered, for it was replete with
what I considered *good jokes*, concocted after tortuous
offences against the rules of the language, and having got
to the end of it — *turned round — and — walked out !*

This reckless act of deceit inflicted on the door keeper, opened the flood-gates of his commiseration for the degeneracy of his race, and induced him to request his brother in solitude to join issue with him in a copious pinch of snuff, when the following colloquy began:

"What's o'clock?" asked one.

"Ten minutes to eight!" was the reply, consulting his time-keeper for the authority.

"When does he begin?" said the first.

"Why, at eight precisely he says," said the second, "and he was very particular this morning in requesting me to be here at seven, that he might have his audience well and comfortably seated before he began, because he didn't like to be disturbed."

"Well, Sandy," quaintly replied the first, "it strikes me that he won't have much reason to complain of interruption to night."

"Perhaps it might be as well to defer it for a week."

"Aye," said his companion, "or till Christmas or New Year's next; as the public seem to have a previous engagement which they are not disposed to break."

My mind began to drift into that pleasing condition I should imagine a gentleman suffers, who is within the meshes of legal constraint, and anxiously waiting the return of the messenger who has been dispatched for his intimate personal acquaintance to become security for his next appearance, when required.

Three minutes to eight, and the idea began to suggest itself that it was more than probable the projected entertainment might turn out a failure.

The money takers returned to the charge with that delightful *badinage* which so pleasantly diversify the monotony of facetious leisure, when it can be indulged in at the expense of another party than those who comprise the company. The style of these mirthful sallies may be judged by the following:

" Well, look here," said one, " what was all this to be about, Sandy, if it ever does come off? "

"I expect it's a kind of definition of the unknown tongue, which language, it is evident, nobody has any curiosity to learn ; because, if they had, they would certainly have come."

" Wonder where he banks his money?" etc., etc.

These, and similar complimentary remarks in relation to the different aspect of the hall a few nights previous, when the city turned out in great numbers to listen to a professor with a high sounding title, who let them into all the secrets of the heavenly bodies, including the condition of the moon's health at certain seasons in its existence, to which they listened with a reverence and stolid assurance, that justified the conviction that they perfectly comprehended everything he had been so lucidly describing.

Time crept on, till at thirty minutes past the hour I should have commenced, being somewhat disgusted with the proceeding, I considered it prudent to capitulate, and beat a retreat. The owner of the building sympathised with my forlorn condition; and, proposing an invitation to his domicile to partake of the hospitality of a family supper, I saw the lights extinguished, took leave of my facetious, but useless, door-keepers, soon forgot my disappointment over the convivial hilarity of the well appointed table, and the following morning left Glasgow with no great regret.

I mention this incident in my career, principally because I never heard of a similar instance where, after preparations being duly and properly made for an exhibition of any sort or kind, *not an individual* had the curiosity to present themselves to judge of its claims to public approval.

The writer was the first person who had the temerity

to occupy an evening on the subject of this great writer's works. He has since had many imitators, and if they have only experienced half the pleasure he invariably feels in discussing so agreeable a theme, they will be well, and amply repaid.

Another evening with Charles Dickens had a more lively and pleasurable result.

About the middle of the month of April, when one of those time-honored storms had cleared the air of its haziness, and the swiftly pacing clouds were traversing the mottled horizon, leaving its alternate reflection of light and shade upon our path in rapid alternation, I was wending my way homeward from Drury Lane Theatre after acting in the farce. Passing the ancient parish church of Saint Giles, a tumult of female voices, in angry conflict, arrested my attention. It was, unfortunately, so frequent an inroad upon the sense, as well as the sight of those in whose way this neighborhood lay, that it may be little wonder I should have passed it unheeded. It was late, and the streets were mostly deserted, save by those whose career of wretchedness and crime cast them out from the comforts shared by the more fortunate of their fellow beings. I reached the entrance gate of that magnificent structure where the *bas relievo* of the Last Supper has so often excited the admiration of the lover of art, when my attention was directed to a gentleman leaning with crossed arms against the post in front of the church. It was the great novelist, Charles Dickens. He was passing, and had been attracted by a pugilistic encounter between two female unfortunates. He recognized me almost before I saw him, and after the usual compliments of the evening, we walked towards the Regent's Park. My way lay to Camden Town, his to Devonshire Terrace.

The conversation took a dramatic turn, of which Dick-

ens was very fond, and was (to us at least) of such an
agreeable character, that I felt an inward regret when I
reached a point where we should separate. Our good
genius was propitious upon that eventful night, for Mr.
Dickens had a small party at his house, whom he had
been obliged to leave for a few hours to attend a public
dinner in the city; and to this party we were kindly invited. I look back to this accidental meeting, with a
pleasure not easily effaced.

As near as I can remember the party consisted of
Douglas Jerrold, Mark Lemon, Angus B. Reach, Geo.
Cruikshank, John Leach, and two or three others not so
well known to fame.

The host was in his happiest and most genial vein.
Jerrold's grey eye sparkled with delight at every grand
coup he made upon the company; and Lemon and Reach
were profuse in anecdote and song. Cruikshank and
Leach drew pen and ink sketches of every one present,
which I regret I could not obtain as mementos of such
men and such an occasion. Leech sent me a note asking
the copy of a song I had just sang, the autograph from
which I am pleased to say I still retain as the only record I was ever favored with from an artist who has
since passed away, after enriching the world with those
matchless productions of his pencil which we may look
in vain to see equalled or approached.

There are in this world of ours, matter-of-fact people,
whose materialism is of such an aspect that they can so
regard the actions and destinies of the human family, as
to view with perfect indifference the (to them) useless
occupation of literary or artistic excellence. They generally appear to live long, as well as to fatten upon the good
things of this life; while what they may have gained by
toilsome routine descends to their thriftless offspring,
who dispose of it with a rapidity far exceeding the pace
by which it was acquired.

I have no desire to exchange places with these, and to look back to such a night is one of the gems we gather upon life's beach, amid the roar of the turgid and troublesome element. It is the sparkling luminary to guide us as we buffet the surf and treacherous shoals which so plentifully beset us.

Young in years, and struggling for a professional foothold, I clung to the words I heard that night from lips so distinguished, with an avidity none but those who have been similarly placed, whether in the field of commerce or the arts, can realize.

The subjects of conversation were, happily for me, of a dramatic and artistic tone; and a joyous relief after a dreary time I had but just passed with a young enthusiast who was studying for the bar, to which position I fear his capacity can scarcely have permitted him to rise to much distinction.

The day had dawned, and the sun was struggling forth in the manner so often sung by our sweetest poets, when I quitted the house of the great novelist. The locality, and the time, were the twin brothers of thought. No wonder I paced those parterres of spring beauty, and communed with my thoughts and their delicious surroundings.

Apart from Dickens, the one whose name and works will ever be remembered, and whose pen has offered up its incense in behalf of suffering humanity with the hand of a master, stands Douglas Jerrold. Oh Jerrold ! thou great and scathing satirist of the follies and heartlessness of our natures, how little did thy legion of readers know thy early and struggling history.

The drama of " Black-eyed Susan " made the fortune of one manager who shall be nameless here, and scarcely obtained *thee* the value of the paper upon which it was written.

Only those connected with thee in the briery path of letters knew thy worth and patient anguish. The author of the "Caudle Lectures," "Story of a Feather," etc. died at the age of 56, in the month of June 1857, leaving to the world the best nautical drama, *i. e.* "Black-eyed Susan," in the language; and also, to my thinking, the most superior comedy in "Time Works Wonders," since Sheridan.

Mrs. Mowatt and Mr. E. L. Davenport made their first appearance before an English audience at the Theatre Royal, Manchester, on the sixth of December, 1847, in the "Lady of Lyons," thus cast:

Pauline, Mrs. Mowatt; Claude, Mr. E. L. Davenport; Damas, Mr. W. Davidge; they played three weeks. The lady's success has received the approval of the public by her very tasty and poetical manner of recounting the incidents appertaining thereto, under her own signature, that it would be indelicate and unbecoming further to allude to it.

Mr. Davenport was received with great favor.

FANNY KEMBLE AND NEGRO MELODY.

There is a stubbornness of purpose about those who cling to an eccentricity, no matter under what guise it presents itself, that is at all times praiseworthy as exemplifying an independence of spirit and opinion, if it has no other virtue to recommend it. The pedantry of Fanny Kemble's illustrious uncle, who would insist in calling *aches aiches* was a peculiarity that gave rise to much discussion; but I must claim for Mrs. Butler the credit of having distanced the classic John, by introducing a verse of a popular negro melody, descriptive of a voyage down the Ohio river in company with a boatman, in the third act of the "School for Scandal."

The audience were somewhat taken aback by this

rendering of the character of Lady Teazle, and stared at each other with mute astonishment and wonder!

This lady's engagement commenced under the most flattering auspices immediately on her return from America, in 1847. Her first performance at Manchester was in the "Hunchback," Gustavus Brooke, the Master Walter; J. S. Browne, the Lord Tinsel, and W. Davidge, Fatham. She played six nights, and it is to be regretted that the number of visiters to the theatre decreased perceptibly at each representation.

CHAPTER XI.

" Ay, and greater wonders than that."

As you like it.   Act 5.   *Scene* 2.

THE PARSON, AND THE PLAYER.

FOLKSTONE, in Kent, had a saucy, rakish kind of look about it, as we threaded the mazes of the circuitous streets about noon in autumn, after a delightful walk over the gigantic cliffs, from Dover.

It was once asserted by a gentleman who found it necessary to migrate to the shores of France very frequently, for the benefit of an exhausted exchequer, that Folkstone was designed, and laid out, by some beneficent ruler who had inbibed an insatiable desire for contracting debts he was unable, or unwilling to liquidate; and certainly the difficulty of penetrating to any given point, by any, save a native, and the further impossibility of extricating yourself, rather favored the idea of its impregnability to the interference of importunate creditors.

In days gone by, the smuggler plied his busy and profitable trade at all available points in its vicinity; and, at the time of which I write, there were those settled down into the outward guise of respectable commerce, who had, in the spring time of their youth, landed many a keg of contraband liquor, the profits from which had raised them to their present pecuniary consequence.

At a small, compact house, the rear of which, when the weather was clear, afforded a splendid view of the cliffs across the channel, I found comfortable, and economic accommodation. The latter, at that particular juncture a most necessary, and desirable negotiation, inasmuch as I had discovered, after reaching Dover by the ordinary conveyacne from London, that the manager, who presided over the destinies of the dramatic establishment there, had suddenly, and somewhat heartlessly, changed his mind in regard to the period of his projected occupancy of the theatre; leaving his company to shift for themselves, in the interim, as best they could.

Folkstone is not a place I would conscientiously advise an enthusiast in art, whether music, painting, or the drama, to visit professionally, with a view to the acquisition of great pecuniary reward. Its population are for the most part engaged in excursions upon the ocean for the capture of fish wherewith to supply the wants of the London consumers, and are frequently, by adverse winds, blown upon the French coast; there to repose until the great Boreas changes the current of his thoughts, and drifts them back again to their own habitations.

The dramatic season commenced in a few days after my arrival, with that negative kind of success which left the members of the company in extreme doubt whether they would receive sufficient to enable them to pay their way for the two months it was proposed to occupy the building. One night, the house would look dreary and deserted; another, it would be honored by the presence and patronage of the mayor, and corporation, or the members of parliament for the county. On the latter interesting occasion, even those who entertained scruples in regard to the propriety of dramatic representations, waived their objections in honor of the guardian of their rights and privileges before the august House of Commons.

In the company was an actor whose name was Moine. He had a wife, and two children, the former somewhat

sickly, and the latter too young to be of any pecuniary
advantage to the household.

Moine was a studious man not only in his profession,
but he had considerable skill in painting, and spent all
his leisure time in sketching the beauties of nature. He
was also a constant frequenter of the Episcopal church.
I mention this not as an exception to those of his class,
but as a prelude to the conduct of the story. The other
members of the company, who paid their devotion to
the same form of religious worship had nothing remarkable in their appearance to attract attention as they quietly took their seats the first Sunday morning after their
arrival, at the church of the Rev. Mr. R——, but in Moine
there was a peculiarity difficult to define; as with his
two children he waited for the pew opener to place him
in some unoccupied spot.

It was evident that the congregation, as well as the
pastor, could not avoid noticing the new worshipper
every time he uttered the responses in a voice of much
power and richness.

Very soon each member of the company became known
by sight to the attendants of the church, some of whom,
being play-goers, rather exceeded the bounds of religious
decorum by the manner in which they would scan us as
we entered the edifice.

The sun was setting on the evening of a beautiful day
in the latter part of the month of August. The ocean
had just recovered from a storm of the previous day,
and now lay sullenly depositing the results of its fury
upon the coast as far as the eye could reach. A fishing
party had just reached the beach, and were proceeding
to haul in the proceeds of their adventure; when, in
turning the corner of a road at the summit of the cliff,
the parson came upon the player in the act of sketching
the picture.

It was a pleasant meeting to both. The parson speedily discovered, that he was in the presence of an artist of no mean ability; while the player found a sympathy in appreciation, common only among intellects of the highest order.

When the darkness came on, and the player closed his sketch book, the pair walked in company towards the town, and separated for the night.

At the circulating library of all watering places, may be found a class of idlers whose *nominal* object for their presence there, is to enjoy rational and social intercourse on matters of public and political interest; but whose *actual* amusement, is to appease their appetite for scandal. Folkstone was not a whit behind in this popular accomplishment, and freely canvassed the impropriety of a recognition by their divine, of a erson so far beneath him as his companion of the previous evening; and it was matter for the deepest concern in the minds of his admirers, as well as dangerous to the best interests of religious teaching.

The winter came on with great severity, and caused a depression in the trade of the town, which had the effect of closing the theatre from lack of patronage; leaving Moine without the means of quitting the place, even could he have found another field for his professional labors, which was doubtful. All the positions worth having were already occupied, and managers are shy of engaging persons of whose name they never heard, and of whose ability they are equally ignorant.

Christmas had just passed, and still no sign of employment. The parson had become by this time quite intimate with the family of the player, despite the parochial proscription, and called frequently to see them, invariably laden with some little compliment for the children, of whom he grew quite fond. He was himself a lover of painting, and could sketch a little. No wonder then that he embraced every leisure hour to watch the painter at his easel.

He saw plainly the embarrassed condition of his newly found acquaintance, but delicacy for the feelings of an over sensitive nature, prevented any allusion to it.

It was snowing hard, and the wind blowing fiercely from all points of the compass, as it appeared to Moine, when he turned the corner of the street near the market place, carrying under his arm a hastily painted picture, then scarcely dry, of a view upon the coast. The same day might be seen exhibited in a window in the principal street of the town a little gem of art, with a label attached to it, to the effect that it might be purchased at a small price; and further, that the author of it would be glad to receive a few pupils for instruction in oil-painting, at moderate cost.

The next day, the player watched with eagerness the several passers by who stopped to scan his last effort, and listened to the comments freely made thereon. When he returned to his lodgings, his eldest child met him with surprise upon her face, and with difficulty told him that a lady and gentleman had called in their carriage to enquire for him, and leaving their address, had requested that he would attend upon them at their residence the following day.

The parson was in his study compiling a sermon for the next Sabbath, when Moine, somewhat elated, conveyed to him the pleasing fact that he had a prospect of employment.

"I congratulate you, Moine, you will doubtless find in them profitable patrons. The gentleman is wealthy, and a man of leisure, as well as a lover of art! His wife, however, is somewhat eccentric, and may propound questions on matters of which she is entirely ignorant. You must, therefore, be prepared for her," said the parson.

Thanking his patron and friend for this valuable hint, the player withdrew to ponder on the chance of success in his newly advertised career, and was up betimes in the morning, working at his easel with brighter hopes than he had indulged in for many a day.

A beautiful villa upon an eminence commanding a view of the sea, was the spot to which he directed his steps at the appointed time.

A philosopher once asserted, that in order to form a correct estimate of a man's claim to a position in the world of taste, it was not necessary to scan the individual himself, but merely guage him by the quality of his pictures. The painter soon discovered that he was beneath the roof of one who could fairly boast the possession of a knowledge of the beautiful, and the good fortune to have ample means to indulge in the luxury.

A bargain was soon made for the work so recently exhibited, and a contract entered into for another as companion to it, with a request that the purchaser have the one already finished the following day, for which a check would be ready.

From this day the star of Moine was in the ascendant. It soon became noised about that the beautiful marine view, by an unknown artist, lately exhibited in a shop-window of the town, had been purchased for a goodly amount by the wealthy Mr. ——, and commissions to an unlimited extent given the painter, for more.

A sudden and irrepressible desire was speedily observed to manifest itself for pictures by the fortunate artist, from persons whose slumbering taste for art had just awoke to the consciousness, that truthful copies of the beauties of nature was a great humanizer of their species, and quite impossible to be dispensed with.

It was not long before it became noised about, that the artist whose pictures were in such request, was none oth-

er than a member of the theatrical company whose presence had been a subject of comment in certain high
quarters; the terrible discovery, like other local afflic-
tions, went through its various stages in strict accordance
with nature's laws, and was superseded by an act of great
atrocity on the part of a portionless, but well favored
youth ; who had, without permission of those (*whom it
did not concern*) taken to wife the first born of a wealthy
resident, and the belle of the neighborhood.

By the kindly influence of the parson, the prejudice
began to disappear to such an extent, that men of high
moral notions commenced a series of patronizing recog-
nitions when they encountered the player in their ram-
bles, and assured him that his position in their esteem
was duly registered.

His fame became a matter for complimentary notices,
and led to an offer from the great metropolis as assistant
to a distinguished scene painter. It was a few days prior to
his departure, that the parson gave a small party to his
personal friends. Moine was one of the number; and
as it was the last opportunity he could have of enjoying
the society of his patron before he left the town, it is no
wonder that he lingered, while the rest of the guests departed, to take his farewell.

They adjourned to the library, where the parson proposed to append his autograph to a volume, from his
large store of literary gems, for the painter's acceptance.

Seated at the table where he compiled the discourses
that so satisfied his hearers of the purity of his nature
and consistency of his religious faith, did the parson, for
the first time during their acquaintanceship, recount the
struggle he had experienced with many of his congregation, on the supposed impropriety of the profession to
which the painter, as an actor, also belonged.

"My dear friend," he continued, " you would be much

amused could you be a listener, as I have been, of the absurd objections urged against an amusement, as well as source of instruction, that millions of our fellow creatures look upon as an absolute necessity. I have been solicited numberless times to deliver what they are pleased to call admonitory sermons on the subject, for the purpose of guarding the youth of the district against the evils that surround them, if they indulge in rational recreation ; and I have always fenced with the difficulty of an attempt to satisfy them of the delusion they labor under, and thus avoided making the absurd attempt. My friend Mr. B—— of Sheffield, one of the most powerful opponents of the stage, and who preaches an annual sermon on the subject, once admitted to me, that he only did so in obedience to a promise he had made many years before, and that no one was more conscious of the fallacy of the attempt, than himself. My acquaintanceship with you has given me what I much desired, namely, it has placed me in a position to be able to scrutinize the social condition of members of the profession to which you belong ; and I am pleased to observe, that I can see no visible difference between them, and persons engaged in matters of trade, or commerce, save that their education is mostly superior, and they are a great deal more artless in their business transactions." "This," said he, "has fully confirmed me in the conclusions I had formed in my own mind, because I saw no reason why it should not be so! Further, I cannot help believing that many of my clerical brethren are not quite as orthodox as they would have the world believe ; for, when I was last in London, I observed two of them at a place of entertainment they would not venture to approach in their own diocese. I am thus impressed with the belief, that the clergy, speaking collectively, prefer to acquiesce in the objections of their over zealous flocks, rather than attempt the fruitless effort of convincing them of their error. Let us however turn to more interesting matter, and before you leave, enter into a compact to correspond with each other periodically and faithfully, and I need not assure you, that no one can more desire to perpetuate our friendship, than myself."

The player and painter grasped the hand of his patron, and, scarcely able to express his gratitude, promised to write constantly a record of his doings.

The moon was shining brightly and, as the player unsnapped the wicket of the gate, he turned, and beheld the kindly features of the parson smiling an adieu.

The compact was most zealously kept on both sides, for several years; and an interchange of thought and sentiment duly enjoyed, and appreciated.

Within the church, that so often echoed with the voice of the parson, is placed a tablet modestly inscribed to the memory of him who was beyond reproach as a man and equaled by few as a theologian; while the player and painter still lives, at the summit of his art, in daily communion with the greatest celebrities of the age.

CHAPTER XII.

" I have seen drunkards do more than this."
King Lear. Act 2. Scene 1.

THE DRUNKEN ACTOR.

THE streets of London were begrimed with the refuse
of a good old fashioned snow storm, swelling its gutters
and gullies to their utmost capacity. A rapid thaw cast
a glow of premature spring over an evening in the month
of February, as a man past the meridian of life presented
himself at the stage door of the Olympic Theatre, and
sought to renew an acquaintanceship that had, from
untoward circumstances, ceased for many years.

He was but poorly accoutred to resist the inclemency
of the season's severity. Yet, from long habit of breast-
ing the terrors of poverty, assumed an aspect of partial
cheerfulness and content.

I was made cognizant of his presence by the stage
door keeper, who sent to my dressing room the following
written in pencil on the back of a play bill:

"Long ago, nearly as long as when Douglas Jerrold
introduced us to a William that married Susan, we knew
a William who wedded himself to our dearest affections,
and regard. Though hard fortune has furrowed our
cheeks, and the implacable and stern despot, Time, silvered
our once raven locks, the recollection of happier days
blooms as verdantly as ever. If our William's memory
be not impaired by the fond caresses of Crœsus, conjointly

with the mythological individual who exercises his musical abilities upon a trumpet, y'clept "fame," and will mingle hearts, one is waiting at the back door to join issue in the conflict.

JOHN J. L."

As soon as convenience would permit, I sought the author of the above, and tendered him a hearty welcome. We had not seen each other for ten years, and his name had disappeared from theatrical circles.

The weather had suddenly veered round, the moon was shining with an intensity that cast all objects outside its refraction into the folds of darkness, as I emerged, with my old acquaintance, from the stage door, and speedily found a warm, and cheerful spot where we sought a retrospect of our past history.

My companion was a man of liberal education; tutored in the early part of his career for the study and practice of medicine, for which pursuit he felt no congeniality; but rather, (as many have done before, and since) courted the blandishments of the tragic muse, who artfully engulphed him in her merciless meshes.

The finer and more acute emotions of an ingenuous nature are frequently placed in array against the chicanery of arrogant pretension, or ignorant vulgarity; consequently my friend was ever in a state of declension with those into whose power he might happen to fall.

He had brought up a large family upon very scanty means, all of whom were dead, save one, whose assistance he could never be prevailed upon to solicit; because he had unjustly, (but as he believed for the best) opposed her union with a person in whom he had no confidence.

When we had exhausted every enquiry respecting the fate, or whereabout of old associates, he extracted a promise that we would pay him a visit on the following day. Taking his address for that purpose, we parted for the night, and as he reached the corner, a violent gust of wind, having a contrary destination, met him at full tilt, and seemed determined to change his course. At the imminent peril of being blown off his legs, he grasped his hat with both hands, tacked against the enemy, and was soon beyond the limits of our observation.

The water side, as pleasure seekers regard it, is a place with associations of healthful immersions during the warm season of the year; or a contemplation of the wonderful power of Nature's laws, while you view its angry foaming, as it lashes itself into fury, during the pealing of the angry storm.

Rotherithe is considered by the genuine, unadulterated Londoner, to be at the water side. It has an aquatic tone about it that affords an agreeable zest to the pent up cockney, who makes occasional forays upon it during the cessation from his weekly labor. It is a suburb that has for years been struggling under the difficulty of gradually using its characteristics as a watering place, without acquiring much landed privilege as an equivalent for its loss. I found myself next day threading the mazes of this amphibious dwelling place, at a time when the air was fetid with the fumes of bilge water, and stagnant pools of rank garbage, in odoriferous conjunction.

A small frame building, or shed, very much out of the perpendicular, and reclining at an angle of about twenty degrees against one of the arches of the Greenwich railroad, contained the object of my search ; where, I could not help reflecting, nothing but the direst necessity could induce a fellow creature to linger out an existence. The approach to it was across a plot of ground digusting to the sight, and clammy to the tread. As far as the eye could reach ran the arches of the railroad company, those resting places for the beggar and the outcast, some of its miserable occupants huddled in corners, and scrutinizing with a wistful aspect, the cold victuals charity had donated them during their morning's importunity. It is to be regretted that the laudable attempts at vegetation here and there manifest, did not appear to be attended with a very fertile result. The population were evidently engaged at their ordinary occupation; but the hogs, those monarchs of luxurious leisure, rambled and wallowed, perfect masters of the soil. A very small girl, wrapped in a very small and gauzy shawl, but wearing a bonnet of such astounding dimensions that it evidently was the personal property of the maternal head of the family, emerged from a side door, carrying in her hand a brown pitcher, crossed my path. Of her, I enquired for the person I had come to visit. She pointed out the place, and as I moved away, a mongrel dog, the color of his skin entirely obliterated from a recent ablution in the mud, came running across an open space, with a growl of discontent at the presence of a stranger.

My friend's tenement I presumed was a fair sample of the rest, and boasted little in the shape of comfort, and certainly nothing in the form of luxury. A common table, and two or three chairs, with a sleeping spot upon an old sofa, formed nearly the entire inventory of the place.

My friend had lost his jovial aspect of the previous night, and was engaged at the table writing, when I entered in obedience to his summons. After finishing the sentence on which he was employed, he rose to greet me and placed a chair for my use. I looked with a feeling of sadness upon the wreck I saw before me, as he proceeded to brighten up the almost expired fire with a few sticks, and a cake of turf. Gradually I ventured to touch upon his present condition, propounding questions relative to the causes that had led to it.

He had hoped, he said, to be relieved from the pain of recapitulating the disasters of his career; because he could find few in the profession who were ready to bestow adequate sympathy for all his efforts to fight the battle of dramatic life against the most terrible odds.

I assured him I was personally desirous to offer my most sincere regrets that misfortune should have so dealt with one for whom, during a pretty long professional acquaintanceship, I had always entertained the highest respect. Striving to admonish him for his good, hoping it might not be too late, with firmness of purpose, to restore himself to an eminence he could so easily assume, by attention and sobriety.

He heard me through without interruption, and when I had finished, crossed to where I was seated, grasped my hand, resumed his walk about the room, as the tears started to his eyes, despite his efforts to check them.

Presently he appeared to be relieved, and proceeded.

"When I first knew you, I had bright hopes of a prosperous business future. My name stood well in all dramatic circles, and I was petted, and caressed by the public. My disposition was not proof against the blandishments of convivial enjoyment, and the misrepresentations of false prophets. To assist, as I then believed, the exigencies of the theatre, I yielded to the wish of the management, and resigned parts that I had long been in possession of, for others of an inferior grade. After a season or two, I found myself gradually, but surely, receding in public esteem as an actor, with the manager, as well as his patrons. In assigning parts, the autocrat of the theatre didn't consider it good generalship to place me in a prominent position, after what I had been lately personating. He was callous to the fact that I had, to spare him a larger expenditure, beggared my fortunes, and ruined my future prospects. My income began seriously to diminish ; with that came the humiliation of dancing attendance upon every speculator who might hire a theatre for a month or two, without the slightest notion of meeting his liabilities should the public fail to patronize the imbecility of his system of management. My wife fell sick during my long cessation from business. I saw her gradually fading from my sight ; my children were often clamorous for food, and I have rushed from the house with a heavy heart and sinking spirit ; hoping in my despair that death would soon relieve us all. Credit, of course, I had none. *I was an actor.* And ignorance had set its seal of doubt upon the honesty of the race.

"My spirit gave way beneath this load of misery ; my wife died ; my children were sinking with the similar affliction that had deprived me of her ; and I flew to drink, to obliterate the misery with which I was encompassed. My professional brethren were sad at the contemplation looming for me in the future ; while some few of them (affecting to symphathize with my condition) were covertly assigning as a reason for my lack of employment, that, hitherto, the force of circumstances had elevated me much above my deserts ; that now I had found my proper level, and must be content with parts of minor importance. I learned this, by letter from a stranger, who had heard me thus alluded to by persons who, in my presence, affected to feel great interest in my well doing.

"My life became hateful to me ! My youngest child was fast sinking. I had no means wherewith to purchase necessaries, and, but for the kindness of a lady member of the profession, she would have cheated nature, and expired from want, ere comsumption would exercise its terrible sway. My stage properties began to disappear one by one. The friends I occasionally met would, unthinking-ly, add fuel to my already heated brain, by inviting me to drink, but none offered me food, which I stood so much in need of.

"One night, the weather was intensely hot, I was alone with my child, without a light, for I had no means to pur-chase a candle. Wearied with fruitless efforts to procure comforts for my dying child, I was dozing heavily; the moonlight streamed, with an opaque mistiness, into the room, and the spirit of my little one was calmly drifting to its ebb. I rose hastily, for I thought I heard the dying one call for drink. The church clock struck two as I approach-ed the window to obtain what I needed. When I reached it, the room was much obscured by dark clouds, but I saw or thought I did, the figure of my wife. My whole body became suffused with perspiration. I tried to speak, but was unable to utter a sound. Actions of my life, long forgotten, came back upon my memory, with the freshness of yesterday, as we are told thoughts crowd upon the mind of the drowning; and I staggered with affright.

"When I came to myself my patient had ceased her heavy breathing, and lay with eyes fixed upon where the vision of her mother was, with the filmy hue of rapidly approach-ing death. I threw myself upon my knees beside her, and thought my heart would break. She stretched out her slim hand towards me, and smilingly whispered,

"'Dear father, you saw her? so did I. You will live happily when I am not an expense to you ; think of dear mother, and me. God bless you, dear father.'

"I took her fragile form in my embrace, and kissed her pale lips. A final adieu left its flickering breath upon my face, as she passed quietly away. I resolved never to touch liquor again, and have strictly adhered to my determina-tion. My character for sobriety has long been forfeited, and no one would give me credit for resistance. I eke out

a scanty living by writing stories of the sensation order,
for cheap publications; but the pay is barely sufficient to
sustain life, and the degradation bitter enough, heaven
knows! For hours do I sit here penning incidents of fashionable life, without very congenial surroundings for the
task. I have been so long out of the profession, that I
doubt if I could fulfill the duties of a situation were I fortunate enough to obtain one."

I entreated him not to despair,— that all men had met
with reverses, and every unfortunate considered his affliction more poignant than his fellow creatures'. I would
exert the little influence I had — it was not much — to relieve him from his present position.

He thanked me, but had no hope of my success. Roll-
ing up the sheets of a manuscript, he accompanied me
on the way to town, quitting me in the Strand, where he
disappeared among the horde of cheap publication offices
that infest Holywell street.

I was successful on my friend's behalf. I found a manager who had himself been the victim of intemperance, but
had bravely conquered the enemy. Under his sympathetic care the "Drunken Actor" lived in comfort and respectability, assuming his former position as an artist, a worthy
exemplar to his brethren of the buskin, whom it is most
earnestly desired will follow in his penitent pathway.

OXBERRY AND THE LEATHER BREECHES.

Little Billy Oxberry, whose happy, genial countenance
sadly belied the bent of a nature suffering under the pressure of inertness and hypochondria, was, in the year
1837, stage manager of the Victoria Theatre, London. I
was engaged on the establishment at the time, to play
second old men. The part of Grainger in the "Miller's
Maid" fell to our lot, Oxberry being the Matty Marvellous.
The two characters in one of the scenes have to blend

their dialogue in the side speeches so as to form a continuous subject, as thus :

Matty. The old woman died when they were very
young.

Grainger. (*singing*) " But love, the destroyer of high,
and of low."

Matty. And poor Phœbe and George went to the
workhouse.

Grainger. Hey Phœbe, and George (*sings*) " That
shoots at the peasant, as well as the beau."

Matty. George went to sea, and Phœbe to service;
after some years miraculously meet, and Phœbe's eyes —

Grainger. Shot the poor cobbler right through the
heart, — derry down, down derry.

The reader may judge the surprise I felt at the following interpretation from the lips of the manager.

Grainger. "But love, the disturber of high and of
low — "

Matty. Bless my soul, what a funny looking old soldier that is, there.

Grainger. " That shoots at the peasant, as well as the
beau."

Matty. That poor old man ought to be taken care
of, it really is a sin for his friends to permit him to wander about with such an attack of lunacy upon him.

Grainger. " Shot the poor cobbler " &c. &c.

At the end of the scene I congratulated him on the ingenuity exhibited, whereby the author's meaning was entirely superceded.

" Ah ! " said he, " I knew it would be so, before I went
on the stage to-night; there's a fatality in 'em. I'm sure
of it."

" Fatality in what, said I ? "

" It's the breeches ! I never do know a line of any
part I play in 'em."

Poor Oxberry, he was a kindly hearted man! totally unfitted for the profession of the stage, where to-day you may be basking in the sunshine of the world's favor, and in a brief period feel the chilling touch of indifference and neglect. For all he had a cheering word of encouragement, regardless of the line of business they professed. He will long be remembered as one of the most comic, and graceful actors that ever trod the English stage, when he could battle with his inertness, and learn the words of his author. His father was distinguished as a comedian of great merit; and his "Dramatic Biography" of the leading actors and actresses of his time, is the only reliable and scholarly production on the subject, it has been my good fortune to peruse. The son possessed much of his father's talent off, as well as on the stage; and has bequeathed to the world several very cleverly constructed dramas. He died in the year 1852, in the forty-fourth year of his age. Let the sceptic, who would look with an eye of doubt upon the avocation of the player, drop a tear to the memory of one who passed away breathing the accents of christian resignation to God, and affectionate solicitude for those around him.

His sickness had been severe and protracted; yet he clung to the hallucination of an ultimate recovery, till an hour before his death. The Melvilles, related to him by marriage, were unceasing in their desire to soothe the last moments of the dying one, who closed his earthly account in the following touching acknowledgment.

Wednesday night, half-past ten, 25th February, 1852.
May my Almighty Maker, to whom I am about to offer up my soul for redemption and his mercy, pardon me for all. Through Jesus Christ, Amen.

To all my friends, I say, Farewell, the few but faithful.

To the best of them, my dear Charles Melville, that kind-hearted man, whom God bless, his wife, his family.

Twelve minutes to eleven.

To Charles Melville I leave all I have in the world, to do the best he can with for my children, to whom I leave the love of a father, which I hope they'll leave as pure as he, in teaching them to be good boys, to study, work, and become honest members of the world. All those who have injured me in the world I forgive, as I hope to be forgiven. For the articles I have by me which are not my own, to be returned to the owners. My wife's gold watch, Ellinor Malcombe Oxberry's, his mother's, I hope my son William to have. My mourning ring to Charles Melville. I have worked hard in the world — tried to do all the good I could — I hope the world won't forget my children when I am gone. I had the honor of receiving her majesty's thanks, on the occasion of her state visit, eight days after her marriage, and in the very part which has caused my death. This is a strange incident. My dramas, as a member of the Authors' Society — I have twenty or thirty new pieces — some of them may be disposed of. My Chronology, contained in my private pocket-book, improved and corrected, &c., may be disposed of to any publisher for the benefit of my children to buy things necessary.

I wish Mr. James Syer to bury me — let this be printed in the morning papers — bury me with my mother in the same grave at St. Peter's, Camberwell, and that Mr. Peters is requested to attend the same, and point out the spot, &c., &c. God bless all my relations.

I should like to lay by my poor old mother; nobody will quarrel with me for that.

Remember me to Miss Grove, F. Mathews, Roxby, Beverley, Charles Mathews, Madame Vestris, Tully, De Vuighi.

I hope Melville will keep my scrap-books for my sake; Ellen's for William till one-and-twenty.

All my family portraits, likeness of my father and myself, for William to keep, also those of my sister, &c.

(Let me sign while I can).

WILLIAM HENRY OXBERRY.

CHARLES MELVILLE, Sen. }
CHARLES MELVILLE, Jun. } Witnesses.

To Captain Walker write, Wellington-road, Regent's Park, of Sandhurst Lodge, lent me £5 7s., as security for which I gave him an original painting of my father, by Drummond, and a little oil, by W. Beverly, bound book, selected autographs (theatricals), and the drawing of myself, &c., the original drawing of my father in *Neversour*, by Wageman, and I hope my friends will get up a benefit for me. I hope these may be redeemed, and kept in the hands of Melville till my boys are of age. I am in debt. I hope funds may be raised to liquidate them. They are very moderate. My long illness has been the cause of all. Once more, God bless my children, and Melville, and his family; the same to my dear Fannie, Mrs. Lancaster, sen., and all the Mr. and Mrs. Lancasters, and their families; the Cullinfords, for their great kindness to me; Joseph Wood, my staunch friend; Richard Flexmore, whom I esteem as a brother. All my playbills Melville will include in his affairs, they are valuable. My regards to William Brew, E. Wright, Mr. Bedford, Compton, Keeley and his wife, Benjamin and Frederick Webster, W. S. Johnson, St. Martin's-lane, printer; Mr. Jarvis, Mr. Donald Nicol, Mr. John Garland, of Oxford-market, a firm friend when I wanted him; Mr. H. Daws; Richards, of Rathbone-place; Mr. Kemp, Stone's banking house (formerly of). I hope my body may be opened for the sake

of science, and a warning to those who neglect colds.
My heart and lungs I know are, I feel, chronically dis-
eased; my liver and my stomach are disorganized. My
heart I wish to be preserved as a specimen of a broken
one, and placed in some medical museum in Surgeon's
Hall, where I was articled to Doctor Septimus Wray, to
whom I leave my sincere respects, and hope he'll pray
for the pupil who deserted him. I can't think of anything more. God bless you all. To my poor, dear Eliza,
my love and esteem as an affectionate brother-in-law —
my gratitude, my last prayer for her happiness and welfare.

(Witnessed)   CHARLES MELVILLE, Jun.
               CHARLES MELVILLE, Sen.

There are five Sundays in this month; I should like to
be buried on one of them.

STEALING ANOTHER'S THUNDER.

Farley, the great genius of pantomime, for so many
years at Covent Garden Theatre, had once introduced a
beautiful effect in one of his productions, by causing Col-
umbine to be lured to sleep in the bowers of Paphos;
and then to ascend on her flowery couch, to the regions
of love.

Some weeks after the success of the piece, Farley was
taking a Sunday stroll, when he was overtaken by a
shower of rain, which drove him to seek shelter in a
Methodist chapel, as the nearest refuge at hand.

Just as he entered the building, the preacher was nar-
rating the particulars attendant upon his conversion, and
exclaimed in stentorian voice,

" I felt, my beloved brethren, I felt as if I was rising to
heaven on a bed of roses, with a pair of silver shoes upon
my feet."

"You have stolen that idea from my pantomime, by heaven!" cried Farley, to the astonishment of all; and rushed from the place instanter, boiling with indignation.

COURT THEATRICALS.

Those of my professional brethren who have taken part in the dramatic representations at Windsor castle, before her majesty the Queen, and her court, will, I am certain, recollect with much pleasure the kindness exhibited to them by a monarch who has shed a lustre upon the British throne, and whose personal recognition of many of the members of the profession of acting, might serve as a bright example to those whose ignorance of the true principles of art prompt them to condemn or remain indifferent to what they have not the intelligence to comprehend, and who can see nothing to admire in the social, or professional life, of the player.

The last of these events with which I was connected, occurred in the winter of 1849. The play was Julius Cæsar, thus cast: Brutus, Macready; Cassius, J. Wallack; Marc Antony, C. Kean; Casca, J. Cooper; Octavius, Leigh Murray; Julius Cæsar, C. Fisher; Soothsayer, Davidge, and Portia, Mrs. Warner.

The reader will please bear in mind that there never has been much regard in the minds of C. Kean and Macready for each other, and the selection by her majesty, of the former as dramatic conductor, and director of the state performances, was not likely to allay the ill feeling. It was the first time Macready had been requested to present himself professionally at the palace, and he would gladly, in consequence of Kean's presence there, have availed himself of a refusal, if it could have been accomplished gracefully, and without offence.

The space allotted for the stage, erected in the Rubens room of the castle, is very limited for the representation of Shakspeare's plays. It is therefore necessary to make some slight deviation from the customary mode of disposing of the scenes and characters. The rehearsals take place at the Haymarket Theatre, the stage being contracted by the side wings in such a way as to present to the actors the exact distance they will have to occupy at the palace.

Macready did not attend any of the rehearsals, being at Birmingham fulfilling an engagement. It was necessary therefore to explain the difficulties by letter. A morning or two prior to the performance, I met Mr. C. Kean in the green room with an open letter in his hand, at which he seemed highly diverted! On complimenting him on his unusual flow of spirits, he said, " I never heard of anything more amusing in all my life."

" As what?" said I.

" I always knew Macready was extremely eccentric, but this beats all I ever knew. Would you believe it! I thought it advisable to explain to him the difficulties we had to contend with from lack of space, and requested; in consideration, that he would be good enough to dispense with the senate sitting, because we had no means of removing their seats without dropping the curtain; and here's his answer. What do you think it is? "

" Don't know? " said I.

" I'm sure you'd never guess it! what an idea! eood, Sir, he refers me to his solicitor, and declines to hold any communication on any subject except through him."

In December 1847, I made my re-appearance in London at the Olympic (destroyed by fire April 4th, 1849) in the character of Sir Anthony Absolute in the " Rivals," and in the following month, Mr. G. V. Brooke,* and Mr. Lysander

* Lost in Steamer " London " in the Bay of Biscay, January 11, 1866, aged 48.

Thompson presented their claims for Metropolitan approval at the same theatre, the former in Othello, and the latter in Tyke. Without vanity, I may say that the debuts
were quite successful, the two latter particularly, but the
concern, by some outside pressure, became involved, and
closed prematurely after a season of six months.

At the end of the year 1849, I joined Mr. James Anderson, at Drury Lane. A short season ended disastrously,
and I accepted an offer from Mr. J. Hall Wilton the celebrated business agent, to join Mr. E. A. Marshall at the Broadway Theatre, New York, for two years. My contract binding me to play the principal old men ; parts in extravaganza
and burlesque, and characters in the Shaksperian drama
where there were two of about equal importance, such as
Launce, and Speed in the "Two Gentlemen of Verona," etc.
The inaptitude, or lack of experience, of the gentleman
who was retained for the comedy, forced me into some
positions for which act of rashness I am duly penitent.

The engagements made in London by Mr. Wilton were
Mr. F. B. Conway, Mrs. F. B. Conway (died in New
York in 1851), Miss Anderson, Miss Richardson, (died
in Australia in 1861,) the Misses Gougenheim, and Mr.
Scharf. In company with these I set sail in the steamer
Canada, from Liverpool, on the 21st of July, 1850.

A voyage across the Atlantic has been so ably and
graphically described by so many writers, that it is somewhat hazardous to venture upon a repetition. As every
one however prefers to tell his own story in his own way,
I propose, nothing daunted, to recount my impressions
of the mighty deep, and some of my fellow sufferers who
confided themselves to its guardianship.

CHAPTER XIII.

" To the wild ocean."

Two Gentlemen of Verona. Act 2. Scene 7.

"Do you ever suffer from sea sickness?" was the question propounded by a dashing looking youth, in a faultless travelling costume, to a young lady of delicate complexion, as we rounded the light house at the entrance of the Mersey.

"Well really, I don't know. I havn't been on salt water since pa took us all to Yarmouth for the season, three summers ago. Pa prefers Yarmouth, because he says the air is better than at Brighton or Hastings; and the lodging-house keepers are not half so extortionate; but for my part, I consider Yarmouth a shocking place, don't you? No style about it, no society that one cares to mix with, nothing but farmers and tradesmen in middling circumstances, and who can't afford to go to the two former, show off their dowdy wives and daughters there. No military either; it's really fortunate almost for me that I was in too delicate a state of health to be much about; but my sister Helen, she's so absurd, she condescended to play two or three games at backgammon with some people who lived in the house, I assure you very much to my disgust! Then she's so free in her manners."

"Yaas, true," responded the youth, "Yarmouth not much of a place — no yacht club there, with anybody one cares to know in it; — very good herrings, — those

bloaters, good things for breakfast! that's all I could ever
see in the place. My fellow knows a man lives down
there, who breeds dogs. When we return, I'll send you
a nice terrier, if you'd like to have one, — good things
for rats, you know."

Lady gives him a ghastly smile of thanks for his offer,
the sky begins to indicate the going down of the sun,
she turns her camp stool to windward, attempts a glowing panegyric on the brilliancy of the scene, and the invigorating influence of the sea air; the description is
suddenly abbreviated by a violent lurch, she rises to go,
staggers into the arms of the captain, who always is on
hand ·when a desirable looking woman needs his assistance, is piloted by him to the companion way, where
she gradually descends to her berth by the aid of the
brass hand rail, and is seen no more till we pass the banks
of Newfoundland, and are in smooth water.

The youth is getting very unsteady about the legs, but
makes strong effort to preserve his equilibrium, — his
yatching experience don't seem to have qualified him for
sea travelling, — and after vainly attempting to light a cigar, takes advantage of a slight cessation of hostilities, and
beats a retreat.

The sailors, denuded of their clean white pants and
shirts, now appear muffled in tarpauling; the pilot takes
leave of the captain, steps into his boat and is soon miles
away. On we go with every prospect of a dirty night;
ladies who have heroically resisted the giddiness consequent on the motion of the vessel, and are plying the
needle with astonishing perseverance under such adverse
circumstances, now begin to change the current of their
thoughts and desires, by artfully recollecting they have
left their scissors below, and are assisted in their voyage
of discovery by an old traveller or two, who lead them
towards the gangway, from which they do not make their
reappearance for several days.

Two or three gentlemen, who affect to be perfect masters of the use of the compass, glance knowingly at that mystic instrument, and closing their left eyes, take an observation of the horizon with a degree of self-satisfaction which affords a source of amusement to the men in charge of the rudder. The ship gives another heavy lurch, the knowing ones say the barometer indicates an approaching storm, and make for the gentlemen's smoking room, amidships. We are delighted to have an excuse to shift our position, and attempt to follow. A strong gust of wind takes a hat belonging to one of the party into its embrace, and it skims the water as far as the eye can reach, on its way back to Liverpool, amidst a shout of derision! The boatswain's whistle is immediately responded to by the sailors who, with a precision and speed quite wonderful to the eye of the landsman, make everything snug and secure for any outburst of the elements.

The rain begins to fall in heavy drops as I am, by the aid of the bulwarks, making my way for shelter; but before I can accomplish my intention, I receive an instalment of the foaming surf full in my face. I reeled a yard or two clinging to a coil of rope, and no sooner recover from the shock, than I get it plentifully from every quarter, and with terrible misgivings of a dreaded infirmity consequent upon travelling by sea, stagger towards the saloon, which I find occupied by many of the most expert at that kind of locomotion, if you are to credit the landation so freely expressed by themselves before the vessel left her dock.

I make every effort of which I am capable, to ignore the bare supposition that I mean to be sea sick. An old friend who had been everywhere, and done everything, humanely furnished me with some most valuable hints in relation to resisting the dreaded malady, and I am resolved to carry them to execution.

The sea begins to lash itself into an extra attack of
ferocity, while I am in the act of unlocking a valise to
search for the infallible remedy. I lose my presence of
mind, become speedily indifferent to the taste of all sub-
lunary things, and would willingly submit to be made a
sacrifice to the insatiable fury of the aquatic monster,
without a pang of fear, or murmur of regret.

The Niagara, on its way from New York, passes us within hailing distance. She carries her flag at half mast.
The captains hold an unintelligible interview through
speaking trumpets, and we learn, that is to say, they do,
for I am not in a condition to be intrusive of other men's
matters, that the gallant warrior, General Taylor, has gone
to his long resting place two or three days before the
vessel sailed.

I took two days probationary service, ere I was able to
devote a thought on the condition of my neighbors; when
I did make the survey, I found them composed of all
shades of society, from the missionary on his way to Cen-
tral America, to the bank clerk and confidential business
agent of a wealthy firm, who usually did a little *sub rosa* in
diamonds and precious stones, on his own account. The
spirits of one lady and gentleman appeared to be considerably relieved, as soon as we were fairly out to sea, and
beyond the possibility of pursuit; and it was ill-naturedly
hinted that the male traveller had appropriated a companion who was by legal covenant the property of some
one else. There were two Milesian gentleman; both,
as a well-established fiction, educated at Trinity college,
Dublin! and whose society was extremely agreeable. One
old gentleman of the Hebrew persuasion, with a very
young wife, but recently elevated to that honor, and with
all her maidenly latitude still a part of her creed. Several politicians from various parts of the States on their
way home, after visiting the points of interest in the old

world; and one officer attached to her Britannic Majesty's army in Canada, who, in order to battle against the *ennui* of the voyage, kept himself in a perpetual state of intoxication.

The first few days at sea are never distinguished for extreme sociability, particularly in squally weather, and our party was no exception to established rule. A Virginian gentleman was the earliest indication of convivial gratification that dawned upon us, and afforded much amusement by proffering his co-operation in an evening concert, in which he took a prominent, and highly acceptable part. Politics was however his speciality; and the zest with which he descanted upon his favorite theme was, to me, both novel and instructive.

The moon was shining with a richness nowhere bequeathed us save upon the broad Atlantic; and the upper deck was crowded with listeners to an animated discussion of the merits of some of the greatest, and best of America's statesmen. When some venturous individual expressed his doubts of the claim to the proud position occupied by Henry Clay, the Virginian was on, his legs quicker than thought. He was a very tall, spare man, and as he leaned upon the stool he had till now been seated on, his shadow upon the calm surface of the waters gave him an almost supernatural aspect. All eyes were turned towards him; even the missionary forgot for a moment his beneficent object of directing the footsteps of the heathen towards his own special pathway to eternity; and faltered in his evening's customary ramble, to become a witness of the scene.

"Gentlemen," began the Virginian "there are moments in our chequered existence which leave an indelible impression; either by the consequence and magnitude of the subject itself, or the grandeur and sublimity of the locality of discussion. In the present instance, it is my good fortune to be able to boast of the purity of the one, and the beauty of the other. Gentlemen, here upon the bosom of the broad Atlantic, with the blessed moon shining in its matchless effulgence above our heads, do I regard with commiseration and regret, the man who shall for a moment indulge in the slightest belief in the charges made by the pettiness of party spleen, against the integrity of that greatest of all statesmen. (Hear ! hear ! and a round of applause from the passengers.) I am not one of those, gentleman, who would look at every trivial action of a great man's life, and point to promises artfully decoyed from him in the heat of debate, for the purpose of falsifying his political position. I cast my thoughts back to the history of past ages; and I take a comprehensive survey of those of our own time who have and are, distinguished by depth of profound veneration, and respect for the honesty of their efforts on behalf of the land of their birth; and I have yet to be acquainted with one man more entitled to the unqualified regard of his own country, and the admiration of all civilized humanity, than Henry Clay. (Hear ! hear !) In time to come, when few, if any, now within the sound of my feeble voice shall exist, America shall tutor her rising generation to emulate the example of him who, despite the factious hordes of slanderers that have ever, from the commencement of his career heaped falsehood and calumny upon his policy, stands collossal like, the interpretation of freedom, rectitude, and the most scrupulous honesty. (Hear ! hear !)

" It would ill become me, here upon the calm bosom of the great waters, just returning as I am from the kindliest hospitality of the mother country, where the intelligent traveller and searcher after the antique and the beautiful readily finds the grasp of welcome extended to greet him, and the overflowing wine cup a cheerful offering at his presence! It would ill become me, I say, to offer invidiously a comparison between the great men of other nations; but, gentlemen, take my word for it, you may talk of your Peels, your Russells, your Lamartines, and a score of others, but Henry Clay's a bigger man than the whole crowd! He's eleven feet high, with a head as big as a hogshead of tobacco!"

A shout of applause followed this panegyric, not unmixed with some surprise at the extraordinary simile employed in its construction. I learned, however, in the course of the evening, that the speaker was from Virginia, thence the comparison with greatness and the hogshead of the staple article of that section of the country. It is also needless to state that no one amongst his many friends, entertained a less regard for the great statesman than he did; and that several of his party had purposely drawn him into an exposition of his oratorical powers for the love of hearing him talk.

He opened ballot boxes for the election of the next president the following day, availing himself of the privilege of descanting upon his favorite in the most laudatory strain.

The Hebrew and his young wife kept up a perpetual family warfare; the slightest mark of attention conferred upon the lady by a passenger of the opposite gender, bringing out the strong points of the husband's character with a boldness of color not at all suggestive of a happy future for one who had, perhaps, to feed her personal vanity, or inflict a pang upon a worthy but offending lover, placed herself upon the altar of misery, and is gradually becoming conscious of the terrors of the sacrifice.

We reach Halifax, land for three hours, and are importuned by the natives to purchase dogs of the most faultless symmetry and the purest blood. One of the gentlemen from Ireland, whose paternal progenitor has an estate

6

of ever so many thousand acres near Clonmel, and has passed much of his youth in the luxury of the field, is well skilled in everything connected with the dog, and its history, drives a hard bargain with a rather dilapidated individual who assures you he is a native of the place; but if his account of himself be reliable, you are firmly convinced that the town and neighborhood must have formerly been the property of an Hibernian monarch who, when he had to flee before the enemy after being robbed of his country and his home, bequeathed, as a pleasing and grateful souvenir, the *patois* already enjoyed by his successors in all parts of the civilized world.

We go on board, the bell rings violently, the passengers arrive in crowds, some on foot, others in coaches, after a drive about the town and neighborhood. The paddle wheels are soon in motion, and we slowly leave the wharf. Our friend is proud of his dog, and is exhibiting him to his fellow-passengers; he is of the best breed, and very large in size; we are on the middle deck near the cook house, and the vessel not far from the shore. Presently a shrill whistle is heard, the dog pricks up his ears, with a desperate bound breaks from the grasp of his new owner, springs upon the guards, leaps into the water, and makes for the shore as if he was swimming for his life. The blank astonishment depicted upon the countenance of the supposed owner, as he saw his property land safely on the bank, is speedily followed by a loud burst of laughter from the pastry cook, who is preparing pies for the day's dinner.

"What, is Mikey at it again?" asks a sailor of the above as he passes towards the saloon.

"Aye, aye, he's made a pretty good raise, lately; two trips since he did a Frenchman out of *two pun ten!* Valuable animal that 'ere"

Our Irish friend, hearing the above, ventures to make inquiry respecting the position occupied in society by the

cunning trader; when all, and every one of the ship's crew
agree that the neighborhood does not contain a more dis-
honest and shameless vagabond than Mickey Donevan;
that the same dog has been his only stock in trade for
two years; that he was once a coal passer in the Cunard
service, but dispensed with by the company for idleness
and dissipation.

We make a rapid run to New York, reaching the
beautiful bay about one o'clock on the 2d of August,
with the thermometer higher than we had ever before
seen it. We reach the dock at Jersey city where, after
the sailors have gone through the ceremony of landing
the mails, being costumed in the most agreeable manner
for the purpose, we shake hands with the congenial ones
we have fraternized with during our brief acquaintanc-
ship, and for the first time tread American soil.

My evening I passed at Niblo's, where I met Hamblin,
Mitchel, Lynne, Chippendale and John Brougham. The
three former have " passed away " some years since.

CHAPTER XIV.

THE Broadway season commenced on the 19th August, 1850, with the comedy of the " School for Scandal," thus cast: Sir P. Teazle, W. Davidge; Sir Oliver Surface, G. Barrett; Charles, F. B. Conway; Joseph, W. S. Fredericks; Moses, Scharf; Lady Teazle, Miss Anderson; Maria, Miss J. Gongenheim.

The inducement held out to me to visit America by the agent of Mr. E. A. Marshall, the then lessee of the Broadway, were of such a nature as led me to understand that the *star system* was entirely ignored under their supervision, and that every artiste stood in a fair and equitable position before the public, who could judge of their merits without the aid of capitals to guide them in the formation of their judgment.

It is needless to state, that I soon discovered that the establishment was the only one in the country where the ruinous *star system* was really carried out to the fullest extent. Seldom, indeed, was anything produced without the addition of some auxiliary aid; but when the management, (at a time when *stars* were not to be obtained) expended some time, and very little money, upon the " Midsummer Night's Dream," and " Faustus," the result was more satisfactory than under a system they espoused at the very advent of their managerial career.

Mr. Beverly, of the Scarboro' Theatre, once related to me an incident in connection with the *star system*, which is worth recording in this place. Mr. B. was for many years manager of the Scarboro' circuit, and died some years since in very good circumstances, without ever permitting a *star* to appear upon his boards.

" During one of my summer seasons at Scarboro'," said he, " my old, and dear friend Edmund Kean, then in the height of his popularity, came down for a week or two, to recruit his health after several months continuous acting. I had a very pleasant residence, where Kean was my guest. After a week or two he gained strength so rapidly that idleness became irksome to him, and with the best intention in the world, he proposed that he should play three nights the following week, beginning on Monday, with Richard. I replied, with many thanks for his offer, that it had always been my settled system of policy to disclaim the aid of extraneous attraction, because I had, from long experience, been convinced that no manager ever came out a winner in the end; and it was only those who lacked the necessary ability to produce their plays in a proper manner, who adopted such means of covering their deficiency."

All writers, from the time of Garrick, have agreed, that bankruptcy is the rule, and success the exception, under such a course of management; and if it were necessary, I could name an instance at the time I write, of a popular manager who has paid thousands, for many years, to " stars " whose position now is most deplorable and distressing.

Mr. Charles Kean has lately shown that the manner in which he has produced his plays at the Princesses' Theatre, London, has done more to sustain the respectability of the drama, than all his efforts for years, as a " star."

The public, or some portion of it, are taught to consider that many years' experience as a stock actor totally unqualifies you for the position of a "star." It is reversing the order of things, it is true; yet I have heard enough to satisfy me on the point, while the novice, especially of the gentler sex, *if pretty*, (this is indispensable) will be readily accepted as a feature, and lauded for the possession of qualities it would puzzle the genuine critic to discover.

Mr. Wallack's style of conducting his theatre, and the success of the system, should convince the sceptical of the soundness of his policy.

In fine, the drama needs what I much fear it will never have, viz : *A school in which pupils can graduate in the several excellences to fit them for the duties of the profession.*

Years ago the drama was the only source of instruction, apart from expensive colleges and seminaries, devoted to educational purposes, to be found not only in towns, but for those in the receipt of a limited income, in the large cities, also. Now, the increase of literary and scientific associations, with their attendant means of access for all classes of the community, render the theatre, as an educational institution, of secondary importance to its position as a means of amusement and recreation.

I remained five seasons at the Broadway theatre, with some pecuniary advantage, and it is hoped with satisfaction to the play-going public. In 1854, "Midsummer Night's Dream" as before alluded to, was produced with great success. This play brought me into a contest with the critics — a dangerous proceeding for one who has so little at his command wherewith to stand the perpetual fire of the unlimited supply of type and space, but from which I believe I did not come out second best.

NEGRO MINSTRELSY.

The great, and increasing popularity of negro minstrelsy since its inauguration as a species of amusement, is a matter of serious concern to the purveyors of dramatic exhibitions in every town or city upon the vast continent of America. How frequently the most eminent in tragedy or comedy, have toiled through the choicest efforts, to scanty listeners ; while upon the same evenings, fantazias upon the bones, or banjo, has called forth the plaudits of admiring thousands.

In 1855, I attempted to play a brief engagement at Detroit, Mich., and am indebted to the wonderful skill and endurance of a gentleman named Dick Sliter (since dead) who exhibited marvellous prowess as a jig dancer, for piloting me through the term alloted, whereby I was enabled to bid adieu to the city, without pecuniary loss.

The late E. P. Christy commenced operations in New York in 1842. At this time the Italian, or indeed, any kind of opera, visited us only in a spasmodic form, like fever and ague. At the present date (1866) it is cheering to be informed that Italian opera is in the most luxuriant condition, enriching managers and artists in such an expeditious manner,— a result very gratifying to all lovers of art of whatever clime, and to America especially, who thereby enjoys the proud distinction of fostering a high and ennobling musical taste with a profitable margin, denied to older and aristocratic nations, whose government in many cases grant a yearly sum of money, for the liquidation of losses which are always anticipated.

The public took some time to tutor themselves into negro minstrelsy, as will be seen by the perusal of the balance sheet of the late E. P. Christy, kindly favored me for reference or copy, a year or two prior to his melancholy death.

Year. No. of Concerts.	Receipts.	Expenses.	Surplus.	Average.
1842,⁶ mo. 69	$1,847,52	$1,652,60	$294,92	26,70
1843, 109	2,653,75	1,875,10	778,66	24,33
1844, 133	3,658,69	2,749,64	909,00	27,50
1845, 118	4,560,25	3,348,15	1,212,13	38,64
1846, 198	13,667,25	8,656,39	5,010,86	69,02
1847, 252	28,752,79	12,585,38	16,167,41	114,09
5½ years. 879	$55,140,25	$30,767,26	$24,372,98	

Thus it will be seen that in 1843, the entire profits only amounted to a trifle over $700, and in 1847 it exceeded $16,000.

1848, 308	$39,432,37	$16,653,00	$22,779,37	128,02
1849, 311	34,295,00	15,765,25	18,529,75	110,27
1850, 305	46,778,50	20,313,00	26,465,50	153,37
1851, 340	43,952,25	23,831,00	20,121,25	129,27
1852, 317	50,019,25	26,022,25	23,997,00	157,78
1853, 312	47,971,75	23,364,00	24,607,75	153,78
1854, 202	43,037,75	39,338,98	3,698,77	213,06
Total, 2,420	$372,140,25	$191,053,25	$181,087,00	191,053,25

Thus from June 1842 to July 15, 1854, Mr. Christy gave 2,420 concerts. The total receipts to which were $372,140 25. The expenses amounted to $191,053 25; leaving a balance of $181,087, or over $15,000 per annum.

I am not cognizant of the amount of yearly profit of Messrs. Bryant, Birch, Backus &c., but believe it to be very much larger than their predecessor; but of this I am from personal experience certain, that great as it may be, it is not capacious enough to sufficiently reward them for the liberal spirit they are ever ready to manifest by words and deeds for all, and every claim made upon them by their less fortunate brothers in the profession of amusement, no matter what style of character they profess to represent.

CANDIDATES FOR DRAMATIC FAME.

The unskilled in the secrets of the dramatic "prison house" are scarcely aware of the persistency of the theatrically inclined, when the notion seizes them that destiny has marked him, or her, for one of its matchless exponents. They are not to be diverted from their purpose by any words, or acts of discouragement ingenuity may devise. Paint, however vividly, your own trials and distresses, while a member of a travelling company, far removed from friends or relatives, with an inadequate exchequer for the liquidation of your necessary wants, they are only the more eager to brave the ordeal in proportion to the difficulties to be surmounted.

Private theatricals have much to do in fanning this Thespian flame, aided as it invariably is by the press, who generally laud the efforts of the novice in the most friendly spirit, hinting darkly that established tragic, or comic actors, must look well to their laurels if the gentleman who was the hero of the night's performance, should persevere in his proposed intention, and throw aside the ruler of commerce for the sword of Richard, or the tobacco pipe of Toodles. The following is a verbatim copy of one of the many letters continually received by managers.

RANDOLPH, Oct., 26, 1857.

DEAR SIR. Having a vary strong desire to adopt the profession of an actor, I now address you for the purpose of secureing a situation in the Theatre, which you have the honor of manageing. I will say that I have attended literary societies considerable, and have practiced declameing some. Consequently I do not think that I shall be much troubled with stage fright. While a member of the Randolph Academy Lyceum, I acted the part of Hob in the play of Hob and Nob, a part requireing

6*

the manifestation of good deal of energy and activity, but still a very easy part to act, at least it was for me. The audeance, (as far as I know anything about it) were universaly well pleased with my acting ; I have lately been invited, by the big bugs of the place, to act the part of Sir Marmaduke Medows, in the play entitled Bamboozleing, and expect to do so in a few days. My friends think that indipendance and determination, is a very strong feature of my character. I do not know that you believe in Phrenology, but the organs which give the disposition and the ability to understand human nature, are marked 6 on a scale of from one to seven (seven meaning very larg) on a chart which I have lately received from Fowler and Wells. Let that be as it ma, I have made human nature my studdy for the last 5 years. In the written description of character and talants which L. N. Fowler has made out for me, he says that I am susceptable of and can endure a very high degree of mental exsitement. But be that as it may, I am very exciteable and when interested in subject speak with great force and energy. I understand that my temperament is very favorable for an actar. Fowler say's that I am naturally well qualified for an actar. My height is 5 ft 5¾ inches with boots off, light build, light complexion, black hair, dark gray eyes, prominiant arched eye brows, somewhat round shouldered. My voice is comparatively strong and good but would be improved by cultivation. I think I could make a good comic acter, so my friends tell me. I think I could represent the passions of grief and dispair as well as any. There is no passion but what I could express, without it is conjugal love ? with a little practice I think I could do that as well as it is generally done. I am willing to commence just as far down the lader as it is necessary in order to do well what

I attempt to do. Please answer this as son as you can and tell me what wages I can get, and whether you can employ me or not.

Please address ·

D. A. P———e

Randolph, N. Y.

CHAPTER XV.

All the secrets of our camp I'll show
Their force, their purposes; nay, I'll speak that
Which you will wonder at.''
All's Well that Ends Well. Act 4. Scene 1.

BEHIND THE SCENES.

[THEATRE. The Ladies and Gentlemen engaged at this Theatre for the ensuing season, are requested to assemble in the Green
Room, at eleven o'clock, on ——day, the —— inst., prior to
the commencement of the season on the ——. By order ———,
Stage Manager. *Vide Herald.*]

THE amusement seeker cannot resist viewing with feelings of curiosity the above announcement of the opening of the favorite places of entertainment for the fall
and winter months. It is a matter of especial interest to
watch for the first issue of a full list of the company,
particularly the names of the ladies.

Every theatre has in its *corps dramatique* some one,
or two, just budding into womanhood, and into the mysteries of their profession, who are subjects of comment
and admiration, among the juvenile portion of the opposite sex,— gents who take especial care of their personal
appearance, and are scrupulous on the subject of neck-
ties, dress canes, and the most *distingue* perfume.'

The more mature admirers of the theatre are not without their cogitations on the approaching campaign. Their
tastes are for the fine old solid drama. They can look
back with regret to the palmy days of the Park, and have
a pleasing and vivid remembrance of losing their coat

tails in effecting an entrance into the pit of that once popular establishment on the opening of the season, five and thirty years ago.

The anxiety *without* the confines of the dramatic temple, are as nothing when compared with the evident uneasiness *within* its portals. The stage manager is daily closeted with the scenic artist, and the prompter; the latter's duty being to furnish a list of the scenes, and properties requisite for the faithful representation of the new drama of startling, and novel interest.

The manager looks careworn but confident, as he emerges from his private office, and is waylaid in one of the passages by an actor whom he has already three times orally, and once by letter, informed, "he can really find no opening for."

The meeting day arrives, and with it a portion of the company, the new members generally putting in an early appearance, and who beguile the time by traversing the stage in pairs, and contrasting the capabilities of the auditorium with the one they have just quitted.

The ladies, smiling pleasantly beneath the pressure of millinery artifice, have seated themselves in the green room, awaiting the important event. Some of the old established members of the company are absent, enjoying their seaside recreations, or enlightening the inhabitants of the smaller cities with the rendition of the choicest gems in their *repertoire* of last season.

Presently, one or two of the new members stroll into the room, hat in hand, striving to seem perfectly at ease, when in fact they are anxious, and diffident, and the counterfeit glares boldly out in spite of their efforts to conceal it. They are probably reflecting on the chances of success in their new, and more extensive field of action; or wondering if the quality of their opening part, will be in accordance with the promises made to give them a " fair show."

"I beg your pardon," says the stage manager, coming into violent collision with a timid youth who is engaged to make himself generally useful, as he is rounding a sharp angle of the passage, near the green room door. Youth smiles upon the manager, and, despite the uneasiness consequent on the puncture of a scarf pin he wears, assumes an aspect of affability, and apologizes in return.

You enter the interdicted apartment, and the ceremony of introduction takes place. The manager, with the gallantry for which his race(?) is distinguished, runs through the opreation as speedily as possible, and hastily sallies forth to find the messenger, who is holding a conference with the back door keeper, on the merits of the several candidates for the next municipal election; but who is speedily cut short in his favorite theme by a request to find the gas-man, and acquaint him that the manager would like to see him in his office, in the course of the morning.

The sun having gone down on the company's embarrassment by the arrival of the first old woman, who resides up town, and always prides herself on her punctuality in all business matters, and accounts for her present delay by assuring the company present that she had not the slightest idea it was so late by at least an hour,—that she had for some time suspected her hand-maiden of tampering with the family timepiece, now she was sure of it. She had submitted to a great deal from that ungrateful girl. "My dear, you don't know!" (addressing herself to the second walking lady,) "what I have done for that girl. Ah, well! have you heard from your sister since her marriage?"

"Oh! dear me, yes. I got a letter only yesterday," says the lady appealed to, and "would you believe it," placing her mouth close to the ear of the first old woman, who starts, with astonishment and pleasure depicted in her face.

" No!"

" Yes!"

" Well, give my kind regards, and congratulations when you write," says the first old woman!

" They were coming on here!" says the second walking lady, " but Mr. ——, the manager, has taken another theatre for a short season, and they are going to remain with him."

Observe the two gentlemen who are looking at the printed list of rules and regulations posted on the wall beside the glass case, wherein the calls for rehearsals are placed.   It is a terrible document, and sets forth at length the several acts of insubordination any member of the company may commit, with the amount of pecuniary punishment consequent thereon,— an exclusive privilege possessed by *one* of the contracting parties, who is, at times, expected to sign, and abide by the conditions, without having to enforce an equivalent regard for its faithful response.

The one in the suit of cocoa-colored clothes, with buttons significant of sporting life, and cravat with pattern of brilliant hue, striped upon the ends, is at present unknown in the metropolis, and has been engaged at the strong solicitation of some friend of the manager, and is under promise to receive a share of some of the comedy. He is a great favorite in his own locality, in proof whereof a grand complimentary supper, and profitable benefit, was lately tendered him by the citizens, dignitaries of the bar, and others high in official significance, to which he responded, brimming over with gratitude and emotion that,

" Through the intricacies of his early career they — his patrons — had, by their encouraging approval, cheered him onward, stimulating him to attain a prominence at the very summit of his art.   Each round up the ladder of fame that he might be destined to mount, would but augment the debt of gratitude he should never be able to liquidate. And whether on the banks of the Hudson, the plains of the El Dorado, or amongst the luscious fruits of the sunny South, fortune might cast him, the present would ever be registered in the tablet of his memory as the proudest moment of his chequered existence."

The other is of more fashionable exterior, and is about to make his *entre* into the capital city after a few months' probation in the provinces. He has already committed sad havoc in *one* female breast, at least, for on his departure from his late field of action he received a pleasing little *souvenir*, in the shape of a watch guard manufactured from the lady's hair, with an anonymous communication to the effect that—

" One who was at present unknown to him desired his acceptance of this small token of her esteem. Hoping that when far distant he would think of his visit to her native town with none other than emotions of pleasure, and pardon her boldness in perpetrating an act she felt it impossible to repress."

Three of the ladies have already decided that he is very good looking; the more youthful of the trio adding as an individual appendix,

" That he is real sweet."

He is to take charge of the young men in the farces, and for which his appearance eminently fits him.

" Hallo, old fellow ! how are you ? " says a gentleman of a rather rubicund tint, and on whom the good things of this life are evidently not thrown away.

" By George, you look well ! Country air, and no bad parts to study, eh ? Ah, they wear out a man's constitution most confoundedly. Look at me ! I believe I've played during the last three years more bad parts than any three men in the profession, but I'm callous to mis-cry, sir. Never got one decent show all last season, but I can brave the storm. Let it rage on for aught I care.

"Ladies, how are you? Glad to see you. Hope you've enjoyed yourselves through the summer. Where have you all been, eh? Breaking the hearts of us poor mortals as usual, I suppose."

This complimentary remark is addressed to the ladies by the comedian; who, without waiting for a reply, takes the arm of the second old man, and enquires where the lady sitting in the corner, with the blue hat, and eyes to match, hails from. The lady thus alluded to, but who is quite unconscious of the compliment, is destined to enact the boarding school misses, who will, in opposition to the parental desire, (as in real life), unite her destiny with the object of her own preference, despite his needy exchequer.

The call boy now makes his appearence, with a slip of paper which he securely locks inside the glass case before alluded to. The same contains the following piece of information.

TUESDAY.—Everybody for reading new piece in Green-room!!

The said "everybody" now begins to take its departure. The ladies in little knots of two's, and three's, to indulge in a stroll by the most fashionable stores, and the gentlemen to satisfy their own *indulgences* in various ways.

If the drama to be read be of native manufacture, the author, or concoctor, will be marshalled to his seat with some degree of ceremony, by the stage manager, who will speedily avail himself of the very first opportunity to escape another infliction he has already been bored with. If, however, he be an actor, or an adept at dramatic upholstering, he will boldly take his seat, unfolding the dreadful document with the air of one skilled in the sufferings of his fellow creatures.

Judges of physiognomy can very readily discover the estimate the exponents of the several characters entertain of the one allotted to their charge. Those having the conduct of the plot, and the majority of the best situations, pay the most profound attention to the ceremony; while the less fortunate, look with a glare of distrust and doubt on the probability of its success.

Those from the provinces, whose hopes have been buoyed up with the promise of a good opening part, betake themselves to their dwelling places with a firm conviction rooted in their minds, that there is evidently a combination to crush them; for who could possibly do anything with such a part as they have each assigned them. "My boy," says an injured one, "there's not a line in it."

_"Why, my dear sir," urges a gentleman, (who has been very well taken care of by the dramatist) "you have a capital scene in the third act, and another in the fourth."

"The third act!" why, my good sir, the scene is simply a feeder to the count, who has every climax throughout the interview; while in the fourth, the low comedy part is on the stage all the time; therefore, what opportunity can there be for quiet, subtle expression, with a buffoon at your elbow! My dear boy, no one can resist the assaults of a clown. If you were acting Hamlet in the most perfect manner, and after the grave-digger had handed you the skull of Yorick, and you made up your mind to produce a thrilling effect in the soliloquy, what would be the state of your feelings if you heard the audience in a roar of laughter, and on turning to discover the cause of their merriment, you beheld the grave-digger playing a nigger air with some other portion of the departed jester's anatomy."

" I don't believe the piece will go; the interest is centered too much in the female character, to the entire exclusion of the lofty grandeur which the author might have availed himself of in the scene where I encounter the duke for the first time. This I consider will be the fatal error, and the audience will not be slow to detect it."

Each day's rehearsal brings the matter more plainly to the minds of every one concerned. The leading lady has a very long part, which she commits to memory as speedily as possible, and is perfect in the text several days prior to the production of the piece. The less fortunate ones in the dramatist's esteem are somewhat tardy in acquiring the words, which invoke from the manager the following peremptory order.

THURSDAY.—New play!!—11.

NOTICE.—The manager particularly requests the same may be rehearsed without parts.

Which manifesto the call-boy, if he be of an hilarious temperament, posts up with a look of ineffable disdain at the delinquents, as he quits the room.

The occupation of this individual, as his name clearly implies, is to summon the *dramatis personæ* from the green-room when their services are required upon the stage. He is not unfrequently the offspring of an actor, with a widowed mother, to whose comforts he cheerfully ministers, out of very scanty materials. Or he may be a resident of the neighborhood in which the theatre is situated, whose instincts from the first time he watched patiently at the stage-door, for an hour and a half, in a pelting snow-storm, to catch a glimpse of the principal tragedian as he departed from rehearsal, have led him, from an irrepressible love for the place, to seek employment within its precincts.

When thoroughly installed in office, the distinctive features of his character are the same, or nearly so, irrespective of his ancestral origin. Punctually, at the hour appointed for the first rehearsal of the morning, he places upon the prompter's table pens, ink, the prompt book, and a written cast of the play to be rehearsed — the latter of which he procured from the call case in the green room, where it has been placed for the purpose of notifying the several ladies and gentlemen of the part they are to assume at its representation.

The Call Boy.

Arming himself with his list of names, arranged in numeric order as they will be required, he awaits instructions from the prompter — who, in due time, and after consulting his watch, to be certain that the usual ten minutes' grace allowed for the first call has transpired, desires him to call *one*. He thereupon proceeds to the green room, and from the memorandum above described, audibly requests the parties whose names are appended to number one, to attend upon the stage for the commencement of the morning's business.

When not actively engaged in the duties of his office, the call boy will frequently beguile the tedium of the morning by a *tete-a-tete* with one of the most juvenile of the ladies attached to the ballet department, or exhibit his dexterity in terpsichorean gyrations by indulging in Ethiopian *break-downs* in a secluded corner, in a selfish manner.

The youthful designation awarded the subject of our sketch, is sometimes as much a misnomer as a similar one bestowed upon the individual who forms an important item in the domestic machinery of the country inn, and y'clept the post boy. He, and his companion of the stable, not unfrequently exercise the duties of their office after they have for many years assumed the trying responsibilities of parental honors! We once knew a call boy who, in stature, was scarcely up to half a score; but in feature, was any age you thought proper to fancy, from twenty to sixty. He was a good, simple-hearted little fellow, much admired by the members of the company, particularly the ladies, to whom he was the very Beau Brummel of politeness. He had a wife of herculean mould, and who added to her other accomplishments the character of the matrimonial martinet.

I took occasion once to question Joe on the nature of his domestic relations, insinuating that I had no idea of finding his name entered upon the connubial list, from the attention he bestowed on the ladies — that his manners and deportment were of that attractive kind that, had I a daughter or female relation at a marriageable stage, I should be somewhat alarmed less his persuasive powers should tempt her to sever the tie that bound her to her childhood's home, and become his exclusive property at the hymeneal alter.

"Oh! that's all very well, and nice sort of talking; but you see, sir," said my minute friend, "man can't help having the natural instincts of his race uppermost in his thoughts."

"Decidedly," said I, "who dares to doubt one of Nature's most peremptory laws."

"Now, look here, sir," he continued, "I have a wife, it's true; but, lor' bless you, there ain't not no congeniality of sentiment between us. She's a woman as is all self; she ain't got none of what you called, in that piece the other night, the ' essential oil of sympathy' in her. Why, sir, I can't ever get a favorite meal's victuals when I want it. Only the other night I took home for supper a dish I'm passionately fond of — pig's fry, sir. Did you ever taste it?"

"Oh yes," I replied.

"Well, sir,— would you believe it? she threw it all into the street, and declared if I ever presumed to bring such rubbish into the house again she would most certainly pitch me after it! She's a frightful jealous woman, too, sir, and so terrible unreasonable! About a month ago I thought, as she was busy down stairs, that I would copy a letter I had to do for the first call in the morning. After finishing I placed it in my hat, intending to seal it at the theatre. I proceeded to indu'ge in my usual afternoon's nap, when I was suddenly aroused by a powerful blow over my head, which nearly stunned me. On coming to myself, I found her standing over me with the letter in her grasp, foaming with rage, and in the most violent terms charging me with the grossest impropriety in keeping up a correspondence with an individual called Jemima Stokes, because the letter was written in a loving strain to a female of that name in the new farce we did. I declared it meant nothing, and produced the manuscript, which she refused to look at, threw a chair at me, and behaved altogether in the most dreadful manner possible. So you see, sir, what can a man do ? I believe in fulfilling one's destiny, sir. Now, I know, as all men must, that we are formed by nature to pay homage to the sex, and as I am debarred exercising that duty at home, by reason of my wife's infirmity of temper, why, sir, I consider the little bits of politeness I show the fair sex here, as we meet in our daily occupation, as part payment of that duty ; and I hope there will not be found a large balance of neglect against me in the next world. Did I call you, sir ? dear me, really, I think the stage must be waiting for you, sir ? "

If impressed with a desire to adopt the stage as a profession, the call boy will occasionally be entrusted with parts adapted to his youthful appearance ; and it not unfrequently happens, in theatres where the number of utility, or small people, as they are called, are deficient, that the subject of our enquiry will be pressed into the service, to assist in the formation of a band of robbers, whose bronzed features, and thickly-set, hirsute appendages, (with the prescribed amount of deadly weapons,) contrast strangely with his smooth skin, and slenderly-knit frame.

Many of the very best actors the stage has produced, commenced their professional career in this capacity. Many, too, abandon it when they arrive at man's estate, and pass the balance of their days in the more profitable pursuit of trade or commerce.

In regard to my friend, Joe, I think it extremely probable that he will steadily cling to the Thespian temple, being too far propelled down the hill of time to adapt himself to any other mode of life.

His early history was a chequered one. It pleased Nature to construct him on so economical a scale, that he was enabled to acquire a decent competence by gratifying the public appetite for sight-seeing, and exhibiting himself as a dwarf. Patronage flowed with acceptable celerity into his exchequer, until he had reached his sixteenth year. Up to that time he had been closely scrutinized by the faculty, interrogated by the inquisitive, and admired by the curious.

At that very impressible period of his career it pleased Nature, who had perhaps woke up to the unfertility of his mould, to suddenly make the reparation, and expand his longitudinal significance three inches and a quarter, in the short space of eighteen months. To this irreparable disaster was added the arrival from a distant land of a distinguished stranger, who was an adept at languages, living, and dead — and, without his shoes, measured six inches less than our friend's professional altitude prior to his recent growth. He quitted the field of instructive usefulness in disgust, seeking refuge in occasional attacks of alcoholic sentiment, conscious that his destiny had been most remorselessly evaded, and that his liliputian star had forever set.

The eventful night for the production of the new piece arrives, and with it the family of the author; who, to avoid the pressure of the crowd, are admitted at the stage door and escorted to a private box, where they are generally very conspicuous during the performance, with the trembling author in their rear, enduring the most poignant torture whenever an actor takes the liberty of substituting a line or word for which he is not responsible.

" Half an hour, ladies," roars the call-boy at the foot of the stairs leading to the dressing-rooms; and after performing the same office for the gentlemen, returns to the stage, where he takes a survey of the audience through a hole in the green curtain, till requested by the prompter to collect his properties for the first piece.

The dressing rooms become a scene of the greatest confusion. The dressers are dispatched to the wardrobe to obtain a belt for one gentleman's dress ; another's doublet wont meet at the back, and has to be ripped up in consequence. The confidential friend, in social pleasure as well as inate villany, of the usurping Duke, has forgotten his feathers. The walking gentleman's patience is getting exhausted, as he intimates to his dresser that he begins the piece ; and he, (the dresser) must be quick sewing those buckles into his shoes, or he cannot be ready when wanted.

The ladies are in a similar predicament. Nobody has any large pins — while a most important article of costume has been entirely forgotten in one instance; the consequences of which would be most distressing if some substitute cannot be provided. The ingenuity of the sex, however, soon surmounts the difficulty, and the boy's voice is again heard, calling :

" Ten minutes, ladies."

If within the proximity of the music-room, you now, for the first time, experience a most unpleasant sensation of musical discords from the gentlemen who compose the orchestra. These paroxysms of internal suffering are persevered in till the ringing of a small bell happily comes to the rescue ; and the instrumental performers emerge from a queerly constructed apartment, and doubling themselves up into the smallest possible compass, disappear into the orchestra, the leader somewhat varying the order of his nominal *sobriquet*, by tardily bringing up the rear, in the hope of receiving the recognition of the audience on taking his seat.

7

"Overture," calls the boy, and while that prelude takes place, let us in the course of our peregrinations enter the sanctum y'clept the

MUSIC ROOM.

This apartment cannot lay claim to much architectural elegance, being disproportioned in size, and deficient of the principles of ventilation to an oppressive degree.

Its furniture consists of a long pine table, and two or three benches of a similar material. Depending from the walls are the hats and overcoats belonging to the band, while the cases in which they keep their instruments are scattered in every direction. The gas burner is in dangerous proximity to the roof, which is entirely innocent of plaster, and guarded from inevitable conflagration by a sheet of blackened tin.

On the table is a pile of written music for the orchestra — a small bottle of ink, a checker board, with some of the pieces missing, but their places supplied with brace buttons of nearly approximating colors — a pack of cards, a piece of rosin, a flute case, a pounce, or sand box, and a newspaper printed in the German language.

Such is the apartment in which the gentlemen of the orchestra while away their spare time during the non-musical portion of the evening's entertainment — in which they take little or no interest — till summoned by the bell of the prompter to resume their duties.

They are generally a quiet, unobtrusive race of men, with a love for their art, and the principles of harmony, highly creditable under the adverse fact of not being in receipt of a very handsome independence for the same, yet they always appear contented, and happy.

The overture is hardly commenced, when the prompter is startled by the information conveyed by a female in a great state of excitement, that Miss —— cannot possibly be ready because, in the nervousness of a first night's performance, the shoes, in which she purposes to enact her part, have been, by accident, left upon the dressing table at her private dwelling. The prompter, — by no means well disposed towards excuses of this nature, — insists that the curtain must rise at the end of the overture, that the lady is not in the first call, that she will have time to send for the missing articles, and that he shall not wait; he is, however, not proof against the earnest entreaties of the handmaiden, and an interregnum occurs, which brings the manager from his office to know the reason of the delay. Prompter explains, manager requests that another messenger be dispatched forthwith; that keeping the curtain down will be of serious injury to the new piece, etc., desires that the band play something, and retires. Prompter calls down tin tube to leader, who turns back two or three pages, and repeats from the allegro movement; the which he has scarcely commenced, when a boy very much overheated, bounds up three or four stairs at a time, with the missing shoes. The prompter is requested to go on — the overture is again concluded, — prompter taps with the whistle on the tin tube communicating with the flies, rings a bell terminating in the same locality, and up goes the curtain.

The first scene is somewhat short, and comprises a dissertion on *Ethics* and *Moral Philosophy*, by three retainers of the usurping baron, clearly proving the acute research of the author in the habits and education of the peasantry of the olden time.

"Call up trumpet!" says the prompter to the call-boy. The latter proceeds to the music-room to request the attendance of the gentleman who assumes the responsibility of that sonorous instrument, and who at once placed himself in such a position readily seen by the prompter, when that individual shall require him to announce the approach of the Duke and his retinue, by a vigorous flourish. "Call two," says the prompter, *sotto voce*.

"Yes, sir," says the boy, and repairs to the green-room, where he delivers himself after the following fashion.

"Duke." "Strato." "Bertoldo." "Marco." "Eglantine." "6 Men at Arms." "6 Ladies." "6 Pages." "12 Guards." All for the Act.

One of the men at arms is also the super-master; whose duty it is to marshall them to their places, see they are properly costumed, etc. He may be very readily distinguished from the advantage in dress he possesses over his companions; indeed, he will often avail himself of the choice habiliments of the wardrobe, regardless of the wants of the principals, who will be startled to discover the lacquey better fitted than the master.

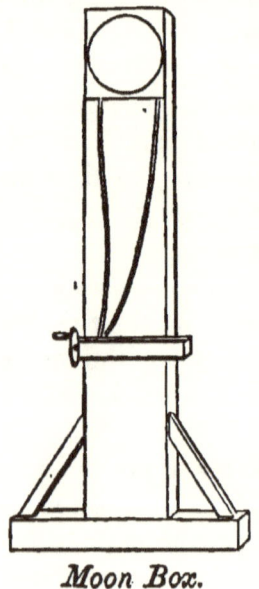

Moon Box.

Boy returns, and the prompter enquires "if Jenkins is ready at the moon?"

This precaution is taken in order that the next scene, which is the *Ducal Palace* with a centre arch through which the moon is seen to shine, may not be discovered before that luminary makes her appearance.

"All right, sir," responds the boy, after satisfying himself of the fact.

The play turns out a success, despite the prediction of the bad part gentleman, and may probably keep the stage for some time. During its occupancy of the boards, let us assist at the rehearsals of its successor.

Behind the scenes of a theatre is not by any means the kind of place the dramatic spectator imagines it to be. You enter the stage door at the back, or side of the building, where you may, if the weather be cold, find the guardian of the premises refreshing himself with a perusal of the morning paper, by the warmth of the stove. This apartment has seldom an encouraging aspect to a stranger. It is neither profuse in its facilities for domestic comfort, nor distinguished for architectural elegance; having in many instances, been surreptitiously appropriated from the general structure; hence its irregular, and unartistic developement.

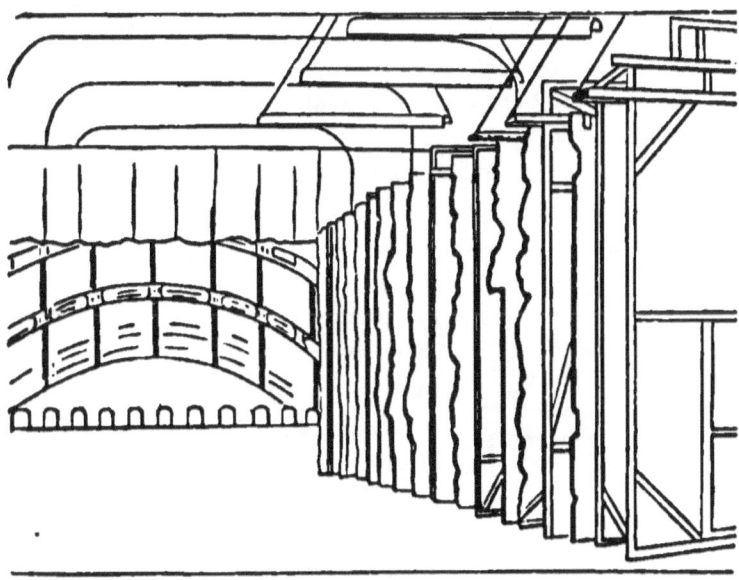

The Flats.

From the wall hangs a small case for posting up the call for rehearsals, an alphabetical rack for the reception of letters addressed to the members of the company; — these, with a clock, two chairs, and a small table, complete the decorations.

The stage itself does not possess much advantage in point of comfort over the apartment just noted, as you will readily find by pushing open the swing door to your left. The momentary blindness you at once experience when you are within its precincts, causes you to falter, lest you find yourself precipitated into some cavernous retreat, with which you feel assured the place abounds. You speedily get used to the darkness, and by the scanty light afforded from two or three small windows, near the roof, you are on the stage.

Rehearsal has not yet commenced, and you have ample time to examine every part of the building minutely.

The first thing that attracts your attention, is one of the carpenters, who is employed repairing the turret window of the Duke's castle,— the said edifice being reduced from its perpendicular grandeur, and lying flat on its back for that purpose.

The scenery is pushed back as far as it will go in the slides, or grooves, so called, and presents in its compact mass, a strange admixture of regal magnificence, and squalid penury. My lady's boudoir is in closer proximity to the laborer's cottage, than their desires are ever likely to assimilate in their journey through the actual voyage of life; and the bright, cheerful landscape, redolent of unfettered .liberty, stands side by side with the dungeon's dark, and dreary terrors, an interesting episode in our morning's peregrinations.

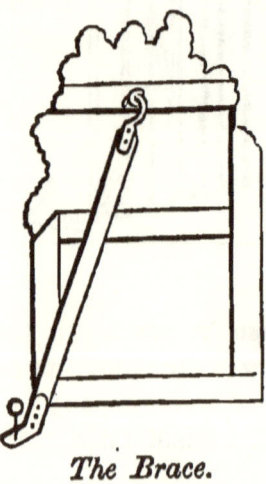

The Brace.

"What are those long rows of formidable looking implements we see hanging on the walls? They are made of wood, mounted with iron hooks at one end, and cir-

cular holes at the other. Are they instruments of torture? They are called braces, and are used for sustaining the weight of cottages, trees, and set pieces of all
kinds. Cast your eyes upward, and what a mass of cord-
age meets your gaze. There are more ropes than would
suffice for a vessel of a thousand tons' register. They are
used for sustaining the borders — the short pieces of
painted canvas that form, to the eye of the spectator, the
horizon, or ceiling, of the apartment represented.

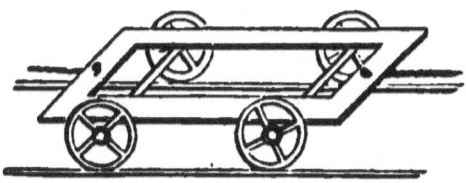

The Traveller.

Elevated some distance above the borders is what is
called the " traveller." This consists of a strong frame
of wood work fixed into a grooved receiver; by the aid
of which fairies or demons are enabled to pass from side
to side, while suspended by very stout wires.

The gas man is employed cleaning the glasses belonging to the lights which surmount the orchestra; these
are called " float lights." His duty is to take charge of
the gas apparatus before, as well as behind the curtain.
The sparkling waters, the transparent windows of the
chapel, the pale moonbeams, are all indebted for their
matchless effulgence, to the gas man.

He disposes of his light to any given point by means
of flexible tubes, some of which are, at the present moment, stacked in a corner at the back of the stage.

The stage itself, when not engaged in the exercise of
its proper, and destined office, has a very forlorn and
dreary aspect.

Where are the splendid suits of furniture that we so much admired only last evening? — the tapestry carpets, the dais of crimson velvet, that carried us back to the period of the middle ages? Where are the rare-looking articles of *virtu* with which the scene was so profusely provided? The property man, (for that is his department) has carefully stored them away in his room on one side of the stage; while the carpet of such gorgeous pattern, is suspended by cords, and run up by pulleys, where it will be kept in a perpetual state of strangulation, till required for use in the evening.

The walls which, from the auditorium, have impressed you with the conviction of their architectural beauty, are now seen destitute of the most primitive handicraft, and are in precisely the same condition as when delivered from the hands of their original depositors.

Our recollection wanders back to the period of innocent infancy; to the interesting occasion of the first play of the sensation order we ever witnessed. It was one of those intensely exciting romances, in which the four seasons of the year are represented.

It is not easy to forget the joy we experienced when, relieved from the thraldom of scholastic tyranny, we watched the mechanical changes with which the drama was plentifully supplied. One section of the play concluded with one of those brilliant displays of colored fire, without which a voracious audience would consider themselves deprived of one of their greatest enjoyments.

I remember trying an experiment with saltpetre, and some other combustible materials, much to the disgust and discomfiture of the family, who were almost suffocated with the nauseous effluvia it emitted, and who couldn't comprehend the motive of the sulphurous visitation.

Who, of my readers, has not witnessed the denounement of a drama, wherein a ruffian in large boots, his waistband plentifully supplied with huge pistols, has, by some unaccountable means, gained access to the castle of the Baron, and is plainly seen ransacking his private papers by the light of the moon ; and subsequently, his figure is clearly discernible making a precipitate escape through the thick foliage of the trees, immediately preceding the discovery that the castle is in flames. How intense is the excitement, as the rightful heir to the estates, (who has been for years, by an ingenious contrivance of the dramatist, engaged in mercantile pursuits in a far distant land) suddenly presents himself, and at the risk of his life, penétrates the blazing ruins ; and rescuing the title deeds of the estates intact and unharmed.

Parlor theatricals have lately become the rage, particularly in the eastern cities. The attempts have been chiefly confined to comedies, and pieces of a light, and colloquial character. It is scarcely to be expected that the sensation spirit of the age will slumber in the bosoms of histrionically inclined individuals. Heart-stirring and exciting dramas must speedily be the repertoire for the festive seasons of the year.

The liberality of the present age is so remarkable, that a man has only to forward three postage stamps to A. B., to be immediately possessed of the secret of acquiring a speedy competence ; or for the trifling sum of twenty-five cents, an ingenious domestic economist will confer valuable hints whereby the entire expense of your household may be easily defrayed, at a saving of fifty per cent. upon the outlay you are at present disbursing. It may with equal certainty be expected, that some humane purveyor will ere long confer upon the wonder-loving public an explanatory volume of the means for parlor enjoyment, under the attractive title of " Every Man his own Stage-Manager."

Should the instructions therein contained, fail to fur-

7*

nish the means to produce those thrilling effects modern
taste craves, as indispensable to appease the general appetite, the following receipts, for presenting scenes, with
all their illuminative brilliancy, may form an acceptable
addenda to the evening's entertainment.

For a confragation of,

RED FIRE.

Strontia,	. .	8 oz.
Potash,	. . .	4 "
Shellac,	. .	2 "
Licopodium,	. .	$\frac{1}{4}$ "

For illuminating a hall of Statuary, make a

WHITE FIRE.

Nitre,	. . .	8 oz.
Sulphur,	. . .	3 "
Charcoal,	. .	$\frac{1}{4}$ "
Alum,	. . .	$\frac{1}{8}$ "
Camphor	. .	$\frac{1}{2}$ "

Should the entertainment embrace an aquatic display,
where fairies are holding their usual revelry, light them
with a

BLUE FIRE.

Nitre,	. . .	8 oz.
Sulphur,	. . .	3 "
Charcoal,	. .	$\frac{1}{2}$ "
Antimony,	. .	1 "

If the Demon of Mischief holds his midnight orgies,
surrounded by his attendant imps, in solemn conclave to
strike terror into the bosom of the fair maiden whose destiny is under the supervision of the good fairy, provide
them with an illumination composed of

GREEN FIRE.

Nitrate of Barytes, . . 62½ parts

Sulphur, ... 10½ "

Potash, ... 23½ "

Orpiment, ... 1½ "

Charcoal, . . . 1½ "

When used, the fire is spread along the bottom of the fire box, composed of sheet iron, and ignited at one end. It is raised six or seven feet high at the sides, by which means a brilliant light is thrown upon every object within its reach. Immediately after use the pan should be placed in the open air or a bucket of water, to get rid of the smell, which is far from pleasant if extensively inhaled.

The piercing cold of the icy regions form frequently a very important portion of the drama. The scenic artist depicts upon the canvas the glacial grandeur of a latitude of perpetual winter with as much fidelity as he traces the lurid intensity of the torrid zone; but even here, the property man must render his assistance to complete the picture.

The flakes of falling snow which, when properly managed, so admirably decoy the spectator into a feeling of reality, are the result of a large quantity of cut white papers placed in a box elevated several feet above the borders over the stage. This box is about four feet long, and three feet broad; it is sustained by two ropes—one from either side, left tolerably loose. On one side is a pole attached, whereby the property man, or his assistant, has a perfect command over the box, and by keeping it in motion is enabled to shake the paper through the bottom, which is only protected by wire placed in such a position, that it is easily scattered in such a way as to strew the stage with the counterfeit snow. This is called the "Snow Box."

By the side of the stage, and not far from the prompter's box, is a light burning in a small nook, or cupboard;
we enter and find there the property man in a canvas apron
and drab felt hat. He is busily employed repairing a trun-
cheon by covering the fractures with gilt paper : and while
he is thus engaged we will take a survey of the place set
apart for his use. Although dignified by the appellation of
property *room*, its disproportioned aspect would fully justify the conclusion that the stranger might arrive at, by
more fitly designating it as a *cupboard*, in which its proprietor stored curiosities of the past and present ages. The
most noticeable of the articles contained in this laboratory are, one dozen combat swords, used generally for
actions on board ship, a stack of muskets for the soldiery,
two or three ash cudgels with cords fastened on one end
only, (these are so fashioned for the secure binding of refractory ruffians, or for the simple hearted peasant, who
most obdurately refuses to divulge his family secrets,)
a few purses, of various colors, containing tokens to represent money, so lavishly bestowed by nabobs and others of
unlimited wealth.

In one corner of the second shelf is scattered loosely a
quantity of artificial flowers; a drum hangs from the roof
with the sticks belonging to it protruding from its sides.
A guitar with two strings wanting, a set of cruets, a pile
of horn drinking cups, two brown pitchers, a few common
cups and saucers, a riding-whip, and a ratan. On the
upper shelf we perceive baskets of fruits of curious devices, with goblets to correspond, such as are required to
assist at the festivities of the heir to his baronial estates;
four pieces of sheet iron, formed like a trough with a
handle in the centre, for the burning of colored fires, as
already described. A caldron, and tripod for gipsy revelry, occupies an obscure corner, while one of the draw-
ers contains a pack of cards, two sets of dice, and boxes,

The Property Room.

a pipe, a bunch of skeleton keys, a do. of full-bodied ones, a clasp knife, two daggers, a piece of chalk, a tape measure, and two or three ends of tallow candle. The other is a receptacle for two table covers, a few sheets of writing paper, a screw-driver, and a pair of scissors.

In a nook, almost obscured from view by two disguising cloaks, hang three pair of convict fetters, in close company with a bundle of stuffed sticks, such as are indispensably necessary to exhibit the hilariousness of the Hibernian character, according to the infallible dicta of the modern dramatist.

The above is the spot where small articles in constant use are stored. In another part of the building we will presently inspect the workshop, where the property man manufactures the several things he requires, leaving the distribution of them upon the stage to his assistant, who presides over the place we have just quitted.

We cannot possibly avoid observing, as we retire from our late enquiry, that we have passed the box where the prompter at the evening's performance stations himself with book and desk, his finger on the passage as it is spoken, and his eye upon the speaker. An office of great trust is that of prompter. He should have a tolerable good education; and be somewhat skilled in heraldry, in order to check any inaccuracy the property man may commit, in placing banners and furniture upon the stage unsuited to the country, or period.

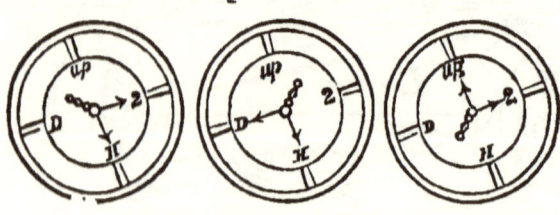

Gas Dial.

What a myriad of bells, and tubes he seems to have at his command. Can he need them all? Oh, yes, without these, the machinery of the department could not be conducted. No action of any kind can take place until he gives the signal. Near his right hand is a dial plate with keys regulated by stops that can govern the gas to the minutest nicety in every part of the house. The bells and tubes communicate in a similar manner. These are in a row in front of him, and are marked thus, *Orchestra, Traps, Flies, Drop, Curtain.* The trap bell conveys the information to carpenters under the stage that an ascent, or descent is to be made. The first ring is called the warning, the second to work the trap, which is done

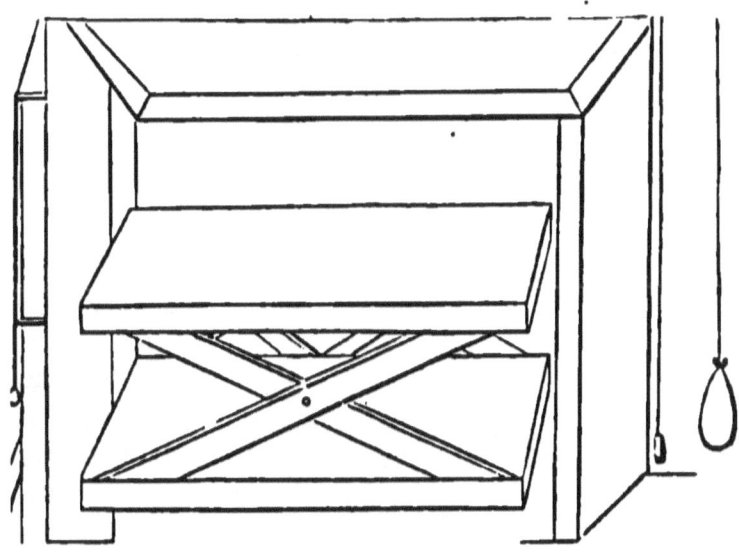

The Trap Open.

by a windlass manned by the carpenters, if it be an ascent, if a descent, an artificial trap is placed under the aperture made in the stage, and the object to disappear sinks by means of a counterweight, the carpenters instantly closing up the trap with the original piece, which slides into its place and is secured.

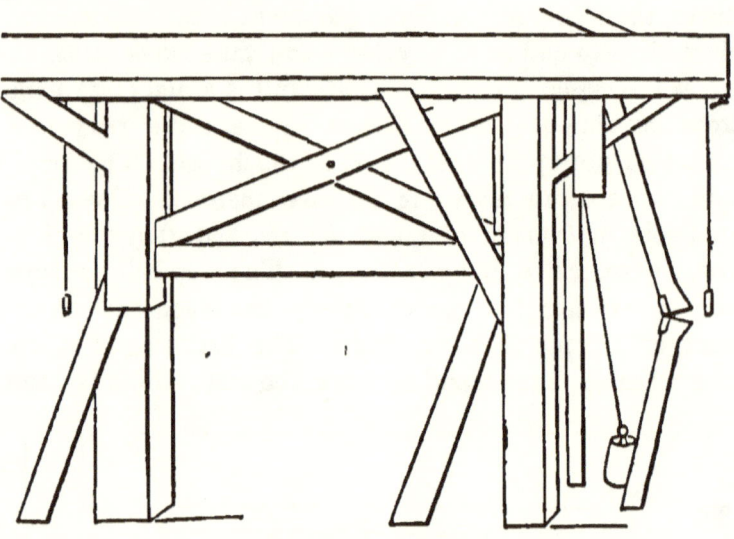

The Trap Closed.

The bell for the drop is used only at the end of an act of a play, the one for the curtain at the end of the play itself. The bell terminating in the flies, where the

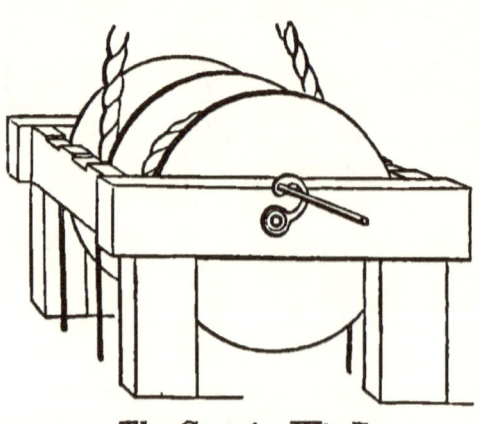

curtain is worked responds in like manner to the duties required of it; and thus the order and regularity, where the prompter is thoroughly an adept at his art, which we see only in well conducted theatres.

The Curtain Windlass.

Before we shift our quarters, let us explain that the circular box with a cord attached in two places and elevated above the head of the prompter, is the "rain box."

It has a goodly quantity of peas inside: its position being shifted by the ropes, the peas rattle towards the bottom, meeting in their course with small wooden pegs, against which they clatter, and give the best, and most perfect imitation of rain that can be well imagined.

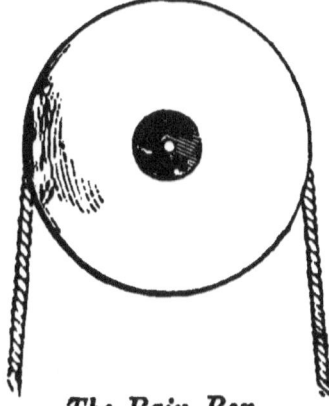

The Rain Box.

One of the two other ropes you see, works the large cathedral bell; and the other, a contrivance for the representation of thunder, similar to the "rain box," except

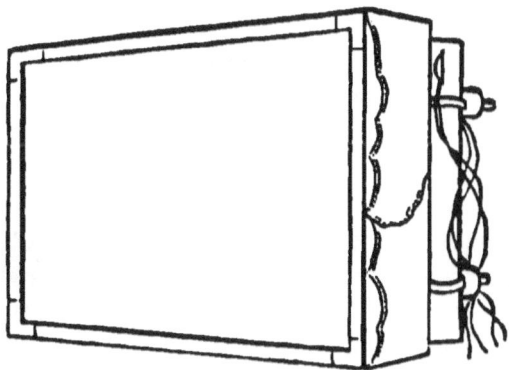

The Thunder Drum.

that the box is long, instead of being round, is minus the pegs, and placed with a cannon ball inside, as near the roof of the building as possible.

Some theatres still use a sheet of thin iron, hung where the prompter can conveniently shake it; but it has a metallic reverberation, not to be compared in effectiveness to the plan above described. If we add a knocker to the fixtures belonging to the prompter, we have noted all his professional paraphernalia.

In some secure nook not very distant from the stage is the *office of the manager.* A small, cheerful, cozy place it is, with an easy chair near the fire, and in one corner two or three pieces of expensive statuary, that have been borrowed for the play at present before the public, and placed there for safety in the day time, when not in use.

On the table are some open letters, from writers burning with a desire to elevate the dignity of dramatic art.

One has just completed, " a play in seven acts, upon an entirely new, and original model, which he desires at the very earliest opportunity to read for approval. The work had already received the very highest encomiums from distinguished private friends of taste and discrimination, and he, the author, cherishes a hope that the day is not far distant when the high and classic drama may break the bonds of modern innovation, and bursting with new-born greatness upon the millenium of ancient versification, stand colossal-like, at the very portals of our private homes."

Another, is from a lady " Who had, at the earnest request of several friends, consented at this festive season of the year to join them in some dramatic representations of a strictly private nature; but whose intuitive ease and talent so astounded the company, that it was immediately voted by every one present, that to longer remain within the seclusion of private life would be an act of positive insanity on her part, as well as gross injustice to the public in general."

There is also one, written with a troubled spirit, and a trembling hand; how differently couched. She who traced those lines was once the idol of the public, and in the enjoyment of position, and esteemed second to none. In the hey-day of her professional career, she looked with an eye of indifference on the members of her own profession who sought her hand. She bestowed it upon one she believed, from his social distinction and private means, competent to guard her through the world, in happiness and comfort. Like many others, she has long since awakened to the painful reality that she has united her fate with one who has no sympathy with her avocation, no sorrow for her sufferings. At all times greedily anxious for the emolument obtained from his wife's exertions, he despises the source from whence it is derived; and readily construes the slightest acts of kindness tendered by her professional brethren, as a violation of his marital rights!

The money she acquired when the bloom of youth and beauty mantled upon her cheek, has long since been squandered upon profitless speculation, or spent for the support of a rapidly increasing family, and she is now driven to the extremity of soliciting an appointment in the theatre at any terms, to avert the dangers of actual poverty.

This is no overcharged picture. The pallid cheek, the sunken, blood-shotten eye, reveal a fearful tale of professional hope blighted by uncongenial marriages.

Turn we now to the room we are examining, and we shall find it, if not very elegant, at least to contain a moderate proportion of comfort. A few pictures of the actors of a past age, with others at present in the meridian of their popularity, adorn the walls; while over the chimney piece, occupying the post of honor, hangs the likeness of the mellifluous bard, who has, with his magic pen, elevated dramatic poetry to the highest apex of human greatness. The piles of two or three past seasons' bills haug conveniently for reference; one or two manuscripts and the last printed copy from the London dramatic publisher, complete the list of items worthy of notice.

As we quit the apartment, the scenic artist passes, and confers upon us the compliments of the morning. Let us follow the bent of our enquiry, and ascend to the sanctum of the gentleman who has just mounted towards the roof, and whose footsteps are still distinctly heard in the distance.

You are suffering with another temporary attack of blindness, therefore have a care how you feel your way up the tortuous flight of stairs at the very back of the stage ; and where you cannot resist thinking, if fortune had favored you with architectural ability, it is the last spot you would select to build such a structure. After smashing your hat twice, and grazing your shins the same number of times, you reach the flies where, at the very back of the building, you find

THE PAINT ROOM.

The presiding spirit of the region has denuded himself of some of his wearing apparel, and now appears in a suit of canvas, tastefully sprinkled with spots of paint of every possible tint, the which give him somewhat the semblance of a human leopard. He has however, no affinity in disposition with the beast he in some measure resembles, being docile, and tractable to a singular degree. He is a great lover of his art, and enjoys a conference with any who will talk with him, on the choice pictures in the season's exhibition, those the visitor has seen in the Louvre of Paris, or the National Gallery in London, and prominent works in collections nearer home.

His boy is busily engaged grinding colors, while the artist himself is selecting from various brown pots, the different ones already fit for use, for a scene now upon the frame, and wanting only the last few finishing touches.

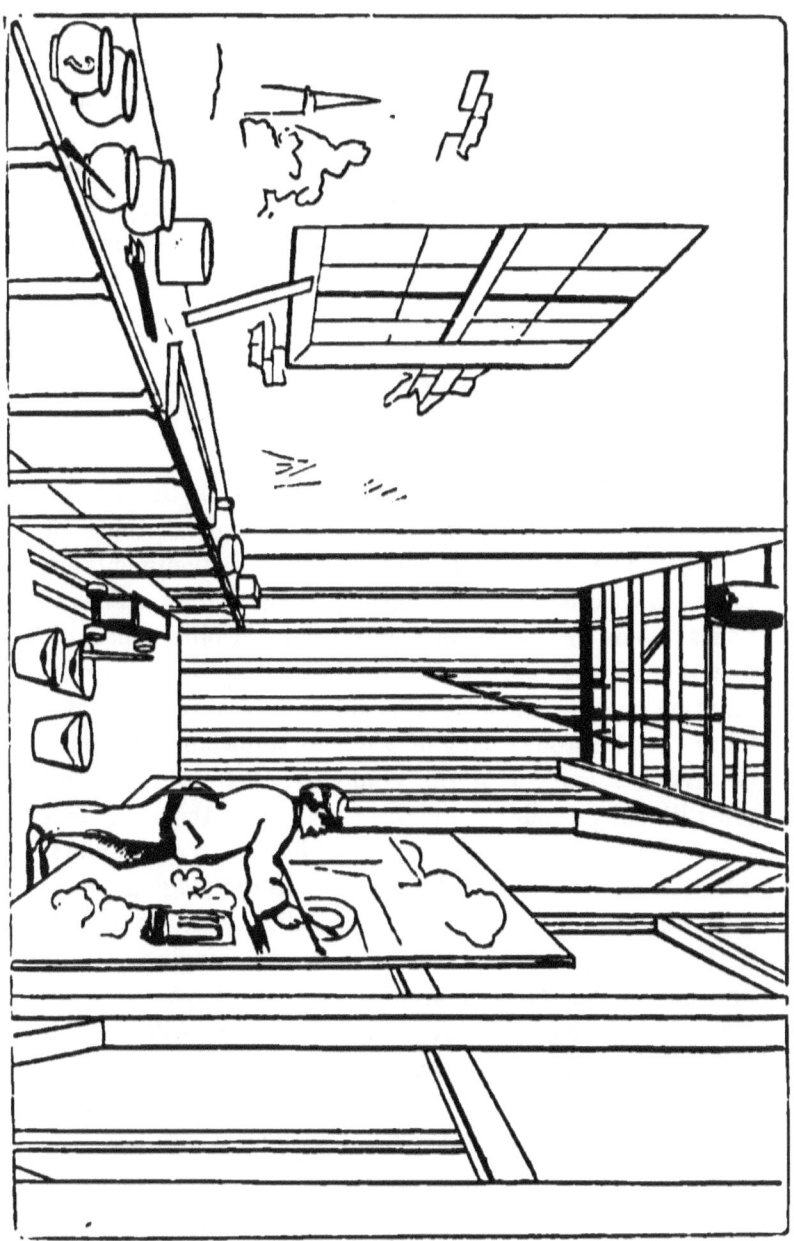

Paint Room.

The frame is the machine upon which the rough canvas is placed by the carpenters below, when it is first made by them, and raised by means of a windlass to its present position, where it will remain till fit for the public gaze, when it will be lowered by the similar means that raised it. This department is very well lighted by day from windows at the back of the building. At night it has two rows of gas-burners down the centre, with a reflector to throw the light upon the canvas.

See how rapidly the artist disposes of the colors; you are astonished, and wonder how such apparently careless work can produce a pleasing result, when viewed from the auditorium.

A cupboard with the door open reveals to us all this place contains. There we find a few rough sketches in charcoal, principally of gothic arches and pediments; a model in card-board of the last scene in a fairy extravaganza; some paint brushes, a meershaum pipe, a pair of overalls, a few numbers of a work treating on the art of painting, and an illustrated newspaper of a recent date. These, with a stone, a keg of size, and some fancy sketches of several members of the company, their weak points most liberally rendered by the artist, form the chief features of a place very rarely intruded upon by outsiders, whose curiosity is generally confined to the stage alone.

In beating a retreat from this locality, your danger is perhaps a little more imminent than you imagine. Hold on tight to the not very secure banister, or you will be precipitated forward with such velocity as will fix the circumstance upon your memory for some time to come. If you achieve the first landing in safety you will find yourself in close proximity with the room where the

PROPERTY MAN

fashions every conceivable article, from a walking cane to an elephant.

If republics be notoriously ungrateful, as the world insists they are, shall the subject of our sketch dare to wail over his neglected condition, when the play-going public, despite the information it constantly receives from those models of veracity — the play-bills — seldom or ever cast a thought upon the individual, who, in the "boudoir of my lady, the countess," has fashioned the furniture of exquisite workmanship, or illumined the fairy in tights as she ascends gracefully through a dazzling vista to tortuous clouds in the realms of bliss.

A good, and efficient *property man* is an indispensable adjunct to a well regulated theatre. One of this kind is preparing to mix the ingredients for a counterfeit eruption of Vesuvius, as we enter. He has received instructions from the manager to be preparing the necessary stuff for a great sensational spectacle for the holidays. *The Goblin Father* is to eclipse all former efforts in the splendor of its production. Before him is a fanciful protrait of his satanic majesty, taken at a time when his digestion was not in a very satisfactory condition, if we are to judge by his facial uneasiness, but to which he must occasionally refer while fashioning a truthful resemblance of that gentleman in clay, prior to completing his medalion in *papier mache*. Near the stove, and supported by a barrel of plaster of Paris, are the heads of the dreadful monarch's body-guard, a dozen in number, who have just received their final layer of color, and whose visages stand out from their white surroundings with the rubicund intensity of a practised glutton after a hearty meal; and as the crackling wood illumines their faces, would, if they were endowed with the power of speech, roar out,

"Ha! Ha! Go it, old boy! Blaze away, we're used to it. You can't roast us."

Around the walls hang implements of warfare, from the combat sword of the valiant sailor, to the cimeter

of the ferocious Turk. Stacked in one corner, leans the
armory of the establishment, while under the window
stands the buck-basket for Falstaff in the " Merry
Wives of Windsor," if not in that state of profuse perspiration described by that *ton of humor*, at least over-
crowded with every conceivable article for stage use.

A hazardous experiment is this property room to peregrinate in ; a large bench, such as is used by carpenters,
occupies the center of the apartment ; move a little to the
right, and you upset a large glue-pot ; turn to the left,
and your head is certain to come in contact with a temporary shelf supported only by small cords, the contents
of which will immediately shower down, crowning you
most unceremoniously with a helmet of the mediæval
ages ; avoiding that, you are face-to-face with the habiliments in which the parent of the Prince of Denmark
takes his nightly stroll.

You are thus placed in a similar predicament to the
inhabitant of a rural district who, after several futile attempts to thread the mazes of Broadway without accident, finally gave up the design in despair, and consigned
himself to his fate. Respectable elderly females, to
whom railway guides are a profound mystery, would find
here sharp practice for their ingenuity, if they attempted
to divine the purposes for which the heterogeneous mass
of articles within this sanctum are intended ; a marine
or junk dealer's, is a well ordered collection when compared with it.

Pending the production of a gorgeous spectacle, our
hero will often take his meals in this dramatic laboratory,
(when he can find leisure to eat it,) the same being conveyed to him by his daughter, a buxom girl of some six-
teen summers, and who has probably commenced her
professional novitiate in the representation of pages, or
attendants on the aristocracy of the classic drama.

He may be seen occasionally on the stage during rehearsal, when specially summoned by the manager, the call boy being dispatched to request his attendance for a moment. After receiving some instruction in relation to the forth-coming novelty, he will, in his slippered feet, glide away to his work-shop, conferring the compliments of the morning, and leaving behind him a strong flavor of glue, with a plentiful show of Dutch metal, particles of which brilliant decorative substance, stand boldly out in meteoric splendor upon his whiskers, as he disappears.

We descend to the back of the stage, and for the first time observe another queerly constructed place. By the dim light we perceive we are in the *carpenter's room*. It is a *fac simile* of the small room above, and boasts little, or nothing of interest. There are two shelves, upon which are scattered tools of every kind, from the gimlet to the centre-bit. Small brown paper parcels with light green labels lay about in various directions; some of these are empty, while from the rest, nails and screws of various sizes protrude. A two foot rule, and one or two articles of wearing apparel complete the display, and we again encounter the *call boy*, who is preparing for the rehearsal. As a general principle, this youth entertains not the slightest concern at your professional discomfiture if pressed for time to acquire the words of a part, but will, with an intense degree of gratification, shout at you while you are reading over your next scene, that you are waited for.

Only keep your eye upon him in the evening when Mr. Battledore, the eccentric comedian, gets into the most interesting portion of his pet story about a pic-nic; where a bear, or a buffalo, he seems hardly to know which, came down upon the company in the midst of their repast, and after poking its nose into everything, finished by gob-

8

bling up a giblet pie, and a young lady's straw hat with green ribbons. Observe the delight he takes in cutting short the story with a suggestion that "the stage has been waiting nearly five minutes, and he dont think the audience care much for a longer delay."

When what is termed a "stage wait" occurs, it arises from one or two causes, viz., either the boy has forgotten to make the call, or the party called has neglected to respond to it.

Every frequenter of a theatre must have observed an occasional mishap of this kind when, after a tedious delay, the delinquent, in his eager haste to reach the scene, will appear from the opposite direction his presence was expected.

It was just past eleven, and the company are arriving, those having the least to do being generally in the rear of the principals. Ten minutes' grace is allowed for the first call, (not for any other) and punctually at the end of that time the prompter directs the boy to "call one," and the rehearsal commences.

It is the duty of the stage manager to be present during this time, to assist by his experience the more natural method of overcoming any difficulties that may present themselves. With established actors, whose position in the public esteem rank them as adepts in their art, the business they may feel disposed to adopt is generally acceded to by the above named official.

It is most difficult to appear graceful upon the stage, without a large amount of practice. The gentlemen who play the small parts are called back several times, and impressed with the necessity of speaking more distinctly, and infusing more grace into their actions.

The play in rehearsal embraces characters for the following performances, viz.

"Leading Man." "Light Comedian." "First Old Man."

" Second Old Man." " Walking Gentleman." " Heavy Man." " Utility Man." " Leading Lady." " First Walking Lady." " First Old Woman." " Singing Chambermaid."

The above are the technical appellations by which the members of the profession understand the several designations of the characters they are called upon to enact.

The duties of each are as follows :

The Leading Man, is the personifier of the principal characters in tragedy, as well as some of the more serious ones in comedy ; as, Mr. Oakley, in the "Jealous Wife," Lord Townley in the " Provoked Husband," etc.

The Light Comedian, is the representative of the fine gentleman of the old school, as Charles Surface, in the "School for Scandal," and others of a more modern date, who stand prominently forward in the play.

The First Old Man, clearly defines itself. They are such parts as aged characters where they assume a similar significance with the principals of other lines of business ; if not, they are only *second old men*.

The Walking Gentleman, is he who enacts all the young men in all sorts of pieces,—youths for whom the young ladies of the drama have a preference, despite the opposition of their parents.

The Utility Man, must appear in any thing for which he is cast, the stage manager being the judge of his fitness for the positions in which to place him.

The Leading Lady, plays all the prominent characters of the drama of the serious kind. Such is however the power of their influence in a theatre, that they not unfrequently absorb many of the comic parts likewise.

The First Walking Lady, is she who must play the parts in both tragedy and comedy that are not claimed by the leading, and the second lady, and has also charge of some very prominent ones in farces.

First Old Woman takes the same relation in the allotment of parts as the first old man.

The Singing Chambermaid is not necessarily obliged to enact chambermaids only, but appears in all the *Soubrettes*, and is called singing chambermaid, to specify her musical capability, and in distinction to those who are not in possession of that accomplishment.

People who mix in society can very easily observe the variable and totally opposite phases of character frequently to be met with in members of the same family. The theatre is no exception to this rule. You have indeed a better opportunity of judging of the peculiarities of the members of the sock and buskin than that of any other pursuit. They are thrown so much in each other's society that there is necessarily an absence of some of the restraint which is not observable in many other professions, or callings.

Here is a most highly respectable gentleman. He takes charge of some of the old men. He is an excellent husband and father, and his manner is bland and affable. He will recount to you how, when attached to the naval service of his country he, in spite of orders from the commanding officer, intercepted the approach of the enemy's long boat, whereby (having succeeded) he was rewarded with a pair of epaulettes, and the favorable mention of his name and exploits at the war department. He will delight to repeat the conversation he had on the subject, many years after the date of the transaction, while on board a steamer on the Mississippi river, with General Scott, and how that great man and good soldier had assured him that "never, throughout the whole of his military career, had he met with a man whose courage he more admired as an officer, or whose convivial accomplishments as an individual, had left so deep an impression upon him."

Some people are addicted to hallucinations, and our friend has one which subjects him to much badinage, and some little abuse, from a few of the members of the company.

For years it has been his practice to purchase a certain number of lottery tickets every month; and although he has never yet been fortunate enough to hit upon the lucky numbers, he still clings to the idea that the day will come that shall see him rewarded for all his anxiety and disappointment.

"Such has been my conduct through life," he will often say, "that I am certain, despite the many reverses to which I have been for years subjected, my lucky star will one day be in the ascendant."

Long after the last auditor has departed, and the tramp of the night watchman reverberates throughout the building, in the deep solitude of sleep will he behold visions of lucky numbers flitting before his expectant gaze. Secretly will he register in his mind the numerical treasure; stealthily will he effect the purchase that is to repay him for all previous suffering! anxiously does he await the result, to be again deceived.

The Heavy Man, has just undisguisedly expressed it as his candid opinion, that his old friend must be cracked. No man in his senses would ever run the extreme risks he did, if he was not in that unfortunate condition.

"Why, sir," he says, turning to the second walking gentleman,

"It's not above a month since I was ass enough to join him in a walk after rehearsal! I never was so ashamed in all my life. What do you think he did?"

"Can't guess," rejoins the party addressed.

"Guess, no! I should think not. I'll be shot if he didn't take a fancy to the number on a policeman's cap, and followed him two blocks, with pencil in hand, in order to obtain it. The guardian of the peace very naturally felt indignant, and demanded to know what he had done to have a memorandum made of his number! Of course he couldn't explain that it was only his lottery lunacy, and the issue was that we were passed through three or four beats by these blue coated gentlemen, and dogged everywhere for the balance of the morning."

The call boy chimes in at the end of this anecdote, that the manager would like to see Mr. ——, the Heavy Man, presently, in his office.

Heavy Man refreshes himself with a copious pinch of snuff, and obeys the summons.

" Come in," says the manager, in his blandest tones, as the Heavy Man knocks at the door with the head of his cane; accepting the invitation, they are speedily face to face.

" Take a seat, Mr. —— "

" Heavy man bows, and does so."

" Excuse me for one or two moments, will you, if you please ? " Affecting to have the weight of empires on his head.

Heavy Man bows again, says " certainly " and fixing his eyes on the portrait of Shakspeare, thinks if he had the assistance of the wig and beard, he should very much resemble the bard ; and it would not be a bad idea to concoct a piece for that purpose for his next benefit.

Stage manager has pretended to write a letter, during this brief interval, and is now prepared for the attack.

" Oh ! by the way, Mr. ——, here is a manuscript I wish you would be good enough to look over. There are two heavy parts in it, one of them very troublesome and of an unusual length. The author was here this morning, and seems determined to drag me into the play. I have quite enough to think of, I'm sure, without the trouble of studying long parts, but this gentleman has a very large and wealthy connection. His name stands well in the best literary circles, and he can influence the houses greatly. I thought that — seeing the position in which I am placed, you would perhaps not object to look over the other part. You will find it short, and pleasant, and I am sure you can make it one of the chief features of the pieces."

Heavy man, not being well able to resist the compliment, and further, not having the same rapid facility for study he formerly possessed, consents at once, "Says he doesn't care, if Mr. ——, the stage manager, thinks it advantageous to the strength of the representations, he would be the last man to contend against a result so desirable."

The manager thanks him, offers him the privilege of an order for two friends for that evening, with a strict injunction not to mention the presentation to any of the company, wishes him good morning, and as the door concealed him from view, inwardly congratulates himself upon his tact and diplomacy, and appropriates the heavy man's part to himself.

All the ladies of the Ballet are about to assemble, and some of them have already arrived. There are two so much alike, that they must be sisters. One is aged seventeen, and the other fifteen. They are fatherless, and are the chief support of their mother and a younger brother, who is a helpless cripple. Their history is somewhat sad. Their father commenced his career with good business prospects; but false friends, competition of a foreign market, with the combination of events that invariably press upon the needy, overwhelmed him; till at length that universal panacea for all ills, death, came to the rescue, and bore his troubled spirit where it could enjoy that tranquility it had long been a stranger to. Left without the means of support, the little knowledge of dancing imparted to them in their infancy, afforded an opportunity for a scanty subsistence. It is whispered that the elder one is about to be married to a very worthy young man with good prospects in life.

By this time the ladies are nearly all in dancing costume, and the solitary violin in the orchestra is indulging in rapid ascents and descents of the chromatic scale, till called upon by the

BALLET MASTER

to begin. A crowd of young girls present themselves, and if ever you entertain the slightest doubt of the fallacy of the belief that they are of the weaker sex, your misgivings are at once dispelled. No stalwart pioneer of the masculine gender could habit himself in the same limited amount of clothing, and keep free from cold and rheumatism.

The stage has just been watered, to prevent their slipping. Their shoes are very thin in the uppers, and a trifle thinner in the soles; they are of various colors, pink being the favorite tint. They are somewhat dirty (the shoes) and have been, when new, used for evening performances, but are now, with the addition of two or three layers of darning cotton latticed across the toes, pressed into service for rehearsals. Their skirts have an etherial, gauzy look, profuse in circumference, but extremely contracted in a longitudinal direction. A jacket, sometimes fitting closely to the figure, at others worn loosely, with the hair well secured, completes the toilet.

The principal female dancer is going through a series of gymnastics in the rear, that would dislocate the limbs of one unskilled in the art of dancing. It consists of forming rapid circles; first with one foot, then with the other,

Ballet at Rehearsal.

8*

finishing by turning *pirouettes*, after raising one leg to a level with the comb at the back of her head.

"Now zen, come," shouts the ballet master.

"Ladies, vy you no make haste, shall I not vait here all day for you? Dis is too pad altogether."

This gentleman has been twenty years in this country, and asserts that he was born in the city of Paris, where his father was a man of great military distinction, and his mother one of the belles of the French capital. Some of his professional brethren have, with the natural jealousy which talent always inspires, insisted that Belfast in the North of Ireland, has the honor of his nativity. Talent is of no country; but it is a singular fact, worthy of observation, that while our friend, the *Maitre de Ballet* has for so many years been an adept at all the luxuries of a foreign locality, he rather retrogrades in his knowledge of the language. If we were in his confidence, he would probably let us into the secret that, having discovered the bent of the public inclination, he was willing to pander to the belief so universally entertained by the masses, that no man can possibly excel in the Terpsichorian art if he speak the English language with any degree of fluency.

"Now zen if you please," turning to the instrumentalist.

"All ready, go along zen."

The violin has only uttered a few bars, when it is suddenly silenced by the slapping of the ballet master's hands, and requesting Miss J—— to change her manner of using the right arm.

"You no graceful at all! Zis is ze way," placing his rotund figure in an attitude, by way of exemplification.

They make another start, and after a few more similar mishaps, the principal danseuse goes through her solos, the *corps de ballet* close in upon her, form a graceful centre piece, with scarfs elevated above her head, and they are dismissed with an admonition to be punctual in the morn ing, and not forget the instructions given them.

· The violinist packs up his instrument, and departs for some resort congenial to his nature. If he be of Teutonic origin, his desires tend towards a spot redolent of the habits and customs of that numerous and thriving race. If the balmy breath of Italy fanned his infant brow, he may be met surrounded by professors of the art for which that charming climate has been for ages distinguished. If of native growth, he may, not unlikely, in his hours of leisure blend the exercise of the commercial with the musical, the cares, and interests of which former will be, in his absence, presided over by his wife. There perhaps, in a thickly populated part of the city, will his partner be seen adding to their little competence.

One of the most important periods in dramatic life is the day on which the salaries are disbursed, and is called

SALARY DAY

At about twelve o'clock on every seventh play day from the opening of the season, does this highly interesting epoch arrive; six nights constituting a week. The choice spirits of the theatre term this the day on which the *Ghost walks.* And the question will frequently be put from one to another in an affected sepulchral tone, whether "That thing hath appeared."

The Treasurer, prior to the hour for liquidating the weekly claims, folds up the amount due to each, writing the name of the recipient on the outside, who signs a book to the effect that he, or she, has been put in possession of the money due to that date.

A code of laws are drawn up in every Theatre for the enforcement of promptness in business, thus :

Absence from rehearsal without proper notice to the

prompter, subjects the transgressor to a graduated forfeit of from twenty-five cents to a dollar.

The profession are in general very attentive, with few exceptions, to this necessary duty, and the forfeits are but seldom enforced. If carelessness is likely to take a chronic form, the manager resorts to the following notice, viz:

> The manager regrets to observe an inertness on the part of the members of the company, which is extremely prejudicial to the conduct of the establishment; therefore is reluctantly compelled to direct attention to the rules and regulations of the Theatre, the terms of which will be most rigidly enforced, without distinction, from this date.
>
> By order of the manager
>
> ——— Prompter.

This notice has the desired effect. Those who are reprehensible, taking the hint.

As the season progresses, the peculiarities incident to every community, begin to present themselves. Some of the ladies of the ballet have a propensity for literature of the sensation order, while all are profusely ingenious in the knitting department. They beguile their spare time at rehearsals with the latter, to a great extent. Not only do the parties above named indulge in this practice, but those of the more prominent of the sex frequently devote much time to a similar pursuit.

THE SOUBRETTE.

After partaking of a hearty and hastily dispatched breakfast, this young lady departs for rehearsal — probably reaching the theatre just too late for her first scene. If the prompter suggests, as he most likely will, that a little more punctuality would be desirable for the better conduct of business, the soubrette will insinuate that she is never by any possibility behind her time — that the clock at home is a model of mechanical exactness, and would be a shining example for the one provided for the green-room, it being an undisputed fact that a timepiece furnished for that apartment never had, from the dawn of the ancient drama, properly performed its functions.

That time honored institution, the British Beadle, is considered by acute judges of his habits and customs, to feel the dignity and importance of his significance, even when not decorated with the official ermine. The subject of our present enquiry has in like manner, become equally identified with the piquancy of the waiting maid, who, on the stage, is received into the sacred confidence of their employer's daughters, therefore seldom accepts an admonition from the prompter in a spirit of content, or thankfulness. This is, however, expanded or diminished in proportion to the position she may, by the influence of her professional ability, occupy in the esteem of a generous public.

When buoyed up by this conviction, the soubrette is not slow to impart to a congenial female spirit, " that she has no desire for Mr.—— the prompter, to dictate to her an inventory of the duties for which she is engaged ; that she believes — for who shall gainsay it ? — that she thoroughly knows her business, and don't thank him for directing special attention to her because the manager is within hearing; while he is ever willing to regard with a lenient eye, the constant derelictions of Miss——, who is retained for the exposition of young ladies of the youthful and romantic kind."

This scathing charge is usually delivered with a negative significance ; but its effect is clearly comprehended by him who, if he perform his duty faithfully, is seldom much admired by the sex whom we are taught to regard as man's greatest blessing.

Having disposed of her part of the dialogue of the play, together with the acrimony which this little incident has begotten, the soubrette joins a small knot of ladies who are seated in the green-room, busily occupied in manufacturing indefinite looking arrangements for the adornment of part of the habiliments of the sex concealed from the vulgar gaze, and enters into a sweeping condemnation of the whole race of prompters, breaking off in the middle of the tirade with a request to know where Miss J—— purchased the cotton she is using, for she — the soubrette — had ransacked every store in town, no later than yesterday, in search of some of that consistency, without success.

The gentleman retained for the comic department, now enters, and after offering the compliments of the morning to the ladies, suggests to Miss —— the soubrette, that it will be desirable for them to try over the new duet they are to sing in the forthcoming drama; a proceeding to which the lady addressed readily assents, but suddenly remembers, that in her hurry to attend that shameful ten o'clock rehearsal, she has left the score upon the piano in her sitting room.

The comic gentleman being summoned for the rehearsal of a scene, the soubrette enters into a most elaborate description of a new pattern of knitting she has just culled from the Ladies' Magazine, the which is received with much interest, till the gentlemen have quitted the room, whereupon she moves an adjournment to a more secluded spot, where she may impart to her hearers the contents of a most passionate epistle but recently received from some unknown source. A young lady, very much heated from her recent exertions in a *pas de deux*, suggests one of the dressing rooms. No one offering an amendment to this proposal, the party make their way to that retreat, encountering at the door of the apartment a slatternly person of their own sex, but of what complexion it is difficult to decide. This is one of the cleaners, whose professional avocation evidently affords no leisure for the exercise of her ability upon herself.

The door being well secured from intruders, our heroine produces a tender epistle, couched in the most poetic strain, wherein the afflicted writer "has seen but to adore her! with ample means, and a heart overflowing with the worthiest considerations, he is madly desirous to link the destinies of two natures which, he felt assured would, on a more intimate knowledge of each other, vibrate with the most ardent sentiments. A record of the melancholy wreck a cruel silence would inevitably produce, might be nightly observed seated in one of the stage boxes, with a small white rose decorating his buttonhole, where he would be faithfully posted so long as his natural functions remained in a sufficiently quiescent condition to enable him to leave his bed. A state of his position would thus be readily obtainable by all who had the curiosity, or charity to enquire, and when his manly essence was so far depressed as to preclude the possibility of his presence in his accustomed spot, it might be taken for granted he was seeking repose to his agonised spirit upon that couch in whose embrace he would nestle with the resignation of a blighted being, and the unhappy victim of a too confiding nature, which an acutely delicate organization would not permit him to subdue."

It not unfrequently happens that these precious missives are posted in the green-room for the amusement of the company. The hapless author regarding the attention bestowed upon his person by the artists of the evening, as a consequent curiosity upon his being the chosen one of her whose seclusion is impertinently invaded by the heartless *roue*, or the unprincipled adventurer.

The lady of whom we speak has been destined by the hand of nature to occupy an elevated position in the calendar of beauty, as a brunette. She holds, however, the object of the original intention as inimical to modern requirements, and by the aid of cosmetics would convert herself into a blonde, — the prospects of achieving a satisfactory result are rather vague and unsuccessful.

The rehearsal over, the soubrette, and two of the ladies, depart to purchase small articles for their sex's use, and during their walk dilate upon the most becoming tints with which to decorate the new boddice now in course of construction for the stage, with an occasional outburst of indignation on some of the last fashions, the head-gear generally demanding the greatest attention, till they separate for their respective dwellings.

After dinner she proceeds to arrange plateaus of ribbon of variegated hues, in double file around an apron of pink silk, with extremely contracted pockets, the same in which she carries her hands while indulging in *repartee* with the head of the family in whose service she is supposed to be employed as a domestic, and whose equanimity she somewhat ruffles by her very free definition of the rights and liberties of the female race.

Toward evening, her preparations being completed for the performance, she reclines upon a sofa, or easy chair, and carefully peruses the words of the character entrusted to her by the dramatist; and about an hour prior to the rising of the curtain, sallies forth, satchel in hand, to take part in an underplot with a flaxen haired youth, whose chief occupation appears to be to pay homage at the shrine of Cupid. With alternate attacks of jealousy and repentance, (as in real life) a union is effected between the happy pair in the third act, their worldly responsibilities dawning upon them with strict conformity to the laws of nature, till, in the fifth, we generally find them established in an hostelry on the very verge of a mountain peak, much frequented by vocal huntsmen, whose sport is supposed to be the chamois. Here, surrounded by family cares, our heroine propounds the principles of total abstinence to her partner, whose chief weakness appears to be a fondness for appropriating to his own use the viands he provides for his patrons.

Such are the duties, professionally, of our subject. Domestically, she may be regarded as imbued with the same womanly instincts as distinguish her sex in the several phases of the world's history. Happy for her, if she be blessed with the protecting presence of parents or brothers, to step between her and the arts of the destroyer. The fulsome adulation of empty-headed foppery she generally receives for about as much as it is worth, and very rarely consummates a marriage with the comedian above mentioned, despite the universal opinion, that professional similitude begets such a result.

Unhappily for her, she at times unites herself to one whose means are not of that positive, or satisfactory nature represented, and awakes to the fact when too late, to know that the evening of her life will be consumed in laboring for the support of him, and his offspring.

However intrepid the assertion be considered, in offering compliment to her general good and proper deportment, both socially and professionally, it is nevertheless true, that very few of her sex would exhibit as much stability of character if placed among the same artful surroundings of false professions and dazzling deceptions as constantly encircle her! And it is no small boast to know, that the *artiste* can look back when, in after life, she shall have become encompassed by maternal cares, to the time when to escape unscathed from the polluting breath of scandal, was considered, by her own sex particularly, quite inconsistent with the character of the soubrette.

DRAMATIC MOTHERS.

This perplexing epidemic disposes itself through most theatres with a virulence painfully distressing to all who

—unhappily for them—come within the pale of its blighting influence.

Worthily desirous to watch over their female offspring, while engaged at their professional duties, they exhibit a duenna-like supervision, spreading anarchy and confusion in every direction throughout the dramatic camp.

Mrs. Plumpley has a daughter, who enjoys the proud distinction of holding captive the hearts of susceptible youth by her personal graces; as well as the more matured auditor by her histrionic superiority. This much coveted privilege would be duly and properly appreciated by its possessor; but that a maternal instinct interposes to dam up the well-spring of her nature! making her, in after life, but a reflex of her present instructor.

No one who has watched with any degree of observation the several phases of character with which the theatre is beset, can have failed to be impressed with the conviction that "Dramatic Mothers" are, in their instinct and habits, a grave and serious offence against the comfort and equanimity of the establishment across whose portal some designing influence has permitted them to intrude.

The door-keeper excites the undisguised hatred of this lady by (before he had the honor of her personal acquaintance) refusing to permit her to besiege the building without permission of the manager, as set down in positive characters within his presiding sanctum.

The dressing room is the favorite *locale* for the exercise of her most popular and personal manipulations; there she can dilate upon the inefficiency of ladies who are the pets of the public at other establishments; and whose personal beauty or dramatic skill are in any way likely to conflict with the ascent of her own charge up the professional ladder.

Great pleaders in criminal law have often been distinguished for acerbity in conducting the cross examination of the witnesses on the opposite side, and when we know the acumen displayed by our heroine on the public as well as private conduct of her friends and acquaintance, we feel a deep regret that the practice of that learned profession should be monopolized by the so called, sterner sex.

In the dressing-room, preparations for the evening's performance are in a state of the usual bewilderment which generally distinguished that apartment, and the subject of our sketch has endeavored to allay an attack of nervousness with which one of the ladies is afflicted, by assuring her that her head looks a perfect fright! that no blonde should wear ringlets in such profusion ; with other remarks of a similar nature. Not having sufficient skill to conduct a battle of words against so expert a professor, the fair one affects to make a different disposition of her much admired tresses, finishes by giving a few touches of a pearly compound to her countenance, and hastily beats a retreat.

The costume of the several ladies of the establishment is a matter of serious concern to our heroine, and it is difficult for her to look with an eye of favor upon any who may be in possession of habiliments that can, by their color or style, excel those belonging to her darling Julia.

The lady who has just entered, and is unfolding a bundle freighted with a satin dress of exquisite tint, and made in the best and most becoming manner, opens the floodgates of the old lady's envy, from which she will not for some time recover.

" Bless me, my dear ! Why I do declare you've got a new dress (grasping it, to test its quality.) A present, of course. My Julia was offered a presentation the other day, of the most delicious thing I ever saw ; a Perkins's purple, my dear. But to my thinking, it isn't proper or prudent for single ladies to receive presents, no matter under what guise they may be offered; therefore I at once refused to permit it to be accepted."

"What, my dear, you bought it yourself? You astonish me! saved it up out of your salary! Oh dear me, *that's very odd!* Oh, yes, I see, it's a last year's pattern. Are you sure it isn't a dyed satin, dear me. Oh — oh! I remember now, it is one of those I saw at Stewart's some time since, among those cheap things on the counter, where the bargain seekers hover about. Eh, fifteen dollars, I think they were marked. I thought they would soon become very common, so made up my mind that I wouldn't have one, but let Julia be properly dressed; for in her position, you know, my dear, it is so very necessary; with you, who play only smaller parts, of course anything will do, and the public can hardly expect that, with your means, you can appear as well dressed as she does."

Such is a fair sample of the friendly admonition meted out by the "Dramatic Mother" to all who are at all likely to divide, or occupy the attention of the audience, in any degree conflicting with her "darling Julia."

During the evening's performance, she plays the part of a corpulent Hebe, and wanders after the object of her solicitude, with an acidulated compound in a tumbler, aiding her with advice on the proper exposition of her natural graces, and an earnest appeal that she convey the tones of her voice with a more audible effect to the extreme limit of the building.

The distribution of the several characters in the various pieces represented, is a matter of the most serious concern to her. The colloquial contests in which her daughter may be engaged, must be conducted with those whose position commands a certain amount of respect and confidence from the patrons of the establishment;

evidencing thereby, either a profound esteem for the wel
fare of the author, or a maternal solicitude for an effec
ive display of the family consequence.

When her daughter shall reach the period that suggests
itself as fitting for the fulfillment of her sex's destiny,
her feelings are much harrassed to decide upon whom the
honor shall be conferred. The pleasure of her who is to
be a contracting party to the ceremony, is not unfrequently made subservient to the future comfort and provision
of the *maternal martinet,* whose prospective affluence is
hopelessly crushed by the fact, that, after repeated fail-
ures to obtain permission to select a partner, she surreptitiously bestows her hand upon a gentleman whose facility for supporting a wife is somewhat visionary; or, it
may be, that being musically inclined, she will seek congeniality in harmonious contact with a professor of that
divine art, who has long looked upon her with an eye of
affection while engaged in the same establishment as herself, as a performer on the *violino secondo.*

THE WARDROBE.

We have omitted to take a peep at the wardrobe
where the costumes of such richness of design and material are stored. As we enter it we find the keeper of
the place engaged in making some repairs to a doublet
and trunks. He is extremely polite, and cheerfully and
with alacrity exhibits all his best dresses, those of his
own make especially. He has them all packed in layers
on shelves, all round the room, with a muslin cover for
each department; in the same manner that dry-goods
merchants preserve their stock from dust during the
night. A tailor's board is in the centre of the room; on
it are implements of the trade, and some dresses wanting
new strings, and buttons. If the wardrobe-keeper be
engaged to go on the stage when necessary, he is easily

The Wardrobe Room.

distinguished, like the super-master, by the careful way in which he is costumed. Propriety is not a matter of much moment to him, and the facilities he possesses of obtaining the costliest dresses, regardless of the position in society the individual he represents is supposed to occupy, will frequently tempt him to present himself to the multitude a perfect meteor of dazzling brilliancy.

As the season progresses, we cannot fail to observe the little bits of attention consequent on the mixing of the sexes in all communities. A shower of rain at the close of rehearsal, or after performances, will actuate the male members to offer the protection of their umbrellas to the opposite sex. The extent to which these attentions are persevered in at times, may result in the startling information that Mr. —— and Miss —— were married the previous day, quite unknown to the parents of either parties.

The gentleman before mentioned, and who enacts the young men, and on whom the ladies look with an eye of favor, does not exhibit the amount of attention the ladies seem to expect, and their jealousy is invoked to an excitable degree, when they learn from very reliable authority, that the only daughter of a merchant residing in the most fashionable part of the city, has fallen desperately in love with him, and their marriage may be shortly expected to take place.

You cannot fail to observe an extremely respectable gentleman, who seldom enters the green-room, but walks to and fro at the back of the stage, carrying his gold headed cane after the fashion of an officer in the army. He plays a portion of the heavy business, but when younger was a tragedian. He has seen a good deal of service in his profession, and in intellectual consequence is far ahead of the entire establishment.

The young men think him odd and cynical, when he

them with a look of discontent at their opinions of the
efforts of certain much lauded performances. He is quite
a recluse in his habits, and the changes in dramatic taste
that constantly occur, seem to bother his conception of
propriety, sadly.   The line of parts he has to play seldom
attract the attention of the critic, but an occasional lover
of art for art's sake, will derive much satisfaction from the
way he delivers the lines entrusted to him.   He is unusu-
ally spruce in appearance this morning, and wears a new
hat.   Only think, he has been highly complimented by
the critic of a leading journal for his performance of *Cassius*, in lieu of a *highly priced* artist, who was taken sick.
It is the first time he has been noticed by the all powerful censor, and with the earnest, but perhaps fallacious,
hope of an increased income, he has effected a purchase.

The gentleman who was to get a share of the comedy,
does not feel much flattered when he discovers that it is
only the worst share that has fallen to his lot.

Some of the new members grow into favor, while some
of them do not.   They all seize with the greatest avidity
every journal that expresses an opinion on their merits.
Those who are adverse to them of course must have a
motive for maligning them, and undervaluing their tal-
ents.

Once or twice, perhaps, the manager may be requested
to relieve some lady, or gentleman, from the (to them)
annoyance of appearing in some character for which they
have been cast, insisting that it does not come within the
terms of their contract to be called upon to do it.   At
times the point is yielded, at others the manager insists
that he or she play the part, or they are fully aware
of the consequences of a refusal.   If they remain obdurate, they probably have to quit the theatre, — this is,
however, a very rare case.

The members of every profession are all more or less

liable at times to be overtaken by sickness or misfortune, resulting in pecuniary difficulties very distressing to all, but particularly to those of an intellectual character. It may not be surprising for the public to know, that the professors of the dramatic art are, at times, visited with the pangs of penury, in common with others whose incomes are more positive and continuous. They have that peculiar delicacy always inseparable from those whose pursuits are of a studious character, and confine the knowledge of their condition entirely within the sphere of their own calling.

THE NEEDY ACTOR.

On a cheerless night when the rain is forming into ice as it falls, may be seen the figure of a man near the stage door. He pauses ere he enters. His hand is upon the latch; voices are heard in conversation with the hall-keeper, and he retreats with the blush of genteel indigence upon his cheek. Why does he dread to meet the gaze of the man whose voice he has just heard? Years past, when he, the needy one, was at the head of a large establishment, he gave employment to the man within, and his pride will not permit him to encounter him. He is sparingly clad, and ventures forth at night only. When the sound of the voices have died away, he seizes the opportunity to enter, and depositing a small note with a person the hall-keeper has left in charge for a moment, requests as a particular favor it may be sent in as speedily as possible to Mr. ——, and say he will call in the course of the evening for an answer.

The party addressed, requests he will wait, and take a seat near the stove. The petitioner, affecting an air of business urgency, declines; says he has a call or two to make elsewhere, and will look in again on his return.

In the neighborhood may be seen, sauntering about to

beguile the time, the author of a letter craving from his brother artists, " The means whereby he may make himself presentable in society; as well as to provide his family with the necessaries of actual need with which they have been for a time deprived. Those whom he addressed are cognizant, from years of professional connection, of his claim to their kindly consideration, and he concludes with an earnest hope that his most bitter enemy may never be reduced to his present painful extremity."

In one corner of the green-room stand a small group of men whose sympathies are very susceptible to the sufferings of their fellows in adversity. But a few words pass between them; a slip of paper is soon well provided with names attached to various amounts, in proportion to the means of the subscribers. The comedian is charged with the pleasing, but somewhat embarrassing duty, of presenting the amount collected. Towards the end of the performance he may be seen taking the arm of the petitioner, and making rapid strides down the street, in order to make his companion feel as much at ease as possible, while he proposes questions of the present whereabout of members of the profession he cares nothing to know. Turning into some convenient locality secure from notice, he invites his companion to partake of refreshment, and in the course of the repast, produces the results of a little collection, regretting it is not larger, but they have many calls upon them, and further, the salaries of the company are not as much as report had emblazoned them to be.

With a lighter heart than when he started on his mission, does the once popular actor return to his scantily provided dwelling, with tears of gratitude for the welcome gift, bestowed in the quiet, unostentatious way peculiar to a class, whose means, however limited, are always freely bestowed upon the needy and deserving.

As the end of the season draw near, the names of the several candidates for public consideration, grace the top of the bills, as recipients of a benefit. The plays each person proposes to present to his, or her patrons, are submitted to the manager, who decides whether it be within the resources of the establishment to do them with befitting credit. If we can not take a liberty with our friends, with whom should we be permitted the privilege? In selecting a character to appear in on the important event, it is not uncommon for the beneficiary to adopt one somewhat above the grade of prominence he or she may be designed for. This pardonable weakness is always kindly overlooked by the public, and mostly acceded to by the manager.

It is an amusing mystery among the company, who are all anxious to be put into possession of the names of the pieces each purposes to present to their friends. At times interests will clash, by two persons wishing to fix upon the same play. This is arranged by the manager. The proportion received by the petitioner at these benefits depends entirely upon the terms specified at the time the engagement is consummated, as a third, or half of the gross receipt, as the case may be. It may not be out of place here to state, that the proceeds, after deducting extra expenses, fall very far below the amount of the public estimate.

Ticket nights are taken by most of the employes of the theatre, these yield the half of the amount each person can dispose of, or rather the half of such tickets as are presented at the doors.

The manager generally takes the last night of the season for his own benefit, which affords him the opportunity of paying a graceful compliment to his company, " who have so ably seconded him in his efforts to secure the public esteem. To the public, for the liberal manner they have responded to it, the which will be an incentive to future exertions ; and during the recess he shall endeavor to provide such an array of talent for the next season as shall far outstrip the present, now concluding. And with an earnest hope to meet them all in the enjoyment of health and prosperity early in the Autumn, he begs most respectfully to bid them farewell."

Prior to the end of the season, the note of preparation in the minds of the company has long been sounded in relation to the succeeding. Those who desire to remain, wait anxiously the result of their letter of application which they have, by the assistance of the call boy, had placed upon the table in the manager's room.

These applications are in reply to the following notice posted in the green-room four weeks before the close of the season, viz :

The ladies and gentlemen of the company, are respectfully informed that the present season will terminate on the —— inst. Those who may desire to re-engage for the season ensuing, will please signify the same by letter, on or before the ——.

—— Prompter.

Now is every one impressed with the same uneasiness housekeepers have, as they approach the period of their emigration to some other domestic habitation. The theatre box at the post office is daily swollen to repletion with replies from provincial managers, who have been solicited to give the subscriber six or twelve nights in the month of August. Some however, who delight in the world's luxurious ease, betake themselves to the more agreeable task of rural sports during the hot spell, and return to their fall duties invigorated by fresh air, and wholesome recreation.

The manager is much employed replying to the applications of candidates for next season's engagements, and members from the rival establishments may be seen quitting the private office with an air of unconcern, as if it were not possible they could be suspected of holding conference with the manager upon any business connected with the theatre, but had simply dropped in to make a passing call, — an act of politeness that never occurred to them till the present moment.

The company themselves are somewhat on the reserve in relation to their future prospects. Those who return next season merely acknowledge the fact as if it were a matter of course, which any one of the smallest capacity must have anticipated. Those, however, whose applications have been answered negatively, assure you that under no circumstances whatever, would they consent to a repetition of the conduct they are at present receiving, — that in no instance through the entire season have they had the slightest opportunity for the display of their ability; and to endure a second edition is out of the question.

The private property of the company is now seen to depart by instalments in boxes, wrappers, and champagne baskets. All outstanding accounts are sent in, audited, and settled.

The manager congratulates himself upon the successful termination of a season begun, perhaps, without any great prospect of pecuniary profit; but happily, by his superior judgment, one of the most paying campaigns since the building was erected. The lessee, (if there be such a person behind the throne managerial) is highly pleased with the tact displayed by his man of business, in proof whereof he is, while enjoying the luxury and hospitality of the said lessee at his little place in the country, complimented by the presentation of a watch of exquisite workmanship, accompanied by a speech teeming with assurances of his personal regard for his public talent and private worth.

The manager receives the treasure with heartfelt gratitude; and as he wends his way to the chamber allotted to his use, cannot help reflecting upon the oft quoted axiom, "that the test of genius is success." How variable must be the emotions in the breast of that donor who can fashion his liberality to the exigency of his subject; for when, during a period of commercial disaster, he endured sleepless nights of anxious thought for the welfare of his employer, *but didn't succeed*, no words of gratitude or encouragement were offered, to cheer him on his next venture.

Falling into a deep slumber, the manager is happy to become oblivious to the intricacies of all matters appertaining to

BEHIND THE SCENES.

I desire to impress upon the minds of my readers, that the foregoing applies to the season's doings within the walls of a theatre conducted upon principles of etiquette and business propriety.

To accurately describe the innovations that have, from time to time, held despotic sway, in antagonism to those as here set down, would be an endless, as well as a humiliating task. Man, philosophers tell us, is a progressive animal, and many eventually establish a code of laws for a dramatic millennium, which consummation cannot arrive too soon for the personal comfort, as well as the pecuniary interest of a numerous class, whose positions at the present time are somewhat indefinite.

CHAPTER XVI.

THE state of Ohio has within its boundary a river still retaining its Indian nomenclature of Maumee; a town y'clept Toledo skirts one end of it, while the other terminates in Lake Michigan. It was ushered into existence somewhere about the year 1836, by some hardy pioneers, who probably conceived the notion that when it was thoroughly drained it might become a pleasant spot for those who sought the invigorating breezes from the river, hard by. When we visited this delicous retreat, it was under the excitement of railway engineering, and is now (1866) the great route from the Eastern states to the West. The country a few miles away is beautiful in appearance, and fertile to profusion ; but the town itself is deficient in every requisite for a healthful location, being filthy to the sight; and subject to frequent attacks of fever and ague in the most virulent form. It was at one of these periodical arrivals, that we reached the place, in the latter part of the month of November. The disease was blooming in all its native joyousness, the river donating its profuse miasma with its customary liberality. The morning sun had commenced to struggle through the thick and poisonous atmosphere, with very ill success, as we arrived from Cleveland, and are shaken to the hotel in a vehicle built coeval with the date of the town's nativity. The resting place for travellers is a fitting companion to the other enjoyment of the neighborhood, and is not readily forgotten by those who, by the pressure of untoward circumstances, find themselves entangled in its meshes. Hotel keeping must be a profitable speculation in many of the western cities, if your feelings can become, after a sufficient course of tutorage in the science of extortion, sufficiently callous to the sufferings of your fellow creatures.

It is Sunday, and the several boarders hang lazily about the house, exhibiting much restlessness at the approach of the hour when meals are served. As the evening draws near, those who are under the influence of the season's severity, hover around the large circular stove, wrapped in thick overcoats, piteously awaiting their nightly attack.

In the morning I repair to the building used as the theatre, and at the entrance and about the passages, encounter some of the company. The leader of the band is on the stage smoking a short pipe of tobacco, and imparting dramatic instruction to a dirty looking French poodle, whom I found a prominent member of the *corps dramatique*, and a great favorite with the public.

The rehearsal of "Paul Pry" is somewhat tardily got through, from the difficulty the manager has in persuading either of the ladies to do violence to their personal beauty, and assume the character of Mrs. Subtle! One is found (at last) bold enough to attempt the sacrifice, and the morning's business is dispensed with after a fashion.

The manager expresses his regret that he is a *little short of people*, but expects two additions from a neighboring city the following day. While I was in conversation, an open van approached, containing a family of female musicians who, as per placard hung around the vehicle, propose to exhibit their musical accomplishments that very evening, in a grand instrumental concert!

Our manager is in despair. Such a powerful opposition will ruin the first night, as all the young men about town would be certain to patronize an exhibition so novel, and with such good looking performers, too? What should we do? Something in the shape of counter attraction must be thought of! I said it couldn't be helped, must hope for the best, and quitted the theatre with no very sanguine expectations of the pecuniary result of our visit to Toledo.

I repaired to the hotel; it was a quarter of an hour past the time for dinner. The majority of the inmates had long quitted the table and had finished two or three cigars each; therefore, I came in with the fourth relay of feeders upon the *debris* of the banquet.

The manager had promised to call upon me after dinner, to show me the points of interest with which, he seemed really to believe, the place abounded. I was seated at the window of my bed-room, fortunately a front one, when I heard the approaching sounds of martial music, and the tramp of the juvenile portion of the populace. I turned my eyes in the direction from whence the sound proceeded, and was horror stricken to perceive my friend pull up in front of the building with four grey horses harnessed to an open van, in which were seated the orchestral performers attached to his establishment, while himself assumed the office of Jehu. A place reserved on his left was evidently intended to be the pyre on which I was to be sacrificed; for, stretched across the vehicle was a huge canvas placard with this announcement:

W. Davidge, the great comedian from the Broadway Theatre, New York, for a few nights only, and who will have the honor of making his first appearance this evening.

Taking a despairing glance at the triumphal car on which I was to be burnt alive for the wonderment of an astonished multitude I barricaded the door, disencumbered myself of my outer garments, jumped into bed, declared I was suffering from a sudden and violent attack of sickness, from which I took good care not to recover till the great advertising Juggernaut car had driven away. In the evening I was informed by this western Crummles of the treat I had missed; for that all the boys in the town had gone frantic with excitement, and shouted so loudly for a comic song, that he was compelled to pass off one of his brass band for the *original Jacobs!* and they made him sing "Villikins and his Dinah," and "I wouldn't be at all surprised if they insist upon your standing on your head, and doing the same this very evening.

The introduction of railroads has greatly destroyed the feature of country life; and it may be readily believed the drama has equally shared in the rapid change that has affected every branch of trade or profession. I do not wish to infer that the art of acting is, in its vitality, injured or depreciated in places where a taste for the better class of amusement ever existed at all; but I do believe that the rapid increase in the population in newly formed cities, produces a style of patrons whose habits and associations afford no opportunity for the cultivation of the arts, but, in the thirst for acquiring money leave them content with a recreation that appeals only to their visual wants, to the total exclusion of the intellectual, which the denizens of older localities yearn for as a necessity.

Before the progressive change above described, the country actor had a totally distinct characteristic from those who were the favorites of the city establishments. He was gradually, by the study of the best authors, fitting himself for his debut before those who were to sit in judgment upon his claims to the occupancy of a niche in the temple of dramatic fame. There was a standard of excellence to be reached ere you could approach that much coveted goal! The historian who shall pen the rise and fall of public taste during the last twenty years, will find ample materials for the exercise of his thoughts, and the variety of the subject.

SALISBURY.

Few of my professional brethren will be able to resist a smile at the reading of the above name.

A genial man was Salisbury, an excellent actor and an inveterate practical joker! The western part of America has not produced a greater character than he of whom I desire to speak.

My acquaintanceship was but slight, when I encountered him in a railroad car at the Detroit depot, bound for Chicago. Before starting, he beckoned me in a secret and suspicious manner, on to the platform, where he hurriedly enquired, If I had purchased my ticket?

"Certainly!" replied I.

"Ah!" he continued, "I never do that."

"Don't you, indeed," I added, "are you on the free list."

"Well, pretty much so," was the rejoinder. "Oblige me, don't take any notice of me through the entire journey, until we reach our destination, and then not until we are clear of the depot." I readily yielded to his request, not without some curious cogitations in regard to the result.

The bell rung furiously, the inevitable last passenger is with his baggage pitched into the car, and we are on the way for the city of wonderful progress, Chicago.

We got on a few miles, when the conductor made us acquainted with his presence by most authoritatively demanding "Tickets." When Salisbury was solicited to satisfy the curiosity of this functionary, the following was the mode in which the attempt was made, and the result.

Conductor. Now, Sir, ticket please.

Salisbury. (Apparently unconscious.)

Conductor. (Passes on, but presently returns and repeats the previous performance.) Come, neighbor, I want your ticket.

Salisbury. (Exhibits the upper part of his face, stares vacantly around, turns over, and sleeps again.)

Passengers. (Are cogitating on the result of these inattentions to such polite requests.)

Conductor. (Gets more anxious to close up his accounts, and gives his unconscious passenger another shake, with an evident show of temper.)

Salisbury. (Assumes a sitting position and hands conductor a copy of an evening paper, which he finds he has been reposing on.)

Two young Ladies. (Give a loud laugh.)

Conductor. (Very much flurried, and looking suspiciously at the two females.)

Conductor. Now come, there's been enough of this. If you don't show your ticket I shall have to drop you here (raises his hand to the check line.)

Elderly person. (Attached to the cattle interest, apparently volunteers to explain to the gentleman the nature of the conductor's demand, bawling in S's ear.) He wants your ticket !

Salisbury. (Still incorrigible.)

Conductor. Here, come! Out with you! (Is going to suit the word to the action, — when, ——)

Somebody, (or something wrapped in numerous shawls interposes.) Say, look here, Conductor, I'll fix him all right, leave him to me.

Conductor. Are you in his company ? Does anybody know him here ?

No one acknowledging an acquaintanceship, conductor is about to carry his threat into execution, laying hands upon the incorrigible passenger for that purpose, when Salisbury, having gathered a crowd around him, got upon his feet, and with a pencil wrote upon the margin of a newspaper the following : " I regret this extremely. I am deprived of the power of speech to express my situation. I have been robbed and ill used by sharpers."

Conductor. Well, I havn't anything to do with this. I want your fare. Come now!

Duet. (Two Ladies.) Oh shameful! poor creature, you wouldn't surely turn a man out on such a night as this. Some people have no more feeling than brutes!

Cattle Dealer. No, nor half as much as some brutes. How much do you want?

Conductor. Why, if he is going to Chicago, I require such a sum, (naming it.)

Lady. (In ringlets very much disordered.) Now really it's too bad. I guess it can be all arranged satisfactorily. I'm sure I'll give a dollar towards the amount with pleasure, rather than he shall be expelled from the car, at this distance from the town, too.

Omnes. Of course, I'll give something too. The necessary sum is speedily collected, and the conductor retires, after receiving his fare, and an addition of universal disgust from all the passengers.

At the stations where we alight for refreshments, our hero is safely conveyed to the dining hall and his meal paid for by one or other of his fellow travellers. We meet with a delay, and it is late in the afternoon before we cross the long trellis work bridge skirting Lake Michigan, and are deposited at the depot.

Salisbury was speedily upon the platform, and as I looked at him in wonderment I see him raise his hat, and in the most bland and gentlemanly manner hear him deliver his adieu to his fellow voyagers in these terms:

"Ladies and gentlemen, I cannot find words to express my sense of the obligation you have conferred upon me. I shall ever consider myself your grateful debtor. Good evening."

SALISBURY AND THE FRENCH COOK.

If I say that the weather was hot, I shall give but a faint idea of the summer of 1854, when I paid my first visit to Chicago, to find that dreadful scourge, the cholera, decimating the population, and driving all those whose means and leisure served them, to more genial dwelling places.

Our hero had never been able to lay in a stock of the world's goods, therefore it was not surprising he should be driven to the exercise of his very fertile ingenuity in order to appease his daily wants.

An opportunity presented itself the morning after our arrival.

A rosy little Frenchman was preparing breakfast in the kitchen of the "Young America," and as he scientifically tossed his omelets and warbled his snatches of song, attracted the willing attention of our adventurer who, with a wistful aspect, was admiring the operation from the window which abutted upon the street. Presently their eyes met, and they smiled in unison. Salisbury, began,

"You sing well, Monseiur!"

"Oh, sare, you too good! much oblige!"

"The songs of your native land, monseiur, are charming, *bien bon!!*

(With a shrug, and an attempted accent. "Oh, sare," (bowing low.)

"Fact. I assure you! I know no country that can excel yours in the extreme beauty of its ballads, especially those where love is the theme !

"Ah! oui! ye love ballad! *magnifique!* you come inside, sare."

" Thank you, I'm tired, I will," and speedily Salisbury is seated in the kitchen. A few more compliments, in order to bring the Frenchman into a condition sufficiently impressible for his purpose, and our hero began a dissertation upon the mystery of preparing coffee, at which he boldly affirmed he was ready to challenge the world.

The *Gallic pride* was wounded in its most sensitive part. His prowess had never, even in his native land, been questioned, and now to have the shadow of doubt cast upon his *cuisine* by a stranger, who had never enjoyed the pleasure of feasting upon viands prepared under his masterly direction, was a serious blow. When he had somewhat recovered from his bewilderment, he continued in as good English as he could collect at short notice, " Sare, *mon amie*, you say mon cafe not good like him vot you have!"

" My dear fellow," rejoined S. " you can have no idea of the way in which I make it, and the secret I have whereby I defy any one to discover how it is accomplished."

" Accomplish! ah! vat is dat accomplish you put in him? sare, tell to me, you never taste mon cafe?"

" Never," said S. " but—"

" Oh! *mon amie.* You shall see vot I sall give to you. Suiting the action to the word, he placed upon the table a cup of delicious coffee, with ham, and omelet, taking a step back while his rival sat in judgment upon its quality.

Our hero took one sip at the coffee, and fixed his eye upon the Frenchman, whose visage was suffused with perspiration and anxiety.

" Capital, monsieur, very good indeed!" (Rising, and shaking his hand.) This is excellent; but confess now, you are not always as fortunate as this."

" Vat you say, monsieur?"

" Why, your coffee is not always as good as it is this morning?"

"Oh! oui! How long you stay here?"

"About a week, perhaps two!"

"You shall see, monsieur, come ye to-morrow and ye day after him, and you shall see mon cafe, him as good, ze same to-morrow as it is ze day before, always ze same!"

"Much obliged," said Salisbury, bowing himself out, "your coffee is excellent. I had no idea it was possible to find a man who could equal me at coffee!"

Punctually at eight o'clock every morning, for the next fortnight, might be seen, with his breakfast before him, a cheerful, ruddy faced man, waited upon by the French cook, whose merry laugh bore ample testimony to the pleasure he derived from the society of one who, but for their fortunate meeting, must have started on his daily mission with an empty stomach.

THE LIGHT COMEDIAN.

Well accoutred for an attack on the impressibility of susceptible female nature, our subject promenades the most fashionable quarters of the city at a period of the day when the *first society* has made up its mind to inspect the stock of those who allure you with articles of costume faultless in design, and fabulous in cost. In common with others whom the gaudily dressed windows attract within their precincts, the light comedian is not proof against the blandishment of the last consignment of expensive dry goods; it may be, perhaps, that he desires to contemplate the purchase of some article that may have taken his fancy; or it is just possible he has heard a pair of sweet lips utter his name, as she is alighting from her carriage. She is in company with two congenial spirits who have often witnessed the professional exertions of our hero, when, after being expelled from the dwelling of his inamorata on three distinct and separate occasions, he has triumphantly, in the disguise of a

domestic, returned and carried off the object ot his affection to the nearest clergyman.

What a source of attraction he is to them! How much
they would like to address him, but dread the imprudence
of such a step! How unconscious he is — or appears to
be — as he turns suddenly to meet their gaze, then slowly moves off with the satisfaction of one who believes
himself somewhat above the common, every-day stock,
which nature has disposed in its wisdom for the propa-
gation of the human race.

Not alone do the fair sex look with an eye of pleasure
upon the light comedian. Men may not unfrequently be
seen to nudge each other as he passes them, adding some
remarks upon his professional capability in the last sensational production in which he has taken an important
part.

The progress of photography has deposited his resemblance with plentiful alacrity in all the more eligible
positions, and in the most graceful attitudes; while any
alteration in his hirsute embellishments becomes immediately the city's talk.

Epistolary effusions of a warm and tender tone occasionally beset him, from all kinds of people, and couched
in every kind of style, from the rose-tinted and highly
perfumed satin paper with its adhesive fastening of the
quiver of the god of love, to the more practical business
stationery of the milliner, or skirt factory.

Wonder not, dear reader, that the crime of vanity be
sometimes laid to his charge ; for who amongst you could
escape the stigma with such an array of admirers as he —
in virtue of his office — draws around him. On the stage,
he is invested by the dramatist with virtues of the highest class, and a spirit of reckless effrontery highly palatable to the taste of the fair sex, whose nature off the stage
as well as upon it, yearns to exhibit its prowess in sub-

duing the exuberance of manly folly, and the turbulence of unsystematic youth.

Pending the production of a drama wherein our hero is to represent a noble of the court of France, at a time when that country was revelling in the enjoyment of uninterrupted pleasure, he may be seen in the wardrobe, holding conference with the designer of costumes on the most becoming blending of colors; illustrating his views by a sketch of a noble of that period clad in all the paraphernalia of regal splendor. There is an earnest desire on the part of the proprietor of the theatre to look with the most economical eye upon the wants of the approaching new drama, and the light comedian is assured by the costumer, that the material he would like to habit himself in will far exceed in costliness the rate as "per his instructions," or, as he quaintly expresses it,

"The governor wouldn't go that, not at no price, he's sure!"

To ordinary people, this would seem to be conclusive, that our hero must be content with the scale of expense as set down by that infallible autocrat, "The manager," but it does nevertheless happen, that when the play shall be presented to the public, he will carry off the palm for the splendor of his costume as well as for the satisfactory rendition of the character.

With becoming grace does he confer the usual civilities of every day life to all who encounter him in the course of business contact; and not unfrequently, will exhibit a fondness for sports requiring an immense amount of physical endurance, scarcely compatible with the public's preconceived notions, from the medium they have been accustomed to contemplate him.

When the announcement is duly put forth in the daily papers, that the public can have the pleasure of assisting at his annual benefit about to take place, he is speedily overcharged with missives requesting that certain boxes, and eligible positions for seeing and hearing, be retained for the use of the subscriber, with kindly expressions of hope that the affair might be a genuine ovation of pleasure and profit.

Perspective mothers, as well as those who have long assumed the dignity of maternal cares, vie with each other to render homage at the shrine of their favorite; while their cavaliers exert all their interest to make the occasion one of the genuine successes of the season. And when these mysterious boxes, which outside innocency believes to be impregnable, are disclosed to the delighted gaze of the recipient, the vouchers assure him of the esteem in which his exertions are regarded. He counts his gains with the air of a man who has received his proper quota of the public consideration; or if he be of a selfish nature, ponders on what an increase might have found its way into his private coffers, if a powerful attraction elsewhere had not occurred on that very evening, or an antagonistic influence had not been exerted to his disadvantage, by copious showers of rain throughout the entire day.

The exponents of the broader kinds of comedy find little, or no favor in his esteem. He is ill-disposed to award them the meed of approval the public voice would seem to consider their just due. Not that he is insensible to the necessity of their introduction into the *dramatis personæ*, but the means usually employed by the dramatist involves an association with the influences of persons who move in the lower walks of life, by no means congenial to the surroundings of one who is constantly called upon to present living pictures of the highest toned people, whose idiosyncrasy, by a natural course of attrition, give him incalculable advantage towards the fulfillment of a high moral and consequential destiny.

When he lays aside his professional armor for the customary recess, he repairs to some spot redolent with the presence of youthful beauty and matured independence — there, by the exigency which a void in the male population sometimes produces, will he find himself in frequent companionship with some of his greatest admirers, whose regard for him and the art he so much adorns, make them supremely delighted at the pleasure of making his acquaintance; though the idea has never before occurred to them, till, being stranded upon the dreary waste of their own invention, they clutch at a rescue with an affected sincerity too transparent for the meanest capacity to pass unnoticed.

It may be that the persuasive tones of the light comedian are at times remembered as they were wont to be uttered when he swore, in the last new drama, to "Break through all edicts, no matter by whom issued, and boldly thunder at the portals of his father's castle, till the reverberation should topple its proprietor from his seat, that Angeline should be his, and his alone, ere the sun should again present his reflective presence upon the apex of the building."

Or it may be, that a totally different sentiment is uppermost in the female breast, and prompts one lonely possessor to seek a defender in the person of our hero; who surreptitiously sacrificing himself on her behalf, becomes the author of several blooming pledges of mutual affection most zealously cherished by one who is regarded with a feeling of sorrow by those whose antecedents may have graced the pages of a criminal register for misappropriation of valuables not their own personal property, but who cannot readily recover from the social disaster that the friend of their youth, whose hand had been solicited by many well skilled in the aptitude for municipal peculations, should have devoted the balance of her days to so indefinite a circumstance as the Light Comedian.

A VERY LONG SONG.

In what has been proudly termed the palmy days of the drama, at the Park Theatre, lived a worthy and amiable gentleman whose name was Cobb. The sea was his occupation, and he commanded a packet ship, sailing between Liverpool and New York. The theatre was his great delight, and when in port he was a constant patron.

One evening, prior to his date for sailing, he entered the Park Theatre, and while there, was accosted by some friends, who invited him to sup with them. The offer was accepted, and they quitted the building at the very moment when Mr. Peter Richings was in the act of singing a patriotic song, and waving his sword in the most approved manner.

The captain departed on his voyage, and on his arrival in Liverpool was dispatched to China, and did not return to New York for nearly three years. The first visit he made when he reached the city, was to the theatre; there, to his great astonishment, was Richings, in precisely the same attitude he had left him at his departure.

Turning to a friend who accompanied him, he said:

" Well, by thunder! if that isn't the longest song I ever did hear; Richings was at it three years since. I've been nearly round the world, and darned if he's got through it yet."

CHAPTER XVII.

My speculative, and active instruments.
Othello. Act 1. *Scene* 8.

THE SCIENCE OF TICKET SPECULATION.

THREE or four of these events in a season, will secure a very acceptable sum to him who is skilled in the method of taking advantage of the popular greediness for novelty. An excitement is gotten up at the retirement of some prominent member of the profession, who, if it be of the male sex, is about to quit the scene of his numerous achievements, to repose upon his well-earned laurels. If a lady, she is probably about to be led to the hymeneal altar by some one distinguished in the political or commercial world ; and the public have, by the outside pressure of social influence, been called upon to bear in mind that one of brilliant talent and unspotted virtue, is about to be torn from their fond caresses, and borne for ever from their sight. The said public peruses its favorite journal, and suddenly becomes conscious of the extent of its deprivation, and cannot possibly refrain making one at the approaching leave taking.

This is the time when the ticket speculator distinguishes himself. He watches the temperature of the public appetite. He and his aids purchase large quantities of the best places, as soon as the doors are opened. The manager is suspicious that an imposition is about to be practised upon his patrons, the public ; and such a course of proceeding being entirely beyond the thoughts or desires of managerial rectitude, issues a notice to the effect that "The public be cautioned against the purchase of tickets of admission from speculators in the streets ; none being genuine, save those procured through the instrumentality of the box office."

The speculator laughs the above proclamation to scorn, and with his aids patiently watches the time when the best seats are all secured. It is then he approaches the expectant pleasure seeker with the information that he has a few choice locations he can dispose of at a reasonable per centage on the original outlay. The individual addressed passes him with the remembrance of the prohibition in the morning papers, and applies at the office for three seats for his party, and is assured that the back row at the left hand side is the only thing he has to offer. A blank astonishment suffuses the face of the enquirer as he consults his watch, and expresses his surprise, that being only three quarters of an hour after the time of opening the office for the sale of tickets, he should be so unfortunate.

The treasurer says he is very sorry, but does not look particularly distressed about the matter; and makes the rejected offer to the next customer who, being from a rural district, is content to take the best he can get. The disappointed one moves a short distance away, and revolves in his mind the consequences of defeat. He has, in a moment of social delight, promised the charming Evelina that she and her mamma shall be escorted by him on the forthcoming interesting event, and to place them in a back seat, where his enviable monopoly of the prettiest girl in town could not excite the envy of every fellow he · knew, would be positively awful! Further, as he had at no very distant day the fond hope of becoming the possessor of the lovely one, it might do him an irreparable injury in the eyes of her maternal parent, should it ever become known that a few paltry dollars had stood in the way of the purchase.

" Better take 'em sir," says a voice close to his ear.

" How much ? " timidly enquires he.

" Twelve shillings each, sir ? "

" What ! "

" Why, sir, they'll be well worth two dollars this afternoon, — or if I keep them till to-morrow, and take them to the St. Nicholas, I can get twenty shillings at the office there."

This being unanswerable, the money is paid over, the cheques for seats duly received, and the transaction realizes a clear profit of *three dollars.*

The next is a youth of ardent temperament, also on the high road to a matrimonial connection with a charming young lady, who, having, as she believes, some taste in matters of costume, and the assurance of her dress maker that no one of her numerous customers have been so faultlessly designed by nature for the display of an elegant toilet, makes frequent donations to society by indulging it with an exposition of her elegant person, the same being more a matter of concern to her than the enjoyment of the entertainment itself.

The speculator, who is somewhat of a physiognomist, can read his wants and desires, and negotiates a very satisfactory sale as in the former case.

This is the *modus operandi* in the more simplified portion of the profession. The scientific method of effecting large profits is much more intricate, and involves a greater amount of judgment than the mere tyro in the business can easily accomplish.

I know a party who admitted to me, that on one occasion, in the city of New York, he cleared nearly *four hundred dollars* by premiums on boxes and seats. He was a man well skilled in all the minutiæ in creating excitements and keeping his victims at fever heat while there was a possibility of a beneficial result accruing by the operation. He had traversed the length and breadth of the land with every novelty, from the brilliant soprano and the mellifluous tenor, to the bearded lady. He is well known on town, speaks two or three languages, English the most imperfectly, and was indebted for his advent into this world to a race whose shrewdness in the science of driving a bargain, leaves the Yankee trader a long way beyond the confines of competition. He is well accredited at all places of amusement, whether operatic, dramatic, equestrian, or Ethiopian, and is personally familiar with every person of importance and good standing in the city.

In the course of his manipulations, he confers extensive patronage on several persons who are indispensably necessary to the successful completion of his plans. It not unfrequently happens that the party who may be about to tear him or herself from the public gaze, will employ him to take charge of the pecuniary portion of the leave taking; awarding him a liberal percentage and a handsome keepsake, for his judicious managerial display.

In the ordinary case all the best boxes and seats are secured several days prior to the date of the entertainment. What is to be done? Mr. Cent-per-cent and family must be there, and is compelled to place himself in communication with our friend, who will of course, with his extensive dramatic and musical influence, be able to suggest a means whereby his desires can be gratified.

Agent is regularly on the alert, and fully aware of Mr. Cent-per-cent's dilemma. He is appealed to, can see no remedy at present; but will make enquiry of the party

10

who has rented the choice box, and endeavor to effect some satisfactory arrangement. The morning of the play arrives, Mr. Cent-per-cent will willingly give twenty-five dollars sooner than be disappointed. Agent, or speculator, says he has called on the parties, whom he thinks may be induced to vacate, but that he, the speculator, will have to effect some counterchange of places at much cost and trouble. "Never mind the expense" rejoins the anxious millionaire, "if it can be done."

The evening arrives! Speculator watches his party as they pay for their ordinary admission tickets, as agreed upon. He joins them at the back of the boxes, and requests they will follow him. They reach the box. Speculator knocks, and the door is opened by a gentleman gotten up regardless of consequences. A conversation is carried on to the effect that "it is very unpleasant, don't like to refuse, ladies, etc., shall expect some good seats elsewhere!" Speculator gives the required assurance — deposed party vacate, — while the reigning usurpers assume their seats, Mr. Cent-per-cent places, unseen, into the ready hand of the speculator, bills to the amount of twenty-five dollars, feeling happy to pay a good premium for so comfortable and elegant a location; but perfectly ignorant of the fact that five dollars was disbursed by the speculator himself for the said box; and that the gentlemen who had occupied it, were placed there only till an eligible customer with a large profit in perspective, should present himself.

Where the ceremony of securing seats is not pursued, but every person takes the best he can find, it is no less profitable to the speculator, and is accomplished in this manner. A certain number of aids are provided with the means of admission, and take up their position at the doors long before the crowd present themselves. When the rush comes, they are all in the choice seats before the eager ones can obtain their checks, because they are all provided with tickets. The house fills speedily, and the speculator watches the late comers, fresh from the hands of the accomplished peruquier, as they regard with looks of bewilderment the crowds that obstruct his view of the stage. Speculator gets into conversation, refers to the large numbers present. Victim feels sorry he didn't procure places by some means, expects a lady and gentleman friend, who were to meet him there, — he had promised to be there early but was detained. Speculator says he had anticipated the sale of three seats, which he has taken from a friend who had lost his mother, and couldn't come, that he had paid two dollars each for them, and would now willingly dispose of them for five dollars, sooner than be stuck with them! Victim sees a good opportunity of redeeming his character for promptness, and offers readily to hand over the required amount, as his friends are seen forcing their way down the passsge. Speculator requests them to follow him, holds up three fingers, when the like number of eligible occupants in the front row immediately give place to the newly arrived trio, and the speculator realizes a profit of three dollars and fifty cents.

THE WALKING GENTLEMAN.

"Have I been called?" is a question not unfrequently propounded to the first professional associate the walking gentleman may encounter, as he makes his way towards the stage some minutes after the appointed time for the commencement of rehearsal. Receiving an answer in the affirmative, he will quicken his pace, silently perusing his part, till summoned by the call boy to repeat it in the presence of the stage manager.

It is not without considerable difficulty our hero has been able to tear himself from his downy pillow, after a very limited companionship, caused by his presence the preceding night at a convivial gathering of the youth of both sexes. Little did he think, while hastily preparing his toilet for the day, that he had lacerated a female heart, now throbbing with its first attack of wretchedness; and whose anguish could never be assuaged, until it was duly considered the exclusive property of the aforesaid walking gentleman. So satisfied, indeed, was the owner of the lacerated member aforesaid, that it confided to a congenial female spirit the startling disclosure of its fixed intention to quit, for an indefinite period, its painful existence, in the event of opposition to its wishes; and further, that any attempt to dissuade it from its purpose would meet with speedy resistance and contempt.

The dramatist must be considered as an accessory before the fact, when he supplies the facilities for a foray upon female nature; and the crime is doubly reprehensible, when the exponent of the author's ideas is blessed with a handsome face, and symmetrical form.

The walking gentleman has apartments not far from the theatre, where, after dinner, you will find him with one or two members of the company, discussing the general topics of the day, as well as the quality of the parts he has been called upon, in the course of his experience, to personate.

"Why, sir, it was fourteen lengths, if it was a line; and not a scene that wasn't a complete feeder from beginning to end.

"Well, sir, I studied it letter perfect from the night before, never missed a word, either, at rehearsal, or at the performance; and the author never felt grateful, or if he did, he never expressed himself in terms to that effect."

"Perhaps he didn't imagine, from his knowledge of the extent or quality of the favor conferred, that a return for what you conceive to be an obligation, was due in any case," chimes in a timid youth, with an unusual quantity of hair, and whose appearance upon the stage, is always ridiculed by the audience.

"Thank you, Charley," says our hero, "if you could only be as clever on the stage, as you affect to be off it, you'd soon be at the summit of the profession. The next time you stick, in the second act, don't expect me to take it up, and cover your stupidity, for I'll be shot if I do it."

Not much abashed by this rebuke, the timid youth, after relighting his cigar, returns to the charge with redoubled zeal, and assures the company that our hero has some little cause, at this particular juncture, to be down upon him, inasmuch as he had lately supplanted him in the affections of a young lady, who was passing fair to look upon; and whose paternal parent was plentifully encumbered with the spondulicks.

Those of my readers whose means enable them to indulge in a suite of apartments, with all the necessary accompaniments of elegance and display, must readily admit that there are more tidy looking places than the bedroom of an actor, wherein he has to store his wardrobe, professional and domestic. The curious can find ample material for enquiry, by a close inspection of this apartment. It is summer time, and the windows are open to admit the air. Its occupants have disposed themselves in every imaginable manner, and are smoking fearfully. Our hero, very sparingly clad, reclines upon the bed, his nether extremities dangling over the foot board. The chairs being the posts of honor, are allotted to the two gentlemen boarders, who are engaged in mercantile pursuits. They are constant patrons of the theatre, and ever anxious to cultivate the acquaintance of those whom they have admired behind the footlights. One of them has a great inclination to become an actor, and has already, by stealth, taken part in an amateur performance; but his mother, being a strict, and very devout patron of the tenets laid down by Whitfield and his disciples, would never permit one of her kith and kin to engage himself in so profane a calling.

Articles having a strong dramatic affinity occupy every portion of the room, obtruding themselves from all points of sight. From the walls hang one Roman and one regimental sword, a pair of yellow morocco boots, a pair of foils, a black velvet hat; a few play bills and prints in lithograph, forming the chief decoration. The chimney piece is laden with books, and written parts of plays, cigars, match-box, two ball tickets, the daguerreotype of a lady with a profusion of dark ringlets, and a pair of boxing gloves.

The afternoon is far advanced, when one of the party desires to excuse himself, for he has a part to read, and his things to look out, and must be going. He has, however, scarcely quitted the apartment, when a voice salutes him with a request that he will not forget the bald wig he loaned the previous evening, as also a red ostrich feather, with boot tops, and sword chain, all of which he assures the borrower are to be found on his dressing place in his room at the theatre.

The *personnel* of our hero is quite up to the mark to satisfy the most exacting of the opposite sex. It is true, there are those among men who are always at a loss to perceive how their female acquaintance can make him the subject of their approval; but, as these are somewhat proud of their own claims to the monopoly of the ladies' favors, their opinions should be received with caution and misgiving.

Beyond the professional circle in which he radiates, our subject has less distinct characteristics than perhaps any of his brethren. The *ornamental* portion of the theatre is mostly divided between the tragedian, the light comedian, and himself; and in proportion as nature has been lavish in her gifts, is he the object of attention with the fair sex.

Outside the theatre, and within the seclusion of the strictest confidence, does he, without being cognizant of the proud distinction, enjoy the honor of having his personal qualifications the frequent theme of admiration by the ladies, who, at his benefit, will muster in strong force to evince their appreciation of his histrionic ability and attractive person. Not only will he be the recipient of a substantial testimonial, but anonymous gifts will perhaps flow in from admirers who desire, in their own way, to show their affection and esteem.

The walking gentleman is usually the worst paid member of the theatre. His outlay for necessary costumes should entitle him to one of the most liberal emoluments in the establishment; but it is very rare that his income equals that of others whose expenses for presentable properties and apparel fall far short of those demanded by the subject of our sketch. This is the only reason we can assign for his general disinclination to remain as the exponent of those very necessary parts of the *dramatis personæ;* but eagerly seizes the first opportunity to obtain a more elevated position, for the purpose of increasing his pecuniary consequence, not unfrequently to the serious disadvantage of the very best works.

So long as our hero has the good fortune to retain his youthful appearance, he is eagerly sought after by managers who have an eye to the *tout ensemble* of their productions, but when obesity exerts its sway, and ruthlessly destroys the romantic form that has so often pined in the anguish of unrequited love or parental opposition, then must he look back to his days of conquest of female nature, and — painful though it be — confess that he must read up for the more adaptable position of the heavy business.

THE DRAMATIC WASHINGTON.

That necessary adjunct of the theatre, "The supers," have, from time immemorial, been the source of extreme amusement to dramatic audiences ; the more youthful of whom delight to assail them, should they be left alone upon the boards, by the appellation of "supe," which opprobrious epithet they generally bear with a martyrdom extremely praiseworthy. The indifference they invariably exhibit to the startling incidents going forward around them, is a striking exemplification of, either the profound contempt they entertain for the profession into which chance has thrown them, or the equanimity of a temperament that cannot suffer itself to be disturbed by events of a suppositious character.

It was an opinion very freely expressed by an old manager of mine, "that supers were the pest of his dramatic life ; " for, he was accustomed to urge, "expend as much money as you will in costumes, import trappings and habiliments direct from the hands of the most skillful manufacturers, and when you have done all this, your hair will stand on end, when you behold the terrible result. One will present himself with a polished steel helmet the wrong side in front, or a colored cravat will peer beneath the splendid gorget of another. Not alone is your sense of propriety shocked at these, and similar acts of absurdity ; but, despite the efforts of the super master, they will occasionally present themselves at most unseasonable times and places, such as resting one of their legs over the arm of the king's chair, or expose their head and shoulders behind the scenic compartments of a transparent lake, where they are sure to be saluted with a boisterous recognition from the audience.

An accomplished actor, well known in his profession, has labored for many years under the conviction that, when appropriately costumed, none can so much resemble the Father of his Country, as himself. When regularly made up for the part, he is disinclined to reply to questions of a trivial nature, assigning as a reason, "that it distracts his mind from the position into which the assumption has elevated him."

To a mind of such poetic tension the herein related incident, in which *the super* plays a prominent part, must have caused the most painful anguish, viz:

A patriotic spectacle had, for its last scene, an allegorical design, representing the great Washington, in company with the Goddess of Liberty, making an ascent, surrounded by clouds, while the populace were to pay adoration in an attitude of reverence; upon which picture the curtain should descend.

When the great man stepped upon the platform, he there discovered a super reclining upon the very spot designed for himself. He was astonished beyond measure,— such a thing had never happened before. There was no time to seek the stage manager, for the tableau was about to be discovered; therefore he was obliged, much against his will, to hold a parley with the intruder, with the following result:

Washington. Hollo! I say, you! This can't be, you know!

Super. Why not, old hoss.

Washington. Never heard of such a thing in all my life! Go down!

Super. Shan't do it. Say, what's the use o' talking. There aint no room down there among that crowd. I was told to put myself near here, and I'm bound to see the thing through.

Washington. But no one can have instructed you to get up here. You'll spoil the piece. My good man, go down at once!

10*

Super.   Not I; I shan't spoil the piece.

Washington.   I tell you, you will.   This is Heaven, and no one goes there but Caroline and myself.

The super was insensible to his appeal, and stood his ground till the curtain descended.

CHAPTER XVIII.

" To be merry best becomes you; for, out of question, you were born
in a merry hour."

Much Ado About Nothing. Act 2. Scene 2.

MOSE IN CANADA.

To be favored by nature with a continuous and un-
wearying stock of happy spirits, is a blessing vouchsafed
to few. Such natures shed a halo of jollity around their
fellow mortals, which cannot be too highly prized for the
blessings it diffuses. They are sunbeams breaking through
the haze of sombre humanity to illumine the pathway of
our worldly pilgrimage. Every wanderer can carry his
thoughts back with pleasure to some period of his history when, amid the gloom of weariness, some genial spirit
has burst upon the scene, and beguiled the tedium of
many otherwise dull and irksome hours.

Let not my readers suppose I am about to indulge in a
dissertation upon that nearly extinct specialty of America, y'clept Mose, in support of the position assumed at
the beginning of this chapter. My subject has a distinct
existence, and well deserves a niche in my kindly remembrance, for his companionship at a time of professional
depression.

Winter in Canada is far from a favorable period of the
year for transmission from place to place, in any given
length of time, despite the extensive appliances at command of the railroad officials.

I turned lazily in my bed on the morning of a day in
the month of January, and peering through the window

blind looked out with a discontented spirit upon the streets of Quebec; with the painful conviction uppermost in my mind that I had, at all hazards, to set out on a journey in order to reach New York as speedily as possible.

Shiveringly I made an attempt to get into my clothes, which, from the extreme severity of the weather, seemed to have been changed in the night, and to be the property of some person of much larger circumference than I was, while the rapidity and ease with which I deposited my right foot into its usually tight boot, sufficed to convince me of the wonderful power of contraction by cold, more satisfactorily than all the scientific asseverations I had heard and read, upon that very interesting subject.

Descending to breakfast, I encounter several brothers in prospective suffering who, after having partaken heartily of the good things for which the Russell Hotel is distinguished, wrap and fold themselves into all sorts of curious devices, with furs and mufflers, and are tucked up in their sleigh to cross the St. Lawrence to Point Levi.

Who is that massive individual with gorgeous side whiskers, of the most *distingue* cut, partially concealed by the ear pieces of his fur cap? He is on the platform, awaiting our arrival, with his leathern bag swung across his capacious body. He receives the compliments of the morning from the majority of the passengers, and returns it with a countenance suffused with such unalloyed mirth, that the perils of your journey are speedily forgotten.

To all who have travelled between Montreal and Quebec, " Mose " is well known; and his existence is as much a matter of the neighborhood's history, as the time table records are of the number of miles you diminish from your starting point, till you reach your destination. Portly in flesh, and plethoric with good nature, he poises himself upon his capacious legs, and reviews the train of voyagers, as they deposit themselves in the carriages of the Grand Trunk Railway, about to start upon their way from the latter to the former named city.

The bell rings to prepare for moving ; our conductor, "Mose," not like the athletic attendant who bounds upon the last platform with a show of perfect security — but having deposited himself beyond the possibility of accident, gives the signal, and we are off.

Who has not a vivid remembrance of being aroused out of a comfortable doze at the end of every quarter of an hour, and being commanded to exhibit those detestable coupons ; and who has ever forgiven the cruel despoiler of his rest, who insists upon seeing " that ticket," after its possessor has, with persistent ingenuity, erected a resting place which he designs to dedicate to " nature's sweet restorer ? "

Rigid philosophers, associates of institutions for the diffusion of knowledge, members of congress, at whose gatherings withering anathemas are wielded in vocal conflict, lose their potency of argument, and become passive sufferers, at the assaults of this barbarous and despotic custom.

The popular impression favors the idea that this mode of torture, being in itself a simple and necessary proceeding, cannot be much abridged or modified without destroying the time-honored privilege of the institution of which it forms an important part. To those who incline to this belief, I would suggest a journey with the subject of my thoughts, and the supposition will be speedily dispelled. By the potency of his *ensemble,* you will find yourself a grateful recipient of the privilege of occupying a seat in his conveyance. Such was my sensation, when I made his acquaintance under circumstances to which this chapter refers.

Two of the strongest locomotives were put into requisi-

tion to give battle against a pelting snow-storm, and for
a time seemed to get the best of the affray; a vigorous
and persistent relay of the enemy's forces, however,
poured such a torrent of ammunition in our path, that
the iron contestants were obliged to capitulate, and
being brought to a state of helpless inactivity, stood
belching forth their yells of despair and mortification, at
a small station about seventy miles west of Quebec.

The snow was packed into mountainous deposits of
such magnitude, that I wondered how many months of
genial warmth it would take to liquify it; when we
were all acquainted with the fact that it would be desirable to make the best of our condition, and prepare to
console ourselves with the belief that our stay at our
present resting place might extend to a period of some
considerable duration.

Loud and violent were the complaints of the passengers; one old gentleman was prepared to take his affidavit that he had never known a solitary instance wherein
the company had faithfully performed their contract to
the public. Another, a lady of very choice material, and
whose back hair was coiled over to the front, and curled
with desperate severity, to aid in a laudable desire to
counterfeit juvenility, was on the verge of epilepsy, but
recanted at the indifference manifested at the project,
and relapsed into an abstraction of the last novel, while
the majority met the difficulty with the spirit of philosophy usually begotten by the exigency of stern necessity.

Darkness soon came upon us, huddled together in a small
apartment used as a waiting room by the few patrons
who resided in the vicinity of the place. It was lighted
with a flickering, but strongly perfumed oil lamp suspended from the roof, which shed a cheerless ray of comfort
upon the faces of the occupants, as they gathered around
the newly ignited stove. Benches and boxes of all kinds

were speedily hunted up, and resting places improvised upon which to pass the night. A store of wood is laid in, and every person is anxious to do something to ameliorate the condition of things, and for the common good.

After conferring with the engineer, our conductor enters the telegraph office, and communicates to head quarters the position of affairs, and solicits assistance; this important and necessary duty performed, he is at liberty to mingle with the company, and be bored with suggestions of all kinds, in relation to our deliverance, to which he listens with great relish, and even makes a feint of adopting, much to the satisfaction of the proposers.

The lady passengers compose themselves to sleep; save one, attired in common apparel, who has a fractious child that continually asserts its distaste of surrounding objects, and is not appeased till its parent, with the untiring heroism of her sex, has walked to and fro, long into the silent hours of the night, and when sheer exhaustion assumes its sway, and holds its revel in forgetfulness.

Mose forms himself into a committee of " one," and taking possession of a small ante-room adjoining the telegraph office, charters a brakesman to provide, as best he can, for the wants of a select number of congenial spirits. The arrangements completed, he issues invitations in person, and prepares to play the part of host for the night. As we enter, we find him at the head of a small table, looking very much out of proportion with the size of the structure, chanting his favorite ditty, complimentary to the other sex, somewhat in the following strain:

> " There are girls, with raven hair,
> And lips, a luscious pair,
> Whose coral richness vanquish us,
> Then jest at our despair.
> Then in anger should we pass
> To some blonde, and sprightly lass,
> Whose glance of witching loveliness
> All others can surpass.

" Fill the cup with sparkling wine,
And while draining, ne'er repine,
But homage pay to beauty,
For tis a joy divine.
So we'll toast the lovely fair
With the light, or raven hair,
Who conquer us poor mortals,
And jest at our despair." &c. &c.

Amidst the jollity of the night, he steals away to assure himself that the lady passengers are as well disposed
of as circumstances will permit. To the more needy
one who, with her fractious little charge, is pacing the
floor, he offers comforts not sparingly bestowed, but lav-
ished with a cheering welcome, that wealth can never
purchase.

There are moments of an actor's career when the programmes of the performances set forth with great boldness, the assertion that " The public are crowding the theatre to repletion, to pay homage to the talent of the distinguished artiste who is at the time honoring the building with his presence, and powerful rendition of character," but when-the luckless one shall divest his mind of
the poetry of this manifesto, he will probably arrive at
the painful reality that his efforts are sufficiently remuner-
ative to satisfy the claims of the landlord and the printer;
leaving him to banquet upon his well-earned laurels only.

It was during one of those interesting episodes of my
adventures, that I found our hero the oasis of a professional desert.

The sun was shining brightly in the month of September. A company of riflemen were going through their
manœuvres with wonderful exactness in the square front-
ing the officers' quarters, inside the citadel of Quebec. I
was watching them with pleasure and curiosity, when my
ears were saluted with,

" What ho! my noble lord. How fares it with your
excellency ? "

There can be no mistaking that voice, thought I, as in turning round, I recognised our adolescent friend, enjoying the refreshing breeze from the river St. Lawrence. He strikes an attitude as I approach, his face beaming with mirth. As I make towards him, he assumes the manner of a well known Canadian manager, and in a loud whisper exclaims,

"Jack's come, by heavens, we're safe, we're all right now! I know it. I was sure he'd be here,— never mistaken in Jack."

This being the said manager's customary manifesto when announcing the arrival of his *property boy*, whose presence in any one of his towns, he considered quite sufficient to inaugurate a season, and carry it satisfactorily and profitably to its close.

We had not seen each other for two years. Sickness had dealt him a heavy blow, from which he had not expected to recover; yet his hilariousness had not forsaken him. For the balance of the morning he regaled me with all sorts of oddities, and during the process of the *donation* of my services to the people of Quebec, (for I cannot regard my visit in any other light,) he constantly smoothed the pathway of my labors, for the which I desire to record my grateful acknowledgments.

Finally, dear reader, if you propose to indulge in a trip through Canada, fail not to travel with *Mose*. If you are a victim to hypochondria he will, by his genial deportment, do much to assuage your melancholy. If your 'nature is inquisitorial, I will venture to affirm that he can impart sufficient information to appease any native of Connecticut who ever quitted his parent state. There are those under the firm impression that, should he adopt the position of purveyor for the weary traveller at any one of the numerous resting places with which this continent abounds, he is just the man of all others who could *keep an hotel.*

While willing to concede any amount of convivial
honor that can possibly be thrust upon him, I most conscientiously affirm that, if unfitted for the above severe
and popular test of excellence, he is just the man who
can *conduct a train.*

THE TRAGEDIAN.

Sensibly alive to the status he occupies in the public
esteem as the expounder of the loftiest creations of the
most distinguished poets, the tragedian unconsciously
wraps himself within the folds of classic dignity, even
when not engaged in the exercise of his professional calling. An habitual reserve would seem to say "excuse me
if I temper my appreciation of your joke with a stolid
regard for high art, befitting the conduct of one who is
amongst the most celebrated of its professors."

Of his early association with the best society we are
constantly made familiar, from his own undoubted, and
unprejudiced authority. How well he remembers, as if
it were but yesterday, the frequent gatherings of high
official personages around the family board; where he
was permitted, in virtue of his great primitive ability, to
occupy a seat at the table, from which he only seceded
to be borne in triumph to the drawing-room — when the
ladies withdrew,— where his extraordinary perception of
character, (for his age) together with his personal beauty,
was the theme of conversation for the balance of the evening.

If it be conceded, as laid down by a great poet, that
the man who drinks beer will think beer, it surely must
be terrible to believe that one, the active part of whose
life is passed in the utterance of the loftiest forms of poetic excellence, should be somewhat imbued with sentiments and affinities of a corresponding character. This
is the only explanation we can offer for the frequent meta-

physical bearing of the subject of our sketch ; though it by no means marks the character with sufficient exactness to establish the affinity of a principle.

Some there are, whose jollity, under the influence of convivial surroundings, would lead the observer to believe they worshipped at the shrine of Thalia, and not Melpomene ; and they not unfrequently rise to greater distinction than their more serious cotemporaries.

" My dear fellow," they will say, " you have no poetical responsibility ; you make the people laugh — and they, unfortunately for art — don't care by what means you do it ; but we tragedians have all the weight and interest of the play to sustain through five acts ; the physical effort of which — apart from any other consideration — is labor of the most distressing kind. With you, it is very different, for how few — even those who set themselves up for critics, trouble their heads about the consistency of your representations."

In the provinces, the tragedian is viewed with a larger amount of concern than usually greets him amidst the din and bustle of a populous city. There, on the natal day of the greatest of poets, he will join a choice circle of admiring spirits who assemble once every year to utter their warmest encomiums on his matchless productions ; and after a wholesome fortification of the good things of this life, he will, in virtue of his office as " the unworthy expounder of the poet's creations, propose a silent ovation to his memory, coupling it with a few remarks on the progress of art, from the period when Euripides bequeathed his gigantic effusions to the world, down to the time when so humble an individual as himself, is permitted to lend his poor ability to the perpetuation of the drama," concluding with a fervent hope " that the sister arts may speedily hail the advent of another mighty mind, to add lustre to its intellectual progression ; then shall the harp of the minstrel, the chisel of the sculptor, and the pen of the poet, blend in educational grandeur throughout the universe."

Having lashed his hearers into that state of imbecile candor they are prone to fall when they feel on the best terms with themselves, the company depart with a firm conviction on their minds, that their dramatic friend would have distinguished himself equally well in any one of the learned professions, had it pleased fate so to have disposed him.

Our hero is frequently clamorous on the decadence of the drama, and evinces his desire for its intellectual welfare, by sacrificing himself within the toils of management, where the productions of the choicest works of the best dramatists shall be his chief and positive aim.

The prefatory advertisement sets out with the assurance that talent of every grade shall, in this "model temple" meet with that fostering care commensurate with its due; but it does so happen, either from the scarcity of ability in the first roles, or that those in possession of that gift have nobler purposes in view, and turn a deaf ear to the pressing invitation, that the public are very seldom called upon to sit in judgment on the merits of any whose success would be likely to conflict with the professional status of the manager, whose unremitting endeavor it is to mould the public mind to the belief that none can so worthily embody the best parts, as he who thus immolates himself upon the altar of their instruction and amusement. The serious characters in the best comedies that fall to his charge are, by no means, welcome visitors. Nor does he very readily admit the same justification for objection on the part of the comic strength of the establishment, who consider themselves ill-placed in the subordinate ones in tragedy.

In most instances, our hero brings to his aid in the ex-

ercise of his professional calling, a gentlemanly deportment on, as well as off the stage, backed by liberal education, and a nice discrimination for the purposes of his art.
His emolument is usually the largest in the theatre, and
many have passed the evening of their days in the comfortable possession of a competence, derived from their
exertions while in active service.

Some there are who, being soured by the imagined
neglect of the public, have quitted their brothers of the
sock and buskin with a dignified disgust which nothing
can assuage ; and after lingering around the atmosphere
of their old associations for a time, betake themselves to
that *forlorn hope of educated incapacity,* i. e., "The
Lecture Room," where they are usually greeted with
frantic exultation by a class who view with an eye of
envy all institutions (save their own,) and cherish a
deserter from the dramatic camp with a tenderness and
regard, typical of that bestowed upon the stray lamb who
sought admittance within the precincts of sancity and
truth.

There, surrounded by a halo of apparent piety, our
hero has been known to descant with a penitential
visage upon the numerous wickednesses he perpetrated
by adapting himself to the exercise of his much maligned
calling, savoring his recantation with the most ingenious
accounts of incidents long grown threadbare in the minds
of adepts of romantic lore. Emboldened by the belief
that a wholesale tirade levelled against the art dramatic
will be seized with avidity by his new found admirers, he
will contribute to the literature of the country a volume
most liberally charged with their popular belief, wherein
he will show for future clerical reference, how the youth
of both sexes can never find so fitting a sphere for the
consummation of their total ruin, as the exercise of a
profession for whose perpetuity the great master minds

of all countries have scattered their matchless gifts in luscious profusion, despite the clamor and warning of the self-elected purveyors of morality and virtue.

It is scarcely competent to believe that the early instruction imparted by an indulgent and highly educated parent, while struggling against the limited income of a provincial position, and more liberally bestowed when he attained to the summit of his art, should have produced, in some singular instance, so uncongenial a result. It is nevertheless undeniably evident, that when the play-going public, with an obstinacy for which it is remarkable, can no longer be induced to believe that the subject of our sketch is the greatest actor of his age; his discontent can find no more fitting channel for ventilation than an immediate secession from the recusant camp.

Few there are who do not, when in the decline of life, cling more closely to the affinity of professional love; and it is only with a view to embrace the several characteristics of those whom I have encountered in my pilgrimage, that I ascribe any personal allusion to "The Tragedian."

THE JOB ACTOR.

In a part of the city where the thirst for progression and improvement has recently erected dwellings replete with conveniences, within the limited resource of the re. spectably disposed, affording the occupants all the outside splendor of the private family mansion, with the internal seclusion of domestic hermitage, resides the Job Actor.

You enter one of these hives of humanity, dignified by the high sounding name of "Hotel," and find yourself in a hall very much contracted in space, but brilliantly furnished with a gaudily printed oil-cloth, and plentifully supplied with gas light. You ascend the stairs, the edges of which are studded with copper-headed nails, or provided with a strip of zinc to economize the structure from the constant wear and tear it is subjected to by the myriads of passers up and down.

The higher you ascend, the lower becomes the amount of payment you are called upon to disburse for the privilege of occupying a suite of apartments in one of these rapidly increasing domains.

An overlooker, or purveyor of the strict propriety of the building, occupies an apartment near the entrance, who unites to the duties of that office, the genteel art of millinery, and dress making. If you are in doubt of the precise location of the party you propose to visit, you solicit her aid in procuring the necessary information, and are there apprised that the back room on the fourth floor, is the point of your destination. You ascend, counting the flights as you go. You reach the landing considerably excited in respiration, and knock at a door. After a little delay the key is turned in the lock, and a lady, whom you have most unceremoniously disturbed at her toilet, presents one half her countenance, and in reply to your enquiry directs you to the other end of the landing. You pause ere you again venture, till approaching footsteps decide you to wait till they reach your locality, and you are soon face to face with the lad who carries a partially concealed loaf of bread under his arm, and from whom you are instructed with the required accuracy.

The job actor is an exotic entirely of American nativity; begotten conjointly by the exigency of the times, and the shrewdness of managerial cupidity. You find him surrounded by his wife, and four children. He is busily engaged in the manufacture of a huge black beard, with which he has to provide himself for the approaching sensation drama of the "Inca, and the Dromedary," and in which he is to enact a recluse who exists in the depths of a forest, and supports himself on berries, and other fruits of a similar kind with which the neighborhood is supposed to be plentifully supplied.

"Aha! old fellow, how are you. Here I am, hard at it, as you see. 'The labor we delight in physics pain.' Mary, give me the scissors, and some more crape hair. Thank you. Well, what's new? Find a chair somewhere, won't you? How are things at your place, — how's the business, eh? The press don't seem to think much of that last piece, rather shaky, I should say, eh? Hope it won't affect the company. Sure to keep open, I suppose?"

You cannot help feeling grateful to our friend for propounding so large a list of questions without waiting for an answer. He is probably aware of the unsettled condition of your respiratory organs, from the distance you have mounted in order to pay him a visit. You are glad to see him, and soon express as much. Times are changed since you first met. He was single then, a favorite with every audience before whom he appeared, and regularly attached to one of the first class theatres of the city. Changes of management brought about the usual exercise of friendly interference on behalf of others, perhaps no less worthy, and he felt himself distanced in his professional position without being able to assign within himself a satisfactory reason. The rapid increase in his family, with occasional sickness, had bound him by stern necessity to the great city, with a hope that things might mend. He was certain his habits were unexceptionable, he had a good wardrobe, was always perfect in his author, attentive to the business of the scene; and the audience, with whom he was still a great favorite, ever ready and willing to acknowledge him by their plaudits. He had a part in the new piece at the —— Theatre, but the duration of his engagement was to be regulated by the run of the play, and he saw but little hope of employment for the approaching winter season ; further, he was compelled to accept about a third of what he was honestly worth ; being assured by the manager, that although he would like to have him in the cast, he should give no more salary to any one, and numbers could be provided who would readily accept the terms.

You suggest, knowing that your old friend possesses some literary ability, that he should endeavor, by the exercise of his pen, to add to his income.

" No use, my dear boy. I've tried that long ago. May be very well for those who have a position, and can get their articles accepted, but the humiliation is not over pleasant to outside talent of whatever grade; I did, some time since, two articles for a popular publication; their scale of payment entitling me to *six dollars*, which I was only able to obtain six months after it was due, and after numberless applications. In another case I prepared an article for a magazine of world-wide reputation, on a subject I was advised to believe of a very interesting character to the general public; but the reader of the concern, who was himself in the habit of writing, and deeply attached to subjects of a metaphysical nature, rejected the contribution, assigning as a reason for so doing, that it was too *Dickens-y* in style to suit them. Thus every avenue appears to be closed against me. However, we must hope for the best; let's have a smoke, and forget our troubles in the fragrant weed."

We lighted our pipes and chatted over past incidents of our career, enlivened by the cheerful presence of one of the best of wives and mothers, who, despite the state of the exchequer, always sweetened the family meal with the spirit of contentment and satisfaction.

I very soon had the pleasure of congratulating my friend on the success of the new drama, and his consequent full measure of employment for the winter ; hap-

11

pily relieved from the necessity of watching with eager gaze the dramatic column of a leading daily paper, to find that a certain establishment is about to fall into the hands of a party who desires to surround his managerial speculation with those who are of acknowledged position in the profession, and that none other need trouble themselves to apply at the box office of the theatre at a stated hour the following morning.

Punctual to the time, may be seen several of the fraternity of the art, who affect a nonchalant air on the subject of their present mission, waiting the result of an application that shall enable them to look the next month or two in the face with confidence, and whereby they may keep the domestic machinery in motion without difficulty.

Those whose employment is continuous, can scarcely realize the full measure of misery such a system is fraught with, to the actor. At best, a profession of great uncertainty, is that of the stage; this system of brief engagements has reduced it to the verge of pauperism, which no one possessing the instincts of respect for himself or an art to whose service he has, perhaps, devoted the best period of his life, can long submit to.

It is pleasing to state, that the provinces have not yet reached this highly ingenious method of professional torture. An opportunity presents itself at any moment for some person of an adventurous nature, to inaugurate the system.

PALMY DAYS OF THE DRAMA.

This is an expression so often used by old play goers, that it leads to the supposition that, in those much and frequently lauded times, it was only necessary to throw open the doors of a theatre, to have the public immediately take possession of the building.

The following illustrations will show that some of the greatest artists have not unfrequently appeared to most indifferent houses, viz:

" In the year 1822, during the season at Drury Lane, London, the receipts for many nights did not amount to more than fifteen or twenty pounds, while the expenses are stated to have been more than two hundred, and this when such names as those of Elliston, Harley, Cooper, Fitzwilliam, Knight, Gattie, Braham, Mrs. W. West, Glover, Oger, Misses Forde, Povey, Smithson, Copeland, etc., etc., of very considerable talent, were often combined in the performance of some of our best tragedies and comedies.

I well remember, for I was a member of a company at the Ipswich Theatre in 1841, that Mr. William Farren played six nights, and the gross receipts of the entire performances only amounted to sixty pounds, ($300). And at the commencement of the season at Colchester, in Essex, also belonging to, or forming part of the Norwich circuit, the receipts to the performance of "London Assurance," and the pantomime of " Sinbad, the Sailor " only reached the munificent sum of £1 10s. ($7,50.)

I have met with numerous instances of a cessation of hostilities on the part of the public, to patronize the choicest performances, while those of a quality that have been universally condemned have met with the most signal success ; indeed, an old and very worthy manager of a small circuit in the west of England, once assured me that all through his career, when he had, with a desire to give the public the full worth of their money, engaged persons of good professional capacity, he had always found his balance on the wrong side, when he came to square up his accounts. But, on the other hand, when his people had been so glaringly inefficient that he felt really ashamed of suffering them to exhibit their lack of talent before an enlightened public, the said public had willingly paid their spare cash to see them ; and while yielding him a good profit, expressed no dissatisfaction at the worthlessness of the repast.

A critic who flourished in New York in 1832, gives a quaint description of that classic temple of the drama, the Park Theatre, in these words :

" The Park Theatre has long been the admiration of every one who has never seen any other, and has invariably met the warm approbation of those who understand not a word about the matter. The beauty of the outside is a matter of serious astonishment, consisting of the best quality of colored plaster, variegated by straight lines, which are ingeniously intended to imitate cracks. Indeed, the munificence of its owners has spared neither plaster nor brown paint, to impart to it a sombre cast ; and anxious for improvement, they have changed it from its former color, which was yellow, here and there blackened with smoke, to one of becoming and unvaried brown." Again,

" The scenery of this astonishing exhibition is admirable in the extreme. The same street answers for New York, London, Paris or Madrid, the most distant part of Russia, or ancient Greece. I was much edified by a banquet scene, where Selim, in the "Bride of Abydos," fires his two pistols, each of which killed his man. The scene changed, but as one of the bodies in the agonies of death had fallen too far out, it was knocked against by the half of a handsome palace, which was just then making its appearance. The poor dead man, seeing no one near to take him away, concluded he had best do it himself, and actually jumped up with great agility, and scrambled out on all fours, upon which the audience were manifestly delighted, and gave him three rounds of applause, accompanied with many gratified smiles, in token of their pleasure at his unexpected recovery."

I was also assured by the late Mr. Wallack, that during one of his performances of "Coriolanus" at the same establishment, one of the principal scenes of the tragedy was the same as exhibited in the afterpiece of "Aldgate Pump."

CHAPTER XIX

This was a venture, Sir
Merchant of Venice. *Act* 1. *Scene* 3.

LOTTERIES.

GAMES of chance have an apt connection with dramatic life, as those who have speculated in the venture of success, and come•out of it, losers both in pocket and spirit, can painfully testify. Accident often yields the sinews of popularity, when years of toil and perseverance never would have reached the coveted goal. The great sensation achieved by Tyrone Power in the compulsory representation of an Irish character, which led to fame and fortune, exemplifies this fact.

If I felt disposed to be personal, which I mean carefully to avoid, I might point to numerous instances where members of the sock and buskin have, *and do* expend large sums upon the several lottery institutions, in the hope of achieving a fortune for the trifling investment of a few dollars.

I beg to assert, that I am not one of these, nor have I ever supposed that the most ingenious astrologer could, in contemplating the date of my nativity, deduce a horoscope that should elevate me to the dignity of wealth, out of the regular course of daily and nightly labor.

Lotteries, although abolished in the Northern states, are still an institution of the South; and it was during the season of 1856, while fulfilling an engagement at the Gaiety Theatre, New Orleans, that I made the casual acquaintance of one of these corporations, with the most gratifying result.

In the house where I resided, lived an English gentleman named Barnet, who had on divers occasions been the fortunate winner of small amounts, just sufficient to whet the appetite for a bolder venture. Vainly he endeavored to persuade the several occupants of the house to join him in investments of large bundles of coupons, but they had carefully registered a debtor and credit account of his transactions, and finding him with only his labor for his pains at the end of every year, felt no desire to speculate. I was "like manna in the wilderness" to him, and, although I never indulged a hope of any favorable result, because I looked back to the period of my pilgrimage when I affixed my signature to raffles for sets of crockery, and other fragile articles for domestic use; which had to be — when won — presented to some stationery householder, because unadapted for purposes of locomotion, I yielded to his entreaties, much to the amusement of the malcontents under the same roof.

The sum of two dollars and fifty cents was deposited in his keeping, as the half of a sinking fund, with which we had a fiendish desire to impoverish the state of Georgia ; and vouchers for the amount in mysterious numerals, duly exchanged.

When the drawing came in, I had won five dollars, being in possession of the concluding number of the capital prize. My friend needed no further confirmation to convince him that this was an omen of certain success at any subsequent investment, and retained the above sum for the purchase of tickets in the Havana lottery. When the result of this distribution became known, I held a ticket within three numbers of the largest prize of one hundred thousand dollars.

Barnet was in ecstacies at the prospect, but I couldn't

see any foreshadowing of success, though I readily assented to a further risk of *five dollars* in the Maryland lottery, drawn at Baltimore, December 20, 1856. I placed the tickets in my writing desk dismissing the subject, in the hurry of business, entirely from my thoughts. It is no wonder that I felt a sense of uneasiness, when on going to the theatre one fine morning early in the month of January 1857, the door-keeper informed me that a gentleman, in a state of great excitement, had been seeking me, and without leaving his name, hurried away, promising to call again.

At the conclusion of the scene wherein Matty Marvellous expatiates upon the luxury of a romantic disposition, I was apprised of my friend's re-appearance, and at the first convenient moment repaired to the stage door, where I found Barnet in a great perspiration, and chewing tobacco in the most reckless manner. No sooner did he get sight of me than he roared at the extremity of his ability,

" We've got 'em this time."

" Got who ? " mildly enquired I.

" 17,108, I tell you," returned he.

" Well, what of that," urged I.

" Capital prize," he gasped out.

" Whose capital prize ? " I desired to know.

My apathy about what at the moment I did not really comprehend, having entirely forgotten the Baltimore tickets locked in my desk, evidently disgusted him, and he walked away a few paces to recover himself.

Dislodging the fragrant weed from one side of his mouth, only to place it in the other, he returned, took me by the arm, and walked nearly a block in silence. While I was cogitating upon the possibility of some commercial eruption having unbalanced his mind, he returned to the charge, thus :

" Look here D., you do not seem clearly to understand the pleasing motive of my visit to the theatre just now! It was to acquaint you with the fact that the Baltimore drawing arrived this morning, and records that 17,108 is the capital drawn prize; consequently, as we each hold an eighth, we are both $5,000 richer thereby. Drawing from his pocket a printed list in confirmation of his assertion, he stopped in an entry to enable us to read it, and give him an opportunity to watch the effect produced thereby.

I will not attempt to deny that I experienced a sensation of pleasure as the truth of the matter became more firmly rooted in my mind, and as Barnet stopped every body in the streets whom he knew, and apprized them of our good fortune, it is no wonder that a highly colored account (in so far as regards the amount) appeared in the next day's journals.

Had the distinguished poet who bequeathed to the world the trite proverb that "The study of mankind is man," been a resident of the western continent, he would probably have seen the necessity to amend his conclusion, and substitute dollars for man.

Such, certainly, were the feelings which impressed me, as I suddenly found I was of so much commercial consequence that skillful agents applied for the pleasure of negotiating the payment of my newly acquired independence. Not alone did the resident *artists* in this peculiar and somewhat indefinite occupation solicit the pleasure of a business transaction, but so soon as the account reached New York, those accomplished traders who understand so well the science of scattering money to the *best* advantage, did me the favor to suggest investments of the most eligible character, which, had I availed myself of, might ere this have placed me upon the high road to wealth; at the same time it is more than probable that a contrary issue might have been the result of my temerity.

11*

The following is a copy of one of four applications I received, having one of these ends in view. It is a fair sample of the proposals; and this is the first opportunity I have had of offering my thanks to the Secretary of one of the firms who most liberally warned me of the instability of a neighboring concern; and presented such a glowing description of the financial condition of the house in whose interest he was employed.

(*Copy.*)
—— Wall Street, New York,
January, 22, 1857.

WILLIAM DAVIDGE, Esq.

Dear Sir, — We beg to direct your attention to a most eligible investment in the —— Mining Association, by which very large profits can readily be made.

We enclose prospectus, and shall feel great pleasure in placing a limited number of shares at your disposal.

An early reply will be desirable, in order to make an equitable distribution of the few shares remaining undisposed of.

We are, Dear Sir,
Your obedient Servants.
—— & Co.

My friend Barnet made a purchase of some Louisiana State stock. The last I heard of him, his investment was down to thirty cents upon the dollar. The present condition of that section of the country would seem to justify the conviction that the principal, along with the interest, is now lost to him, and his heirs, forever.

The following summer I was at Laura Keene's Theatre playing an engagement, and was waited on by a gentlemanly looking young man, who said he had business of some importance with me. I requested him to wait a few

moments, and, as soon as I had finished rehearsal, joined
him at the stage door; and while walking to and fro at
the back of the building, the following colloquy took
place.

Stranger. I believe, Mr. Davidge, you are well acquainted with the lottery business?

Davidge. There you are in error, Sir. I know nothing at all about it!

Stranger. Indeed, you surprise me, I thought you had
won a large prize in New Orleans, last winter.

Davidge. True, Sir, but I know nothing of the matter, save that, by accident, as it seemed to me, I became
the winner of five thousand dollars. May I beg to be
put at once in possession of the object you have in making the enquiry.

Stranger. Certainly! As you have been in the habit of
playing at lotteries —

Davidge. Excuse me! I have not been in the habit
of doing anything of the kind. I was a winner, as I told
you; but since that time, have never invested one dollar in
any similar venture.

Stranger. (Evidently disappointed.) Well, I have
a proposal to make, by which each of us might possibly
realize something handsome.

Davidge. Indeed! what is it?

Stranger. I am an agent for the sale of tickets. I
have had a place in Bleecker St. for several years, and all
I have ever got, has been simply a slight commission on
the sale of the prizes that I might happen to sell. The
Mayor seems determined to stop us, and before I give up
I should like to make a few hundred dollars for all the
trouble I have had.

Davidge. By all means, but in what way could I aid
in so desirable a result? "

Stranger. Why, I have a friend in Delaware, who understands how to communicate with me in secret signs; I have also a friend in the operating room at the telegraph office here, and the three of us perfectly understand one another. I have to deposit the unsold tickets in a sealed envelope at 12 o'clock each day of the drawing. Now, there is a difference of nearly fifteen minutes in the clocks at the two places. My friend at the other end of the line would transmit (as I have explained,) the lucky number to my other friend here, who will meet me on my way down Broadway, and by a preconcerted signal apprize me of the result. I retain the numbers, if not already sold, and still reach the office time enough to lodge the package, and the same night could bring you the fortunate ticket, which you could regularly present on the following morning, and deducting a small percentage for my friend's trouble, we could share the consequences.

Davidge. Yes, it strikes me that the consequences might be rather unpleasant than otherwise! Be good enough to tell me why, if you have arranged this combination in such a masterly way, you don't complete it so as to keep it entirely amongst your personal friends and acquaintance; why confer the favor upon an outsider, and more than that, why select *me* as the chosen one?

Stranger. Why, if I were to try any one I knew, it might arouse suspicion; and further, knowing how the thing was arranged, they might refuse to give me my share, and I should be compelled to bear it in silence.

I left him with the assurance that he was in error in making me the recipient of his very ingenious device; and suggesting that he possibly took an illiberal estimate of the character and probity of his acquaintance who, whatever their natural failings might be, could scarcely resist doing justice to the great master mind that had begotten such a method of recruiting an exhausted exchequer.

DEFEAT OF THE AMERICANS, AT THE MIMIC BATTLE OF MONTEREY.

Soon after the success of American arms in Mexico, a drama was produced at the Bowery Theatre, entitled the " Battle of Monterey."

The master of the supers was in the habit of engaging for Mexican soldiers gentlemen of the Hebrew persuasion, from the neighborhood of Chatham Street, to whom he paid fifty cents per night for their services; while those who personated the Americans, were more easily obtainable from the ordinary supers attached to the theatre, and who only received twenty-five cents for a similar service in their nation's cause, being well satisfied with the honor of victory.

On the first Sabbath of the Jews, the usual soldiers were not to be relied on for punctual attendance, consequently some Americans had to be enlisted for the night.

The opportunity for a joke was too good to be lost, and the new recruits availed themselves of it, by refusing to be beaten, or surrender, but gave their opponents a sound drubbing, tore their flag from them, and scattered them in every direction, much to their astonishment, and the enjoyment of the friends who had been apprised of the intention, and who witnessed the scene from amongst the audience, with much gratification.

THE WESTERN ENTHUSIAST.

The members of any profession or calling must at all times be flattered by a favorable recognition of his powers, regardless of the terms employed for the utterance of the eulogium.

The familiarity of the genuine Western traveller has long been a matter of notoriety to those who have visited that extensive section of the country.

In 1856, I acted twelve nights at the theatre in Louis‑
ville, Ky. The commencement of the engagement prom
ised a profitable and satisfactory termination to my visit,
and in anticipation of pecuniary delight I was inhaling
the aroma of a mild Havana at the door of my hotel, when
I was accosted by a good looking specimen of the Western hunter, with a desire to be made acquainted with the
present state of my health, in the not very original expression of,

" How are you ? "

Adopting the usual method of meeting one question
with another, I rejoined,

" How are you ? "

This seemed to satisfy him conclusively, and drawing a
chair beside me, and arming himself with a formidable
quid of tobacco, he commenced the attack.

" I seed you last night ! "

" Indeed, did you ? Hope you were pleased," replied I.

" Pleased ! well, I guess I war ! — Say, do you remember Kirby ? "

" Perfectly," said I.

" He were a rouser, he were ! I sold him a dog once ! "
" Indeed ! "

Before I had time to reflect upon the singular circumstance of my friend's disposal of one of the canine race to
the once popular actor, my informant placed me in possession of the numerous points of excellence for which
the animal was distinguished; with the method he had
employed for his instruction from his infancy till he
reached the proud altitude of dog's estate; together with
the exact amount of money expended in the purchase.

I had a desire to contribute to the enjoyment of this
accidental encounter, and began to take a retrospection of
my past history, in order to furnish a parallel to the event
just recorded, but nothing of similar importance recur-

ring at the moment, I (as a subterfuge, I admit) sought information in regard to the statistical history of the city, past and present, without elicting much knowledge on the subject. I had evidently not sounded the key note of my friend's specialty, and while I was beating about for a congenial theme, was desired by him to adjudicate between the relative merits of two prominent members of my profession.

There was little time to evade the enquiry, for my companion went into a glowing panegyric of his favorites in dramatic art, giving no quarter to those who were not so fortunate as to hold a place in his esteem, till he signified his positive intention of quitting his present mode of life, and at once assuming the dignity of tragic grandeur.

"Now look here!" he began. "How long would it take to learn your trade?"

I assured him that that would depend entirely upon the aptitude of the student. For myself, I had been more than twenty years in harness, and I was frequently reminded in my own estimate, of glaring inefficiency in many things. Further, — talent did not at all times command success, or ensure position and profit. Those who labored under the impression that acting was simply a trade, confounded the art itself with the practice of it.

Though I was willing to admit the oft quoted axiom that "the test of genius was success," in its pecuniary signification, I had in numerous instances witnessed talent of the highest order languish and decay, from lack of encouragement, while those who were not encumbered with more than a certain modicum of business tact, or the privileges of their sex (if of the female gender,) have soon distanced their accomplished cotemporaries.

My friend readily acquiesced in this conclusion, and as an earnest of his faith, announced his determination to devote the balance of his days to the best interests of the tragic drama, as he felt conscious of a brilliant success.

"I'm a great hand at learning anything, said he," I've seen a great deal of acting in all the Western cities. And though I don't believe I could, at first, come the Macbeths; I'll bet any man five thousand dollars I *could run the Macduffs clean up to the handle.*"

I never saw him after the expression of this threat, therefore am not aware if he perpetrated his design. Neither has any information reached me that the conqueror of the Scottish monarch has ever been placed in the unenviable position above referred to.

A CONVIVIAL AUDIENCE.

Columbus, in the state of Ohio, is not distinguished for its profuse patronage of the drama even at the present time, when they are in possession of an extremely elegant and convenient theatre. Years ago, before the building was in existence, attempts were periodically made to create a taste, but seldom with much pecuniary success.

It was during one of these doubtful investments, that the following unusual scene occurred.

The play commenced to a very limited number of patrons, and proceeded with that dull aspect of solemnity which always characterizes a scanty attendance, till it came to the second scene in the second act, when Mr. Parker the manager, who acted one of the principal parts, advanced to the footlights and addressed his patrons in the following manner:

"Gentlemen: You have done us the favor to assemble here to-night, for the purpose of extending your patronage to the exponents of an intellectual entertainment. We feel deeply the compliment you have thus generously designed, and individually and collectively tender you our thanks. That you have not been more extensively emulated by the inhabitants of a location that proudly rears its head as the capital of a thriving and intelligent state, is matter more for pity than wonder. Your object is to seek a pleasing combination of the two essential ingredients of our nature, for without a blending of the intellectual with the social, so imperatively demanded by our physical and mental organization, how dull and monotonous would be our existence. It must be painfully evident to you as it is to me, that with the present influences that surround you, such a desirable consummation is totally impossible. The important, not to say educational mission, with which we are charged, cannot be faithfully disposed to such a limited number of recipients. Desirous as I am to add to the amusement of my fellow man, particularly under the pressure of unforeseen disaster like the present, and to curtail as much as possible the monotony of the time, I do myself the pleasure of bringing this very uncongenial meeting to a close, and invite you all into the saloon next door to "Take a drink;" and they did it.

CHAPTER XX.

" I will persevere in my course of loyalty."

King Lear. Act 3. *Scene* 5.

THE LOYAL MARINE.

MANY amusing incidents are recorded wherein persons on the stage have positively refused to utter sentiments, or perform acts contrary to their feelings. I have heard a leader of an orchestra declare that he would not occupy his seat, if expressions were uttered reflecting upon the honor of his native land.

Some years ago the late Mr. Burton produced the "Battle of Waterloo," at the Arch Street Theatre, Philadelphia, at considerable expense, but was at his wits' end to find efficient men for soldiers, for the several engagements with which the piece abounds. Chance made him acquainted with the captain of an English man-of-war, whose vessel was then lying in the river, who politely offered to send his marines to the theatre, and thus relieve him from a great difficulty. Rehearsal came, and the piece proceeded with satisfaction till the last act, where an incident happened in the dramatic version which gave rise to this story.

The scene was a corn field, where an engagement took place between the French and English, the former making breast works of the sheafs of corn, and after a pretty heavy melee, the English had to retreat and leave the French masters of the field.

All this was fully and clearly explained by the manager, who superintended the rehearsal in person. When, all on a sudden, one of the crew most resolutely, and with powerful saline expressions, refused to comply with the business of the scene. The manager expostulated as best he could. "My dear fellow," said he, "it is necessary for the business of the scene, that it should be so arranged."

"He didn't care about anybody's arrangements, but he'd be darned if he was going to retreat before any infernal Frenchman." The manager was in despair, and again begged, for the sake of the performance, that the marine would waive his objection, for the piece couldn't be done without it." "To the devil with the piece, then," said he, "for what I care, for never shall it be said, that I ever beat a retreat before a Frenchman."

"Well, then," said the manager, "I'm very sorry, but your services are really of no use to me."

"All right," said the marine, "heave ahead, boys," and proceeded to quit the theatre, followed by his crew, when one of the party stepped up to the despairing manager, and assured him it should be all right at the performance, and that he would appease the malcontent.

"Leave him to me, I'll lead the way, and he will be sure to follow." The manager permitted the incident to pass, hoping for the best, and proceeded to the conclusion of the rehearsal.

In the evening the house was crowded, and all moved safely and satisfactorily. The two first acts terminated with deafening applause, and the audience were enraptured with the military skill exhibited by all concerned.

As soon as the third act commenced, the manager repaired to his room to dress for the last piece, inwardly priding himself upon the great managerial skill he had displayed in the production of a piece that was sure to replenish his exhausted treasury, when a tremendous shout of laughter intruded itself upon his ear, and his expressive face went through a long list of contortions at the supposition, that a serious scene he had himself penned, in order to give time for a heavy set by the carpenters, was exciting the risibilities of the audience, when he had designed it for a contrary result.

He stood aghast, with a portion of his wardrobe in his grasp, as the prompter burst into the apartment, livid with fear and dread. Seizing his important officer by the throat, the manager desired to know the meaning of the disturbance.

"Oh, sir, pray come, that marine!"

"What of him?" screamed the lessee.

"Oh! sir, he'll murder somebody."

Pushing his way towards the stage, the first thing that met his astonished gaze, was the malcontent of the morning, beating about him right and left with the butt-end of his musket, upsetting the miniature breast-works, and as an incentive to the act, singing "Rule Britannia" at the top of his voice, totally regardless of the efforts of his companions to subdue him, or the bursts of laughter from the audience

The above is but a slight illustration of the various mishaps which sometimes occur, either from ignorance or design, upon the stage. While writing, I am reminded that one evening during the performance of the Octoroon at the Winter Garden, a child, who represents a negro, during a serious scene deliberately dismantled itself of its woolly hair, for the purpose of scratching its head. The audience laughed immoderately; at which the child, quite unused to the stage, grinned in recognition, and made a low bow for the supposed compliment.

READING A PART ON THE STAGE.

The task of reading a part on the stage in such a manner as to give it the tone consistent with its character, is a difficulty very few actors have been able to surmount. To one at all practised in the profession it is much easier to improvise the dialogue necessary to conduct the plot, than have recourse to the book.

During one of Mr. Barney Williams' successful engagements at the Broadway Theatre, a piece called "Crossing the Atlantic" was produced, in which he enacted an Irish peasant, who took passage from Liverpool for New York, in search of his sister. The second or third day after it was first acted, Mr. Williams was taken so seriously ill, that his appearance before the public was an effort impossible to accomplish. It was on the fourth of July, I was quietly attempting to keep as cool as convenient, when the messenger arrived with a request that I would be on hand at the theatre in the evening, in order to assist as well as I could in the dilemma. When I reached the Broadway, about three quarters of an hour prior to the opening of the doors, I was solicited by the manager to read the part assigned to Mr. Williams.

I declined to do so, but offered, if they would furnish me with the following items, I would go on the stage and say something to the purpose, viz: The name of the character. Where he came from, and what his object was in coming to New York. The name of the sister he was in search of; and, If he spoke the tag of the piece, what was the purport of it?

With these materials I managed to get through with apparent satisfaction, and without serious annoyance to those concerned with me.

Not so when Mr. Goulson, at the Bowery Theatre, had to read a paper in which the name of "Claude Frolia," occurred. The stage carpenter, in order to increase the dilemma he saw Goulson was laboring under from his inability to dicipher the writing, turned down the gas light at the wing where he stood, and when the unfortunate G. came to the name, he called it "Claude Duval!"

Mr. Stevens, the stage manager, whose play it was, rushed upon him as soon as he quitted the scene, to know what he could mean by spoiling the piece with such nonsense.

"What's the matter?" said Goulson.

"The matter!" screamed the infuriated manager. "My hero was a monk, but you have made him a thief!"

"Sorry for that," said G., "but I couldn't see very well, I only knew of two Claude's — Claude Melnotte, and Claude Duval. I felt certain it wasn't the former, and therefore thought it must be the latter."

BARNEY WILLIAMS AND THE INDIGNANT PATLANDER.

In the early part of Barney's career, he occasionally acted at the Chatham Theatre. In the neighborhood of where his mother resided, there lived a lad who was frequently employed by him to assist in placing his baggage on board when he left the city for provincial engagements, but who had not the slightest notion of the nature of his occupation.

On the evening he was to commence at the Chatham, Jemmy was entrusted with the wardrobe required, and was asked "if he would like to see the play?"

"To do which, sir," said Jemmy.

"To see the play?" said Barney.

"Faith, I would, sir."

"Did you ever go to the play?" was the next question.

"Faith, I never did, sir."

"Come along, then," said Barney, and off they started

for Jemmy's first visit to tho theatre. Entering by the usual stage door, Jemmy was relieved of the bundle by Barney, who instructed him to ensconce himself in a private box, near the stage, with full instructions to remain till the people had quitted the house, and he would join him.

The play was the one in which Ragged Pat appears. No sooner did Barney make his *entre*, than Jemmy fixed his eyes upon him with the greatest wonderment, but without the slightest scintillation of pleasure. Barney observed this, and mistook it for the natural diffidence of his disposition, but concluded he'd have him when he danced his celebrated jig, in the next scene; his surprise was by no means lessened when this act made him more stoical than before. The song will not fail to fetch him, mused Barney, he can't resist that, I'm sure. Even there he was mistaken! not a muscle of his face moved, but still kept its blank expression, while the audience were apparently delighted, and signified their approval by a rapturous encore.

The entertainment over, Jemmy was in waiting, in obedience to orders, when the following colloquy took place.

Barney. Well, Jemmy, how did you like tho play?

Jemmy. Ah! well, Mr. Williams, I'd rather you didn't ax me now.

Barney. Why, Jemmy?

Jemmy. Ah, sure now, I'd rather be excused, that's what I would.

Barney. Nonsense, I should like to have your opinion.

Jemmy. You'll not be offended, sir.

Barney. Offended, not a bit of it; out with it.

Jemmy. Well then, since you insist upon it, if I must tell you my mind; it strikes me it would be more to your credit, if you'd be imitating the dirty Dutch, than making game o' the Irish.

CHAPTER XXI.

THE LAST ONE.

" God'ild you for your last company."
As you like it. Act 8. *Scene* 8.

THE incidents that have crossed my path in the course of a long and laborious servitude, as here set down, are those only of a nature that could be likely to afford amusement to the general reader.

It would afford me more pleasure than I can readily express if I could, without violating the sacred precincts of private correspondence, recount the numerous instances of social gratification I have derived from so many sources since my arrival in America.

It is at all times flattering to one whose pursuit is either of a literary, or inventive character, to find a congeniality with his mission, and a due sense of his presumed usefulness.

The members of the profession to which I belong, have perhaps a better opportunity of judging the various and distinct idosyncracies of society at large, than those whose pursuits are of a less observant necessity. Accustomed to the close study of peculiarities of our fellow-men, we are ever ready to detect the counterfeit from the genuine, burnish it howso'er they may.

It is often with regret that we find that faculty intruding itself upon our notice. Still a large proportion of our brethren exist entirely in a world of their own creating;

Their life is one long round of rehearsal in the morning, and acting in the evening. Many can find little leisure for mental culture. It is no uncommon thing during a novitiate, for an actor to study and act in the space of one week as much at forty lengths* and at times even more than that.

It is recorded of Munden, an actor of great ability, and the original old Dornton in the "Road to Ruin," that on Dibdin, the author, explaining to him the nature of the part of Dozey in "Past Ten O'Clock," and referring him to the then highly popular novel of Tom Jones, for the counterpart of the old watchman; he admitted he had never read it, and further, that he couldn't find time to peruse anything save a play book, and then only the part he was called upon to enact.

The struggles and privations of an actor's life have become a matter of peculiar, and frequently exaggerated history! The bright lights of their characters have too often been most sparingly presented, while the darker shades with which ignorance and bigotry delight to robe their victims, have been laid on with a vigor of color, unrivalled for the disposition of the details, and unapproachable for the profundity of its imagination.

It is only just that a proper respect and regard should be paid to the dignity of labor, yet it is notorious that while a large portion of the public evince a profound esteem for mechanical excellence, they look almost with an air of indifference on artistic, or literary superiority. This aversion is more strikingly evident where the mind is, early in life, impregnated with an intense desire to acquire affluence, to the utter and total exclusion of that wealth of the mind which is the key stone to civilization and advancement; and it may be matter for serious re-

*Forty two written lines constitute a length.

12

flection, whether customs of traffic, with all the unavoidable misrepresentations or adroitly concealed facts with which commerce is always surrounded, do not harden the sensibility of many natures which never can be overcome. It would be an uncongenial task to trace causes to effects, with metaphysical obduracy. The truth forces itself upon the notice of every artistic observer, intruding with unmistakable severity into the domestic precinct, with an arrogance as unjust as it is ungenerous. Presuming this position to be accurately sustained, it must be admitted that the public is at fault when it regards literary and artistic pursuits other than an indispensable necessity for the perpetuation of human greatness.

A review of the lives of the members of the dramatic profession will exhibit as many phases of excellence as that of any other pursuit; while their infirmities bear no analogy either in extent, or heinousness. As a class they are charitable to profusion, affectionate sons, and loving daughters, willing to aid and assist at all times, their fellow laborers, even beyond their available, or consistent ability. The crime of thoughtlessness and improvidence may with truth be laid to the charge of some few ; but it is a matter for serious reflection, whether these failings cannot be more readily atoned for at the "Great Judgment Seat" than the practice of selfishness, or the arrogance of wealth, with which many of their most strenuous enemies delight to invest themselves.

A pamphlet entitled "The Drama Defended "* very extensively noticed by the press of America, was written by me in 1858, with a desire to place the members of my profession in a proper and equitable position with the public.

It cannot surely be urged with any amount of justice

---

*Published by S. French, 122 Nassau Street, N. Y.

that, while the clergy, the bar, and numerous other professions,— the first named most particularly — are amenable only as *individuals*, for their crimes or misdemeanors, that the children of Thespis should, from the dereliction of any of their brothers, or sisters, have their *entire race* tabooed and stigmatized as a class unworthy to share or take part in the socialities of every day life.

That the profession of the stage has its black sheep, no one will attempt to deny. Where is the flock without these despoilers of their fair fame? Yet, it is notorious, that their errors are but venal ones, while statistics will undeniably prove that there is no calling extant, taken numerically, that can present so few instances of offence against law and order, as the members of the dramatic body can proudly boast.

It is sometimes considered that the only tangible objection that can be advanced against the stage is, that the surroundings lead to a mixture of the sexes, dangerous to morality, and fatal to the interests of society at large. Yet, with a singular inconsistency, as it appears to me, no similar charge is levelled against the factory system, Sunday evening services, and many others where the sexes mingle, and where more impropriety is constantly exhibited, most glaringly evident to any observer who will take the trouble to watch the retiring crowds from the several churches.

Is it somewhat paradoxical that such a sudden and virulent attack of *theatre preaching* should have broken out a year or two since. Reader, what doth it portend? Is it with the benign intention of bearding the lion in his den, or is it with the hope that the theatre, being accustomed to receive a *fixed tariff*, the devotionals may be induced to donate the usual play-house prices rather than satisfy their consciences by the very popular three or five cent offerings? If this be so, it proves incontestably that the *love of dollars* burns as effulgent in the heart that beats beneath the clerical black, as under the commercial blue, or mechanical grey.

To those who look with that degree of charity on all classes and degrees which should ever distinguish the liberal mind, it will not be out of place to adduce a specimen of bigotry, and supreme ignorance, almost unparalleled.

It is an opinion proclaimed from the pulpit in one of the churches of Kingston-upon-Hull in the year 1792, (verbatim from Wilkinson's Wandering Patentee) a very popular manager of the York circuit, where many of the most celebrated actors that have graced the London stage, graduated :

" No player, or any of his children ought to be entitled to a christian burial, or even to be in a church yard! Not one of them can be saved. And those who enter a playhouse are equally certain with the players of eternal damnation. No player can be an honest man."

It was from such mouldy and absurd *trash* as this, that the Romish clergy of old imbibed their presumptuous audacity to withhold christian burial from actors, and the Puritans have contended for the extinction of the most popular and humanizing amusement, (not to say instruction) extant.

If the church could be a little progressive, it would at once see this absurdity to be quite as great as the old Grecian legislative act, familiar to most of us, of suppressing the study and practice of physic, with the declaration that honor and life ought never to become matter of dispute. Nearly one hundred years elapsed before Aristrato, who was a nephew to Aristotle, re-introduced the medical art with any hope of a favorable reception.

The defects of the stage are only excrescences, they

disgrace the trunk, but cannot vitiate it. It has sufficient strength to permit the eradication of all and everything that is objectionable and flourish with tenfold vigor! It is not composed of the deleterious qualities which bigotry, fanaticism, and ignorance would endeavor to persuade the world it is.

The charity of some of its members is fully established in numerous ways. Among the most prominent, stands that magnificent structure " Dulwich College " founded by Edward Alleyne, where the indigent, to this day, offer up their prayers to heaven for the comfort and shelter afforded by the donation of a profane stage player.

When I had examined its several apartments and sauntered into the trimly arranged garden which surrounds this peaceful dwelling place, my thoughts led me to the substance of a sermon delivered by the Rev. Mr. Best of Sheffield, then fresh in my recollection, in which the actor was unconditionally despatched to perdition for his sinful calling.

A very old man came hobbling along, but newly risen from dinner. I watched him as he took his seat beneath the shade of a large elm tree, and putting on his glasses composed himself to read from a book he drew from his pocket. After a few moments I approached and addressed him. He rose immediately, and politely offered me his seat, which I declined. As delicately as possible I drew from him his history. It was the usual torrent of misfortune that had pressed him down in the financial scale, till, with advancing years upon his head, he had been compelled to avail himself of the institution that so fitly administered to his comfort.

As I walked away with the words of the divine ringing in my ears, I cherished a love for good deeds, and wendered with Othello, whether, "There were no stones in Heaven, but what serve for the thunder."

I am somewhat prolix upon this subject, because I desire to lend my poor ability to aid in establishing amongst the liberal minded, a feeling of generosity towards the profession of which I am a member. In doing so I am influenced by no vain gloriousness, or idle antagonism towards the really devout and christian churchman; conceiving as I do, that as there are in our frail natures "weeds of every soil" so there are abundant evidences of meekness, humility, and unerring zeal in the cause of charity, probity, and devotional usefulness. I am pleased to be enabled to record the pleasure I derive from two good and charitable spirits whom I frequently meet in social harmony, and from whom I always part with a feeling of regret.

I expect to be asked why I make these pointed allusions to the maligners of the stage in this place; and if it be necessary, or politic so to do.

In reply I would say, that so long as I have been in a position to judge of the merits of the subject, I have never shrunk from the defence of my craft from the attacks of the cowardly assailer. The many occasions I have committed my thoughts to paper on this theme, both in America, and England, must be fresh in the recollection of all who take an interest in the subject.

Forming, as these controversies have, a portion of my professional history, it is presumable that my readers should expect some allusion to the motives that have led me to pursue it, with a dogged perseverance somewhat akin to the earnestness exhibited by the opposing parties. Thus then it was.

When I was about fifteen years old, the church I attended had for its pastor a resolute old gentleman of an austere visage, and a pair of eagle eyes which seemed to strike terror into the hearts of refractory boys, and late arrivals. It was his wont to adapt, with the most ingenious sophistry, any incident of every-day disaster that happened to turn up, and so interweave it with his text, that you found yourself corporeally, as well as spiritually at Rome, striving to catch the analogy of his application to the eternal city, during a carnival week, and the burning of a ship-yard on the banks of the Thames, where two men had unfortunately lost their lives.

An individual, callous to the science of natural laws, had, while in a balloon, conceived the notion of taking a downward trip in a parachute, and killed himself in the attempt. This was a splendid chance for our friend, the parson, who made the best of it on the following Sunday, by sending his congregation home with the assurance that they were all in the condition of the man in the parachute.

When the Brunswick Theatre in Goodman's Fields fell, on the morning of the 23d of February, 1828, while the company were at rehearsal, he saw in this conclusive evidence that it was Heaven's judgment upon a number of wretched sinners, whose occupation was adverse to every form of Christianity; which he attempted to show by a reference to the history of Sodom and Gomorrah, or the parable of the unjust steward, I forget which. He was a good solid hater of amusements of any and every kind. " If you want recreation," he would say, " you shall find it in prayer. If you desire music, you can enjoy it in the delicious song of the bird — Nature's own chorister." I have since heard a gentleman in Brooklyn, while descanting upon the enormity of opera amusement, laud the brilliant execution of the mosquito, with similar enthusiasm.

" Do you need intellectual nourishment; listen to me three times on Sundays," he would continue.

About this time I conceived a notion that, in order to attain to the summit of dramatic art, it was necessary to acquire a thorough knowledge of the science of elocution. I have, long since, made the discovery that no person thus trammelled has ever reached that coveted goal; for this purpose I made the acquaintance of an actor who lived in the suburbs of London, and was then under engagement at one of the minor theatres on the Surrey side of the Thames. He was a jovial, honest hearted fellow, teeming with anecdote of odd incidents connected with his professional career, and with a wife and about half a score of children, had to exercise great prudence and economy to keep the domestic machine in motion. I watched this man's habits for months. I scanned every action of himself and family. I saw with sorrow the struggle of a generous, noble nature, against poverty and prejudice. A pious friend, with the best intention for my welfare, had furnished us with Jeremy Collier's tirade against the stage; the parson at our church had been pounding a similar doctrine into me, from his pulpit, whenever opportunity served.

Then it was that I began to peer into the intent and purport of these defamers; then to look upon those more searchingly who bore in silence, and resignation, with the avenues for their defence barred by the taint of prejudice the stigma that ignorance had cast upon them. Then to compare by statistical research the relative proportion of offences committed against the laws; and the result — with shame be it known — exhibits a terrible record of every grade of sin against those whose text should be in imitation of their divine master: "Peace, charity, and universal love."

It is no disparagement to our natures to assert that curiosity is one of its most formidable, and distinctive peculiarities! and there is no class, or calling, that presents so many opportunities wherewith to indulge, or gratify this passion, as the theatre and its connections. Impressed with this belief, I have essayed to furnish materials that, it is hoped, have tended to appease this voracious desire; flavoring the meal with such sprinklings of incident and anecdote as should impart to it an agreeable zest, and relish.

The time honored supposition that has for ages pervaded the minds of many persons, in relation to the birth, parentage, and education of the children of Thespis, as we are poetically termed, is not attempted to be dispelled, for the reason that, to destroy or strip a delusion of its mystery, and clothe it in its materiality, would only embarrass, but could scarcely hope to satisfy the cravings of a class who delight to indulge in the speculations of the theorist.

The vanity of placing this book before the public, in an autobiographical shape, was suggested by a friend of literary aptitude, who, in his zeal for my welfare, has probably inflicted an injury upon his own best patrons; which years of unremitting ability may not enable him to liquidate.

The book, such as it is, was commenced during a vacation of professional labor; it therefore afforded me the pleasure of being in sympathy, as it were, before my numerous friends, *the public!* And it is most earnestly desired, when it shall be placed in their hands, that the affinity of the delusion may not be dispelled.

Opinions of the merits of my contemporaries I have most carefully avoided; in like manner that in sketching the peculiarities of my professional brethren I have dealt in generalities rather than personalities, which I with submission consider only conjures a resemblance in the minds of those who are the most likely to feel piqued at the portraiture.

If the list of my dramatic friends be augmented by this evidence of my desire to speak on their behalf it will afford similar satisfaction to that I shall experience, if the public will henceforth *on the stage* regard me with no less favor for this very small addition to the ranks of literature.

THE END.

www.ingramcontent.com/pod-product-compliance
Lightning Source LLC
Chambersburg PA
CBHW030620030726

47497CB00006B/1577